Nine Meals To Anarchy

The EMP

Farrell Kingsley

Copyright © 2014 MediaWorks Publishing

All rights reserved.

ISBN: 978-0-9905644-1-6

an·ar·chy /ˈanərkē/

Noun

A state of disorder due to absence or non-recognition of authority.

DEDICATION

This book is dedicated to all those who diligently prepare for the unexpected. I am what you call an advanced prepper and I love my family but many of them think I am crazy for preparing as much as I do.

I have to admit it is an addiction that I cannot shake.

Farrell Kingsley

Nine Meals To Anarchy: The EMP
Copyright © 2014 MediaWorks Publishing | www.mediaworkspublishing.com

All rights reserved.

No part of this book/manuscript may be copied in whole or in part, stored in a retrieval system, transmitted, photocopied, digitally copied, digitally reproduced, or other record created or used without prior agreement and express written consent from MediaWorks Publishing or the author.

ISBN: 978-0-9905644-1-6

MediaWorks Publishing has attempted whenever possible throughout this book to distinguish proprietary trademarks from descriptive terms by following capitalization and style used by their respective owners.

MediaWorks Publishing and its author(s) make no representation or warranty of any kind as to its completeness or accuracy of the content and accept no liability of any kind as to the performance, merchantability, fitness for any purpose, or any losses or damages of any kind related caused or alleged to have been caused directly or indirectly from the use of this book.

MediaWorks Publishing accepts no responsibility from the opinions expressed in the book to any entity and the opinions expressed are those of the authors and not of MediaWorks Publishing, its publisher, or assigned. Any names in this book are fictional and are not based on real people, places, or events.

Cover images licensed for print from Fotolia US.

CONTENTS

DEDICATION 3

Chapter 1: Awaking To A Nightmare 6

Chapter 2: Deciding It Was Time To Go. 28

Chapter 3: More Bad News 46

Chapter 4: Bug Out Time 61

Chapter 5: Things Just Got Worse 104

Chapter 6: It's Only Day 4 139

Chapter 7: Day 10 175

Chapter 8: A Town In Crisis 192

Chapter 9: You Can't Plan For Everything 216

Chapter 10: Who Can You Trust? 231

Chapter 11: Society Tampers With Being Civilized. 249

Chapter 12: What Makes a Hero? 265

Chapter 13: Overwhelming Circumstances. 307

Chapter 13: Banding Together. 334

Chapter 14: The Crisis Ends. 351

EPILOGUE 358

Chapter 1: Awaking To A Nightmare

'It was just another Monday morning' is the thought that went through Robert's head as he laid in bed. Just like all the others or so he thought as he was hitting the snooze button for the third time and his wife Sydney turned over to poke him in the back.

"Take care of her." Sydney said groggily.

"Who?" Robert asked with his eyes still closed.

"The little one over here, who do you think?" she asked.

"What's wrong Rylee?" Robert said to his little two year old holding a sippie cup and a little pink blanket she couldn't live without.

"Daddyyy.... my cartoons aren't on." she sniveled.

"Did you change the channel?" I asked.

"Daddyyy...C'mon....It's not working." Rylee cried.

Robert slowly got up and walked with her pulling him down the stairs in to the living room. On the TV was a satellite view showing a large cloud of smoke covering much of the center of the United States. A scrolling bar at the bottom of the screen was streaming the breaking news and telling viewers that all flights in and out of the

Portland, Oregon area were cancelled by most carriers. Yellowstone, the super volcano had erupted with all its overdue fury and already four hours later the ash and debris had covered most of the center of the United Stated and the southern part of Canada.

"Daddyyy fix it!" Rylee screamed.

That sentence tore Robert from his thinking of the ramifications of what he had just learned from the television screen.

"Hold on honey. We may not have cartoons today." Robert told Rylee as he ran back up stairs yelling for my wife.

"Sydney, we are in big trouble!" Robert said.

Sydney barely moved. "What do you mean? Didn't you pay the satellite bill?"

"No! Yellowstone has erupted and it's bad."

"Yellowstone is thousands of miles from here. Who cares? I want to go back to sleep."

"No it's not. It is less than one thousand miles from here and it's a super volcano!" Robert screamed.

"Oh, you blow everything out of proportion. Let me sleep, please!" she hollered covering her head with a pillow.

Rylee walked up next to the bed. "Mommy can you turn on cartoons for me? Daddy won't do it!" she told Sydney in a low voice.

"Robert, can you just turn on cartoons for her so I can sleep?" Sydney begged.

"Sweetheart, there are no cartoons. Only news and emergency alerts on every single channel." Robert replied.

"Robert. You mean to tell me that with seven kids channels there is not a single one with cartoons on at 7AM? Really? Really?" Sydney yelled at Robert.

Robert grabbed the remote and turned on the TV in the bedroom. The channel it was on showed two newscasters talking to a geologist on the TV.

"Mr. Perry you are a geologist monitoring Mount Hood just outside of Portland. What do you think this eruption of Yellowstone means to us?"

Mr. Perry on the screen took a deep breath and paused before he spoke. *"Stan I think this means a change of life for us and the whole world. One of the things we have always dreaded was Yellowstone erupting. We knew it was 40,000 years overdue and could erupt sometime. The last eruption plunged the world into darkness. The region's most recent eruption which was about 640,000 years ago when it created a*

35-mile-wide caldera that was over 50 miles long.

What we are most concerned with in this part of the world is the tremendous volume of volcanic ash that is being blasted high into the atmosphere. Ash clouds will be forming and causing havoc around the world."

Suddenly Stan the lead anchor interrupted. *"Mr. Perry this is great information but right now we need to move to Stephanie Sorenson who is reporting that rocks the size of basketballs are actually falling on cars on Highway 84 in the Gorge and may be responsible for up to twenty accidents there....Stephanie.."*

For a moment Robert turned his head to see the astonished look on Sydney's face.

"Wow!" Sydney said.

The satellite view came on the screen. "Can you turn that up Robert?"

Robert quickly grabbed the controller and saw that the plume of ash was now much larger than he had seen just twenty minutes earlier on the downstairs TV.

Robert turned up the sound to hear Stan. *"This is a satellite view from one of our weather satellites. Most likely if you were within a few miles of this eruptions you are probably not faring so well..."*

Suddenly Mr. Perry interrupted. *"From the looks of*

this, if you were 400 miles in any direction from Wyoming you were dead before you even knew there was an eruption."

Stan interrupted again. *"Now we want viewers to know that we have no information on the status of those close to the volcano at this time. We don't want people to be alarmed or concerned about those friends or family members who might be closer to the volcano than we are here in Portland until we have actual confirmation."*

Mr. Perry spoke up loudly over Stan's voice. *"Stan! You have to let your viewers know that at the last measurement it was estimated that there was enough ash volume to bury the entire United States in thirty six inches of ash. And it's coming. The reason why volcanic rocks are landing here on the West Coast is that the earth spins to the right at about 1,000 miles per hour. When Yellowstone shoots debris miles and miles in the air the earth moves underneath it and the debris comes down here."*

Stan kind of chuckled. *"Well there you have it. It looks like we will be seeing some ash and we may be able to collect some and have it as a..."*

Again Mr. Perry yelled angrily. *"Stan, you don't understand! Ash is more dense than dirt. It is acidic, it weighs more. Not only is ash coming here, it will create breathing problems, darkness....our way of life is changed forever! Just twelve inches of ash on a house weighs enough to.."*

Suddenly there was a pause and Stan spoke up. *"We are sorry but it seems we lost Mr. Perry who is a geologist on Mount Hood. He was concerned that some of the ash might be coming here. If you are just joining us..."*

Robert turned to Sydney. "He was telling the truth and I know they deliberately cut him off. He was about to say that just twelve inches of ash can crush a house because it is so dense and heavy."

Sydney turned to Robert. "Switch the TV to channel 12."

Robert grabbed the controller and changed the channel.

"Here is what we know so far, our network affiliate based out of Denver Colorado reported to our station that Yellowstone had erupted about 3:24 AM this morning Pacific time and we have had no communication with that affiliate since 3:45AM this morning about twenty minutes after they reported the eruption. Satellite images from NASA currently show that a cloud of ash is scattered from Canada to the North, Idaho to the West, New Mexico to the South, and Iowa to the East. This is just a little over four hours after the first report of the eruption."

Just at that moment there was a loud crash from outside of the house but the impact of whatever it was shook the house like a strong earthquake. Seconds later a scream could be heard from outside the house as both Sydney and Robert rushed to the window in Rylee's room to see what the commotion was out front of the house. Both of them looked out on to the street from the second story window but could see nothing outside but a black, dark cloud and both of them rushed downstairs to open the front door to get a better look at what was happening outside.

Robert paused to open the door just long enough for Sydney to finish putting on a white robe she had grabbed on the way down the stairs, opened the door and stepped out on to the wooden front porch. The dark haze seen from the window above was beginning to clear and through the haze both of them could make out a five to six foot tall rock buried in the street in front of their house.

"A meteor came down?" Sydney asked.

"No, I don't think so. I think it is a giant volcanic rock from the volcano." Robert said.

As both of them looked up they could see the sky was filled with streaks from other large rocks and debris raining down from the sky. As the haze cleared even more you could see there were thousands of them in the sky for as far as you could see. Behind all the streaks coming down looked like a beautiful red colored sunset. Sydney thought about what a great picture the sunset made and then suddenly snapped back into reality and remembered it was now only about 8:30 in the morning. Her and Roberts attention to the sky was interrupted by Claire their next door neighbor dressed in her bath robe screaming.

"My husband is gone! My husband is gone!" Claire screamed in a panicked state.

"Where?" screamed Sydney back.

"Under that rock! Under that rock, Oh my."

In Claire's hysterics every word she said after that were not understood by Robert but as he neared the rock he could feel the heat and see parts of a Smart Car protruding from the far side. He could also see that the rock was embedded into the street in front of their house. Only the front grill, bumper and headlights on the ground were all he could find of the small car. The occupant or occupants were now somewhere under the rock below the level of the street.

Robert turned around and could see Sydney with her arms around Claire. Sydney seemed short next to the tall petite blonde who could barely stand by herself and seemed to be going into shock. Sydney who was only about 5' 4" could barely hold up the over 6 foot tall

Claire and struggled to walk her into the garage where Claire's twelve year old son Thomas grabbed a folding camp chair and opened it up for his mother to sit in.

As Sydney reached the chair she dropped Claire into it and then seemed relieved it was over. Sydney put her hands on her knees to take a quick breath as Robert ran into the garage hoping another rock wasn't targeted at him.

Claire screamed again. "We have to call 911! We have to save Greg!"

"Mom I called and I called no one is answering 911!" Thomas yelled.

Robert grabbed Sydney's shoulder. She looked at Robert and locked eyes while he shook his head in a no direction. Sydney caught on and immediately knew he meant that Greg was gone. Knowing the state that Claire was in he felt it was the wrong time to announce that calling 911 was not going to save Greg and he was gone.

Thomas however ran out of the garage hovering low while moving quickly out in to the street worrying another rock would hit him as he walked closer to the rock embedded in the street. A few moments later, he came back running back in to the garage.

"Mom, mom. Dad is dead! Dad is dead! I cannot believe this. The car is smashed! I mean the car is literally gone!" Thomas yelled.

Robert looked at Thomas and Robert slowly lowered his head and shook it no while holding up his index finger in front of his mouth gesturing that his mother knew and he should stop. Thomas locked eyes with Robert and then moved his head up and down in a yes motion and then got a frown on his face. He paused for a moment, started to tear up and then ran in to the house screaming. This alerted Claire's other two kids Kylie who was ten years old and Jillian who was six years old who came running out to their mother wanting to know what was wrong.

Suddenly Sydney started walking away.

"Where are you going Syd?" Robert asked.

"Did you forget about Rylee?" Sydney snapped back.

Robert followed Sydney out of the garage and back to the house. Rylee had her pacifier in her mouth and was holding her favorite blanket against the side of her head just standing in front of the small little window next to the door staring out. She seemed to be in a trance staring at the rock in the middle of the road oblivious to her parents walking up the steps.

As soon as the two of them walked in the door, Rylee looked at Robert. "Momma Daddyyy...I think the street got an eye-ya"

She could not say. "ouie." She said, "eye-ya" instead.

Sydney scooped up Rylee. "It sure did!"

For the next hour or so Sydney and Robert made breakfast and watched the news. It seemed like a repeat of the same news every fifteen minutes. Nothing new seemed to be reported. Occasionally a rock could be heard falling nearby or an impact sound from outside could be heard. Each time they showed the satellite view of the black cloud in the middle of the United States it seemed to be getting bigger and bigger. It also seemed to have stopped stretching to the west and south and started to stretch to the east. After a while or so the sky started having less and less streaking and it was turning out to be a nice day outside.

Robert looked outside and a fire truck was outside of their house and several fireman were looking at the rock embedded in to the street poking it with a fire poker and trying to push the rock over. Robert could also see Claire talking to a fireman and the fireman pointing toward the ground next to the huge rock.

Robert and Sydney both turned around because they again heard the audible tones for an emergency alert start emanating from TV. Sydney who had been in the kitchen was drying her hands sat down and relaxed on the couch with a towel wiping her hands to watch the emergency alert in the living room. Already she felt like the weight of the world was on her shoulders.

A little late for the emergency alert Robert thought to himself.

"Shouldn't they have had one of those for the falling rocks all over town?" Robert said to Sydney while they listened to the broadcast to start.

"This is the Emergency Broadcast System. This is not a test. Local, state and federal authorities in your area have determined that this message should be broadcast to all residents of the State of Oregon. At approximately 3:30AM Yellowstone a volcano erupted sending plumes of ash and debris throughout the central United States and Oregon. Residents are asked to shelter in place and not venture outside unless it is necessary until 4PM Pacific Standard Time.

Please call your local emergency number or 911 if you have an emergency or are in need of medical assistance. Please stay tuned to this station as messages will be updated if the situation changes or you need to take additional steps to ensure your safety."

The newscasters then came back on analyzing the message. Robert turned the sound down.

"Guess I will call into work today and let them know

I won't be coming in."

At that moment Robert's phone vibrated and he looked at the incoming text. The text was from John Miller, his boss at the office saying that the office would be closed today due to the volcano. He decided that he didn't want to risk everyone's safety trying to drive to work with rocks falling down.

As Robert looked at the TV again he could see a list of streets and highways that were closed because rocks and debris had fallen and damaged the streets or directly on trucks or other vehicles. They then viewed a camera which was on top of the KOIT Tower in downtown Portland. From the view from the camera which could see for at least thirty miles Robert could make out dozens of plumes of smoke littering the city. The city of Portland looked like a war zone. It reminded Robert of a scene from the movie Black Hawk Down.

Robert turned up the TV again and the female newscaster was listening to a phone call from a viewer who was asking if anyone knew how the City of Boise was fairing. Her parents lived there and she was unable to get through to anyone there. The newscaster let her know that there was no word on any city whatsoever and said good luck to the caller.

A guest geologist came on. *"...Boise was about 440 miles from Yellowstone. Just right outside the 400 mile range where folks were probably obliterated instantly.*

The problem is that they are not out of the range of the mountains of ash currently falling on the city. Boise simply being so close that if you hadn't made it out of Boise already by some miracle, it's probably too late and sad to say. You probably aren't going to make it. I would guess that due to the amount of ash already fallen most of the structures in Boise have probably succumbed to all the weight of the ash."

The newscaster spoke sad and slowly. *"That's really too bad. We need to pray for those in Boise...and hopefully the callers parents found a way to get out of there. We need to get to Ted Michaelson who is outside of Fred Meyers in downtown Portland...Ted."*

Ted Michaelson was one of the better known newscasters and was best known for a his clowning antics while visiting morning show sponsors and advertising their products or services while humorously trying them for himself.

"Hi Stephanie, I am sitting outside of Fred Meyers watching as hordes of people are already stocking up on supplies. I saw one lady walk out of Fred Meyers with two shopping carts. Her name was Sharon and she had one shopping cart filled with batteries and one filled with bottled water. She said that was all the water they had left on the shelves. She also told me that her husband had called her from work and let her know he was on his way home and getting supplies as well. Apparently they

are both stopping at stores to stock up on emergency supplies because they fear that the disaster at Yellowstone might affect us here in Portland to. Here is another person with a cart full of batteries and gas jugs. Let's take a moment and see if we can talk to her...Maam...Sir..."

Robert turned to Sydney. "We gotta go to the store while we still can too!"

"You really think that we need to go to the store right now? You gotta be kidding me."

"I don't know for sure but I am certainly going to the store to stock up on more things while I still can. How about you stay here and I will go to the store." Robert told her.

"There's not enough crap in my garage or your bug out trailer?" Sydney complained.

One thing about Robert was that he had watched the first few shows of first season of the TV show 'Doomsday Preppers'. The first few episodes had taught him of all the different possible needs to be prepared for. These included droughts, pandemics, earthquakes, nuclear war, economic disasters, and even Yellowstone erupting. During every show Robert took notes and collected almost everything he thought he might need.

Sydney never really said anything much about it.

She would tell him that our neighbors thought he was crazy on occasions and mainly used his spending on things for survival to her advantage to get what she wanted.

Robert had spent over seventy thousand dollars on preparing. Originally his plan was to have just one year of food stored away. He started with getting canned foods and other things. Then it went to two years using five gallon buckets of food, then it went to three years buying buckets of freeze dried foods that would store for twenty-five years or more.

After he had acquired what he thought was about three years of food, he started getting medical supplies, personal items, then camping gear, and then guns. After a while he had amassed fuel, generators, gille suits, toilet paper, Kevlar vests, thousands of batteries, and much more. Virtually anything you needed to live on for three years or more.

When he was done with that he started upgrading by buying portable solar panels, HAM radios, fully rechargeable gear, night vision equipment, expensive water filtering and sterilization equipment. Next he got canning equipment, dehydrators, smokers, and even started stocking firewood.

Soon he had a huge stockpile and created a 'bug out trailer' to store two years of his preparations in. He then purchased an acre next to a creek near Bend, Oregon in a city called Sisters which was a small resort town with very few people to bug out to. He next purchased a mobile home to put on the property, put up a seven foot wooden fence, and then installed a root cellar in the ground and made the new root cellar look like a hill on the property.

If this wasn't enough already, without Sydney knowing, Robert had purchased fifty bottles of vodka to use for bartering. Robert and Sydney didn't even drink alcohol. He had also put together four seventy-two hour kits for his neighbors to supplement his own kits. His thinking was that he wanted to make sure he was friendly with his neighbors if crap ever hit the fan and it could afford him some additional protection.

"Go ahead, call me if you need anything." Sydney said as she laid back on the couch holding Rylee who was acting tired and not as she normally did this time of the morning where she was usually wide awake. Usually she would be in the corner of the living room where she had two small toy baskets playing with her toys.

Rylee acted sleepy and just put her head on Sydney's shoulder and rested while sucking on her pacifier not making a sound. It was obvious she could sense something was not right and kept clinging to her mother. If Sydney tried to put her down she held tighter and started to cry.

As Robert pulled into the parking lot of WinCo, he was amazed to see that there were no grocery carts and the line to get in the front door extended around the entire front of the building. This was something that Robert had never seen before. As he stood in line he overheard people talking about the latest news and mentioning that Yellowstone was a super volcano. Then he overheard a woman saying that a geologist on the news said this could get worse and this was a possible extinction level event. Most people overhearing her just shook their head in and smiled thinking the woman was crazy.

As other people passed by them in line, one lady was returning a cart and Robert asked to take the cart which she was glad to give. Robert took the cart and people standing next to Robert were congratulating him on getting a cart. A few minutes later a cart went by with bags of batteries, stacks of water bottles, soda, canned goods and cereal. The cart was so full that while the husband was pushing the cart, the wife was guiding it and picking things up as they fell off and putting them back on. Robert smiled as he watched the same items the wife had just picked up off the ground and put back on the cart fell right back off because the cart was so full.

It was an hour before Robert finally made it through the first set of double doors of the entrance to get inside of WinCo and enter the store. As he walked in the double doors a checker was posting a sign that said they were now out of bottled water, batteries, bread, matches, lighters, propane, and as he walked in the door the checker was adding aluminum foil to the list.

A few people read the sign and made a scene and they visibly showed their displeasure. A few threw papers in the air, others said choice words at the checker and walked out even after having stood in the line for so long.

One of the checkers at the door said it was 'hoarders' that came in early and cleaned them out. "Some got shopping baskets full of batteries and water." he said. "We put everything we had out on the shelves. If the shelf is empty we do not any more. Sorry."

Robert thought to himself, batteries are not what I really need anyway so I am ok. As he got past the main aisle where droves of people were blocking him in he rushed straight to the aisle with flour and rice in the large bags. To his surprise the shelves were already bare. He then decided to go to the canned aisle where there were lines of people and carts. As he put his cart at the end of the line to get into the aisle he noticed an employee pushing a cart loaded with bags of white rice to the last aisle he had just been in. He got out of the line and rushed over to the employee.

"Mind if I take some of these?" Robert asked with a smile.

"Be my guest mister. I didn't want to lift all these on to the shelf anyways." the employee replied. "In fact I was hoping I wouldn't have to."

Robert pulled his cart over and by the time he had picked up his second fifteen pound bag of rice, the box boy had been surrounded by other people and hands were grabbing bags of rice from every direction. Some people even grabbed the bags of rice right out of Roberts hands after he had already picked them up. Every time Robert grabbed another bag of rice another person forcibly yanked it out of his hand from the other side.

Robert was learning from his mistakes and as soon as the next person grabbed a bag from the other side of the cart Robert quickly grabbed the one underneath and threw it in to his cart. Someone else dragged the entire cart carrying the rice away and by the time Robert got back to where the cart now resided all the rice was gone.

It had become a mad rush and in the end even though Robert saw the cart first he only got two bags of rice. He decided he mostly needed canned goods anyway so he started walking back to the canned aisle. To his surprise again the line was gone. He looked down the aisle and found only a few shelves with cans on them and they were mostly for things he had never heard of. All the soups were gone, gravies, even the cans of vegetables were gone. He noticed several people going by with entire cases of cans in their cart.

As he walked down the same row he saw spaghetti noodles at the end of the aisle but all that there was left were a few packages that were half opened and the noodles were strewn everywhere. He walked back up to the meats and grabbed the last box of precooked bacon. Even though it was in the refrigerator section he knew it didn't need to be refrigerated. He pulled the empty boxes on the shelf and found two more packages hidden behind them. He grabbed the three packages of bacon that were left and placed them in the cart.

As he picked up a missed package of salami he found underneath the mess at the bottom of the refrigerated shelf he heard screaming from the next aisle over. Two woman were fighting over the last 300 package of paper plates. He approached the commotion and overheard the employee explaining to a manager that he was trying to restock the paper plates and both women grabbed the package at the same time and decided it was worth fighting over. In the end each woman's husbands grabbed their wives off the other and the paper plates wound up in the hands of a man not even involved who grabbed them and ran.

Robert started getting scared and when he saw there wasn't even toilet paper or paper towels left on the shelves he decided to cut his losses and go check out with what he had. He was only able to move up three aisles from the back of the store because the line to check out extended half way through the store. Most of those in the front of the lines had more than one cart all filled with about as much as you could place in them or stack up.

As he waited Robert witnessed several people grab items out of other peoples carts when they weren't looking or collect items that fell off overloaded carts without telling the person who lost the item. It was shear madness and the level of noise and yelling was almost maddening. As Robert was in line he saw an employee come out with a few cases of Cream of Mushroom Soup in cans. Robert left his cart and grabbed a whole case before the employee could even reach the canned food aisle. When he returned to his cart he realized that his cart had been ransacked and he only had his two bags of rice left in there.

A man just a few carts up in a line next to him seemed to have the same items that were just in his cart a few minutes ago included exactly four boxes of precooked bacon but Robert didn't want to make a scene. It took about an hour to get up to the checkout line to finally purchase his two bags of rice and twelve cans of soup.

Chapter 2: Deciding It Was Time To Go.

Robert finally made it out of the parking lot of the store when his cell phone rang. It was Sydney wanting to know what was taking so long. Robert told her the story of what had happened at the store and she told him she needed to put gas in her car. She was concerned because there was pretty much an hour or more wait to fill up at every gas station according to the news reports. She said she had gone to the closest station by the house and was in line but at least forty people had walked up with gas cans and blocked cars from entering.

Robert looked down at his watch and saw it was only a little past noon. A little past noon he thought to himself and already there is this much chaos.

"What is tomorrow going to look like if it is already a little past noon?" he repeated to himself several times.

As he got in to the traffic jam on Pacific Highway to head back to his house which was about seven miles away, he noticed the sky was starting to turn red and it looked like it was starting to get dark outside. So dark in fact the people driving on the road were starting to turn on their headlights.

Robert picked up his cell phone. He dialed Sydney

back.

"I think it's time to get the bug out trailer. At least have it close to home." Robert told her.

"I thought you would have done that already. I think you're right though. All those times that I thought that you were a crazy Doomsday Prepper TV show fanatic, well I may have to eat those words. I am sorry. Go get it! We need it now." she said.

It took Robert forty-five more minutes to pull into the trailer storage lot where he stored the trailer. It took him another ten minutes or so to pull up to the hitch. No one was there to guide him so he had to get out every minute or so to see how close he was to the hitch and make adjustments. Finally, he was close enough and turned the jack until the hitch covered the ball on the back of his Honda Pilot. He removed the 4x4 pieces of wood keeping the trailer from moving and hooked up the 6x12 trailer and started pulling away.

Several years earlier Robert continued to watch every season of the TV show called 'Doomsday Preppers'. In that time he had saved about a year of food storage but had no idea how many bad things might happen or how many things he needed to prepare for. He learned that stores used a program called 'Just In Time (JIT)' delivery so they rarely stocked more than what would normally be sold in a 2-3 day period. He also learned that even if there was a pandemic that lasted a month it would take up to eighteen months to get things moving again and for the stores to be restocked. It was at that point he made a conscious effort to prepare.

Robert had spent twenty five hundred dollars to buy an enclosed trailer and started spending about five hundred per month on preparing for anything that might come. He had amassed an incredible amount of survival and preparedness items in that amount of time. Pretty much anything someone needed to survive for up to three years including food, shelter, weapons, fuels, clothing, medicines, and almost anything he could think of that would be needed for himself and his family to survive any doomsday scenario short of the earth being destroyed he had collected and stored in that trailer. The only exception was water and only because of its weight had he only stored about a month's worth on board but he had enough supplies to purify about 50,000 gallons.

Close friends and relatives were always impressed with what he had all ready to go at a moment's notice. They would always be telling him how great it was at what he had gathered and had told him numerous times. "I know where I am going if the end of the world comes." Robert would always let them know that he had enough supplies for his own family and they would have to get their own supplies.

Robert knew when the doomsday came that being in or near any big cities including Portland was what he called 'bad juju'. About six months earlier he and his wife had spent twelve thousand dollars from their savings to buy an acre of land in the middle of nowhere near Bend, Oregon. Robert had planned to install a well and an underground bunker where he could live out any doomsday scenario all alone in safety. Completely hidden with his family from the rest of the world.

Unfortunately he never got the well done, he never got the shipping container purchased that he wanted to use for it, and he never got around to stocking it up and getting it ready for just this situation. Even so, Robert knew he would get his bug out trailer and go there before it got any worse. He knew in his heart time was not on their side.

On the way back to the house, Robert was listening to the news and the announcer came on after the latest news update. *"We have just received word that the president will be addressing the nation personally at approximately 6PM Eastern Time which will be three our time. We will bring the president's address live as soon as he begins his address."*

As Robert came up to the light that crosses the highway he was stopped by a line of cars which was unusual for this light. He looked around and noticed that the traffic was being held up in each direction by the gas stations on each side of the street. The lines extended outside of the gas station and on to the highway. People in cars were stopped as far as he could see. Even though there were three lanes, cars were stopped all the way through the intersection and cars in the far lanes were stopped with their turn signals on trying to cut into the line to get in to the gas station. Those already in line were blocking the intersection and were refusing to let anyone cut in the line leaving those trying to cross blocked. People were yelling, honking their horns, and giving threatening gestures.

All this was happening and it had been less than twelve hours since Yellowstone had erupted. Robert was sitting about twenty cars back waiting for the light to change green and hoping that the cars would clear so he could cross the highway and get home. He was about to call Sydney and let her know he couldn't get there because of the cars. As he picked up the phone he noticed a Sheriffs SUV turn on its lights about four cars back and start making its way forward by going in the opposite directions traffic lane.

As soon as the Sheriff got to the highway he parked in the bike lane exited his SUV and walked over to the first person blocking the intersection. He motioned to this motorist and all the cars who were blocking the intersection to move on and forget staying in line. Even though the drivers were cussing and yelling he told them very loudly that it was illegal to block the intersection and if they didn't move he would cite them.

An overweight man in a Mini Cooper was immediately in front of the officer and refused to move. The officer got on his radio attached to his collar. The man yelled to the officer. "I aint movin! I have been here waiting for forty friggin minutes. You can give me a ticket but I am getting gas!"

"You're not getting cited sir, you're going to jail!" the officer responded.

The man punched the gas after that and drove away flipping the officer off as he drove away. The officer smiled as the man drove off and got back on his radio. Robert realized from the officers actions and his smile that the officer actually had no intentions of arresting him. The officer just wanted to scare the man in to moving out of the intersection. Soon after that the officer was directing traffic long enough to allow all the traffic in Robert's direction to go through the intersection.

When Robert got home, he backed his silver Honda Pilot with the trailer in to his driveway. He then got out, unlocked the door of his wife's white Toyota Sequoia and backed it into the driveway as well next to the other SUV and trailer. Without letting Sydney know he was home he started loading up the food storage from the garage and packing it into the back of the trailer and in to the back of her SUV.

A short time later Sydney opened the door to the garage and saw Robert had returned.

"Oh, I didn't know you were here yet. I have been working upstairs packing the baby. I will be down to help you in a few minutes." she said.

Robert said nothing and continued loading the cars as Sydney closed the door. He was busy playing a real life game of Tetris and trying to figure out how to put as many boxes of number 10 cans of food, soup, and wheat as possible in the smallest amount of space. Number 10 cans are the large food storage cans that only fit about six to a case and he had about forty cases to find space for. He then started packing the five and six gallon buckets which contained salt, rice, sugar, and wheat in to the trailer. After that he pulled the three carefully packed 72-hour-kits from the top of the shelves in the garage. These were packed in to suitcases with rolling wheels and had backpacking straps in case they had to leave in a hurry. Over time Robert had expanded the kits to include warm and cold clothing, several more MRE's than were needed for 72 hours, diapers, and thermal underwear.

Inside the trailer there already was everything they needed to survive with for about three years but Robert wanted to extend that amount of time as much as possible and include anything he could load on. He next went out to the backyard and started pulling out his fourteen gallon gas cans and bringing them out to the front yard. He had four of these and they had plastic fuel hoses similar to the ones you see at the gas station. He had last filled these up about six months before and put Sta-Bil gas preserver in the cans so the gas would stay good longer. The Unleaded Gasoline inside should be good for about two more years he thought to himself.

After he had pulled all four of the fourteen gallon gas canisters to the back of the Toyota, he went back and started carrying the five gallon gas cans which he has four of. He used one of the five gallons cans to top off the gas in his Honda Pilot then estimated that he had about seventy or so gallons left because he didn't think all of the cans contained exactly fourteen or five gallons which they were made to hold.

Next he grabbed the two five pound propane tanks he had in the backyard. Both were full and he placed them in the trailer next to the one hundred pound propane tank he already had in the trailer. He then quickly added up how many gallons of Kerosene he had in five gallon cans. He counted twenty-four of these in the back of the trailer for a total of one hundred and twenty gallons of kerosene. Plus he had eight one gallon cans and two half gallon jugs which he intended to barter with later if he needed to.

Not a bad start but it will only get us through two winters with what he had he thought to himself. He had the chance at one time to buy a fifty-five gallon drum of kerosene but could not convince Sydney to spend the six hundred dollars for it plus fifty dollars for the drums deposit. Instead of getting the drum, he went to work buying a five gallon can each month.

A year before the stores stopped carrying five gallon cans and he had to start buying a box that contained five gallons in two plastic jugs. Some of the jugs leaked and they weren't very good quality but that was the only way he could get them. The first one he had bought in fact had leaked and made everything in his shed including the Cup of Soups he had saved smell and taste like Kerosene. He had to get rid of all of them after that.

Sydney had refused to go in the shed for months because it had smelled like Kerosene ever since. However, for about the past two years he had bought five gallons per month. Well at least the months he remembered to go buy some. Five gallons had cost him forty five dollars. About three times as much as it would cost him per gallon if he had bought it by the drum all at once. Robert was mentally kicking himself now for not getting more because he would most likely need it now and it would cost much more even if it were available and now it wouldn't be.

Robert next got a folding ladder to place the roof

mounted plastic storage bin he would use to store all the suitcases as well as pillows and sleeping bags he would take with him. After he had fastened the storage bin, he next attached another storage bin which connected to the hitch on the back of the Toyota Sequoia. He began filling the back area of the Sequoia with more food storage buckets, shoes, his guns, and fishing gear. Robert then closed the back tailgate door and mounted all the five gallon gas cans on to the hitch storage bin.

As soon as he had finished, Sydney carried Rylee out to the Toyota and fastened her in her car seat. After Rylee was secure, Sydney loaded all Rylee's things including her stroller, baby blankets, diapers, formula, toys, bottles, snacks for the trip, and her Pack-In-Play which would be used as a crib next to her in the back seat. With the storage rack on the top, the back of the car looked exceptionally loaded.

Robert then looked at his car and realized that he had room in his back seat and the back storage area of the Honda Pilot. It reminded him of a game he had played when he was younger. His brother would imagine a scenario where they could only bring three things to a deserted island or some other far off place and what would he bring. Back then Robert would usually want to bring his baseball card collection, his bike and his Walkman cassette player. Or a variation that mostly included those three things.

Robert next grabbed a plastic storage bin that had been full of painting supplies to paint the house. He dumped the contents into a pile in the garage and went to the freezer and started loading all the meat.

"Why are you grabbing all the meat?" Sydney asked.

"It will just go bad."

Robert smiled. "I bought a smoker and wood chips and they are in the shed. Can you go get them?"

Sydney didn't know what Robert had in mind but went to the shed to get the smoker and wood chips. She had never smoked anything in her life but thought they would still need a refrigerator for the smoked meat when it was done. But she went ahead and got them anyway and followed Roberts instructions. As she was rounding the bend from the backyard she saw Robert dragging a generator from the bottom shelf of the garage. It was a small generator about the size of two toasters and she had never noticed it before. As he passed her Sydney read the box and saw it was a propane generator.

Sydney was never into his being a prepper and so Robert constantly bought things without her knowing. She knew he was buying things and when she wanted to buy something expensive and Robert didn't want to part with the money she had her argument ready. To get her way she would often bring up the fact that Robert spent money like it grew on trees to buy stuff for his precious bug out trailer or for food storage but when it came to something she wanted or needed he wouldn't give it to her. She often got what she wanted just because Robert didn't want her to suddenly say he couldn't buy anything else for his trailer or prepping anymore.

Now that they were definitely in a situation where all of his preparedness was going to benefit her, she was certainly happy her husband was one of only a few who had prepared. Robert was probably in the top 1% of the preppers in terms of how prepared he was, how much he had invested in prepping, as well as how many disaster scenarios he had prepared for.

As Robert was putting the generator in the car he heard Sydney screaming that the president was coming on the TV in just a few minutes. Robert started the Toyota both to hear the president's speech and to make sure cool air was blowing on Rylee. Even though it was only about 67 degrees outside the sun slowly increased the temperature in the car even with the driver's door opened.

As Robert adjusted the radio to the AM news channel he heard the announcer summing up what was known thus far.

"For those of you just joining us, we are waiting for

a news briefing directly from the White House. So here is what we know so far. At approximately 2AM Eastern Time a large earthquake estimated to be an 8.3 struck two miles south west of Yellowstone Park. About thirty minutes later at 2:33AM an 8.7 earthquake struck what is known as the New Madrid fault centered in Dyersburg Tennessee. Thus creating a huge area of destruction in Tennessee, Illinois, Missouri, and Kentucky. Some reports of damage have been reported as far as Arkansas from the earthquake. Approximately forty minutes after the New Madrid quake another quake registering 8.9 struck in the same area as the first earthquake just a few miles from Yellowstone which triggered a huge eruption. So far we know there is an ash cloud over 1,000 miles across and it has thrown debris all the way here in Portland....And here is the president..."

Robert could hear the microphone rattle and some feedback before someone spoke.

"My fellow Americans. This is the vice president acting under the authority of the president. It is with a heavy heart that I must tell you that the president boarded Air Force One and attended a fundraiser last night in Boise, Idaho. At 3:38AM local time in Boise, Air Force One was notified of the disaster in Yellowstone and it was decided that Air Force One should immediately fly the president to a safer location. Within minutes the plane in the air heading to the Cheyenne Mountain also known as NORAD.

Air Force One never arrived and there has been no communication from Air Force One since 3:38AM. As you know Boise was hit hard almost immediately by the eruption getting pummeled by ash and debris spewed out by Yellowstone. In fact there has been no known communication from anyone in or around the Boise, Idaho and all the other cities and towns within 500 miles of Yellowstone National Park since just shortly after the eruption. At this point there is no confirmation as to the whereabouts of the president and I have assumed control of the government under the authority of congress and that is why I am addressing you here today.

We have so much ground to cover and I want every American to know I have consulted with and will continue to consult with an extremely good team of experts. These experts have been used to weigh in on some of the topics I will be addressing here today. First off I want to confirm that satellite images are showing an ash cloud over fifteen-hundred miles long and over one thousand miles wide. As of now the ash cloud is still growing in size and the atmosphere is moving the clouds expansion in an easterly direction over the United States and south over Canada. It is too early to tell how badly this will affect the U.S. and even the world for that matter. It will have a large impact on the climate worldwide for our immediate future. At this point Yellowstone has not stopped erupting and it could be days or weeks before we know the full extent of the volume of material blasted into our atmosphere.

Now let's address the New Madrid earthquake. The last New Madrid earthquake erupted in the early 1800's and was an 8.2. It did considerable damage to all the states surrounding it. This Earthquake was fifty times stronger than that earthquake and we expect to hear that it was much more widespread. We are expecting there will be a great need for assistance from FEMA in Tennessee, Illinois, Missouri, and Kentucky. Sadly we are already hearing reports that there are over ten thousand deaths in Tennessee alone and I expect this number will go higher as the minutes and hours go on.

Just before this broadcast it was reported that a 7.8 aftershock has affected this region and the quake lasted almost six minutes. Further increasing the damage. I want to assure you that this earthquake was predicted and FEMA is already reacting and getting as much support as possible in to the affected areas.

Next, I want to address concerns of many Americans throughout the United States. Many Americans in almost every city in the United States have grown concerned that these two events of today are going to become global catastrophes and they should be worried about food and water. Some have even gone to stores and cleaned out the shelves. Some have gone to gas stations to hoard gas and done a run on the banks. This is just not necessary.

These are localized events and you need not worry about having food in the stores and gas for your cars, or money in the bank. If you are not in the affected areas you should go to work tomorrow and pray for those in the affected areas. Give donations and aid if you can to those less fortunate as you.

I want to personally thank all the first responders and I want to keep the American public informed of what is going on as we get more information. Therefore, I will address the nation again tomorrow at the same time, 6PM Eastern Time. I pray for all those in harm's way and I promise you, your government will address any need or issue that might arise. I will not be taking any questions after this address. Thank you."

The radio switched back to the local newscasters after the newscasters from a local station in Washington DC accidentally came on.

"Absolutely incredible speech from the vice president. We learned a lot about what happened today. We also learned that Air Force One is missing...."

Sydney ran down from the porch. "So did you listen to all of it?" she asked Robert.

"Yes I did." Robert replied.

"So are we still going to Bend?" she asked.

"Absolutely" Robert replied as he closed the car door and walked away from the car.

"But you heard the president. He said there was no reason to."

"It was the vice president and everyone knows what the eruption of Yellowstone means. In a few days to weeks the ash cloud is going to travel around the earth and in a few more days block out the sun." Robert replied.

"But you heard him he said there was nothing to fear."

"He only said that because he has to make things sound okay so that law and order can be maintained. If everyone goes and does a run on the banks, buys all the food up, and what not the supply and demand will be crazy and cause inflation. Not to mention shortages of everything. Secondly, if everyone wants their money from the banks the economy is going to crash." he replied as he was carrying another box of food and placing it in the Honda's back seat.

"I guess you're right. Maybe we should just wait to go until tomorrow and see what happens." she said.

Robert felt in his heart they should go now but Sydney could be very convincing and she was not wanting to give up her comfy house to go live in a mobile home just yet. Especially if she didn't have to.

"OK, if that's what you want to do. I don't think it will hurt to wait a day and I can probably pack a little better to." Robert told her.

Sydney started to walk back up to the house.

"Where are you going?" Robert said with a smile.

"Back inside. Why?" she smiled back as she spoke.

"Rylee is asleep in the car." Robert pointed out.

"Oh, I guess better get her, huh."

"Probably a good idea." he replied.

Chapter 3: More Bad News

As the afternoon progressed Robert packed up cans of food and started smoking some of the meat from the freezer. They kept the TV on CNN watching as the death tolls rose and expert after expert examined every part of the day's events. Around 9:15PM Robert heard the tone sound of Breaking News come on the TV even though the sound was turned way down. He couldn't hear the news anchor but he read the news scrolling at the bottom of the screen.

"Air Force One found. President confirmed dead. Vice President to be sworn in within the hour."

This took Robert by surprise. He paused a moment then said to himself. "wow just wow."

Moments later Sydney walked in the living room carrying a laundry basket to put in the car full of towels and socks. She too saw the television. "Well that's too bad. He was our best hope at getting rid of Obamacare."

"Sydney, there is going to be no more Obamacare. There is barely going to be a country left. When this is over with we will be lucky if one-third of the United States and maybe even the world survives. Everyone who is educated knows it. There has been too much information on TV on what is going to happen if Yellowstone erupted.   We are just in the early stages."

Sydney raised her eyebrows and spoke. "Robert, there is an issue but I don't think it's going to be that bad. Two-thirds of the country dying? Right..."

Another bar scrolled on the screen. "*Stock Market drops 42 percent before trading halted.*"

"Sydney, it hasn't stopped erupting and I wasn't talking about the U.S. I was talking about the whole world. Yellowstone is pushing enough material up in to the atmosphere to darken the sun for maybe a year or more. There are almost eight billion people in the world. If you put all the food in the world in a great big pile there is maybe five weeks of food to feed everyone.

With no sun light there will be no grass, no grass means there will be no food for animals, no vegetables, no animals, means no meat, and it goes on and on. The stores are already empty and it's only been twenty hours since the eruption. That means what people have right now, that's what they have to live on for maybe years." he responded.

Sydney turned around. "Okay Mister Pessimistic."

She then walked out to the garage to get away from Robert. This was a battle she didn't want to get in with him. She knew he had researched a little more and probably had a much better understanding than she had.

Robert had studied a little more virtually every day on disasters on TV, the web, and in books. He bought nearly every affordable item for preparing for a disaster. Robert had lived every day of the past four years preparing for this day and she knew it was pointless to get into an argument about it even if she thought he was blowing this way out of proportion. Also in the back of her mind she was starting to question just how bad this really could get. Things were going downhill just so fast. Especially since the President was dead and he was over four hundred miles from the eruption.

Robert got up and turned the TV off and decided it was time to get up to bed. As he turned to walk up the stairs he heard shouting and glass breaking outside. He looked out of the window next to the door and saw four figures that seemed to be teenagers up to no good. This unnerved Robert as he was now coming to the realization that everything he had to live on for the next three years was sitting in both of the cars and a trailer out in front of the house. If either of them got stolen it would be a huge impact on his security and survival. Even if they only got broken into and some of the stuff were stolen it would be terrible.

Sydney came out of the garage and paused behind Robert looking out the window.

"What are you looking at?" Sydney asked.

"Some teenagers making a ruckus. I am worried about the cars getting broken into tonight."

"What are you going to do sleep in the car?" she said rhetorically.

"That's exactly what I am going to do." he said.

"Okay. Well have fun with that. I am going to get in my nice warm bed. Good night sweetheart." Sydney said, turning to go to bed.

Robert knew she was trying to dissuade him from going out there but he wouldn't have slept well all night knowing that someone might be breaking into the cars. Robert and Sydney lived in a small town right outside of Portland. The city was somewhat rural and had very little crime. Their house was hidden in the right corner of a court at the end of a dead end street. Rarely was there traffic or teenagers out late at night in front of their house. He knew however that he had to protect what he had from here on out though and he decided to sleep in the Honda Pilot and that way if they got anything it would be out of Sydney's SUV which held mainly baby stuff. Her car's alarm would sound if anyone opened the door though. Not only that, but if they saw him in the car sleeping the assailants might think twice about trying to break in.

He walked out to the SUV carrying a huge load of blankets and a pillow. Before spreading out his pillow and blanket in the back seat of the SUV he got out of the car and ran a bicycle lock and chain through the gas cans on the back of Sydney's SUV just to make sure they were safe and wouldn't be stolen easily while he slept.

The next hour or so Robert tried to get comfortable but couldn't. Around eleven thirty or so he again heard the teenagers outside laughing and another was bouncing a basketball down the street. He suddenly realized how annoying a basketball can be bouncing on the street. He sat back up and watched the teenagers as they went in and out of a house several times and then another house at the end of the court. He had never met any of those neighbors and they were the only neighbors that kept to themselves and never came out to meet anyone.

In fact the only contact his family had ever had with any of them was when the wife opened the door to yell at the kids next door because they were being too loud late one night about a year earlier. Robert continued to watch the teens as one by one they went back into their houses and the house lights went off about an hour later.

Robert had moved to the front seat and again moved to the back seat and laid down. Before he knew it he was waking up again only this time because it was so cold inside of the SUV. Even in his blanket the temperature was too cold to be comfortable. Instead of getting up to go in to the house and get another blanket, Robert instead leaned through the two front seats and put the key in to the ignition and started the SUV.

Immediately the lights came on for the stereo and he read the clock which read four thirteen. He jumped through the center between the seats from the backseat to the driver's seat and sat down shivering. The front window looked like it had snow on it. Since he was so cold he slowly turned the parking lights on so the dashboard would illuminate. He continued to adjust the controls for the heater. After turning the heat all the way up and changing the vents to the blow on the floor, he then turned on the defrost settings along with the windshield wipers so he could see out of the front window.

To his amazement the windshield wipers moved away the debris to reveal a car hood covered in white and grey powder. Everything he could see out in to the distance looked like it was covered in white snow. At least he thought it was snow. He thought to himself that maybe the volcano had created global cooling. Of course he was still half asleep and shivering.

A few minutes passed and Robert sat there kind of in a daze not really processing what was going on until he felt the first hints that the heater was starting to work. At this point he realized that he needed to go to find a bathroom and it was going to force him go out in to the cold. It took him several minutes to finally force himself to move.

He slowly opened the car door and expected it to be cold. But it wasn't. A white and light grey sand like substance fell on him from the roof of the car and he immediately realized that this was not snow. This was ash from the volcano. And not just a little ash. There was now two to three inches of it on the ground, his cars, and his house. A view in front of his car from the parking lights allowed him to see it was coming down like a steady snow storm.

He ran up to the front porch to open the front door but realized Sydney had locked it after she went to bed. The keys were inside of the car and the car was running. It was four-thirty in the morning. Who is going to be up he thought to himself. Robert scurried around the side of the house, unzipped his pants and started to relieve himself behind a bush in the backyard. About thirty seconds later as Robert was getting the chills as he heard a huge crash from his next door neighbors house and a cat howl.

Robert thought to himself. "What was that?"

He quickly zipped up his pants and ran to the fence next to his neighbor. His neighbor had also heard the crash too and had his lights on already and was opening his window to investigate.

"What was that crash?" Robert asked to the figure who opened the window.

"It looks like my aluminum shed just caved in. What the..." His neighbor shouted.

Robert's neighbor Harold was a short bald older man who was a retired forestry officer who used to work for the U.S. Forest Service and a former deckhand on the USS Forrestal.

Robert could tell that from the sound he made when he yelled that he had walked away from the window. A few minutes later both Robert and his neighbor were in the neighbors backyard with flashlights.

At about the same moment as both neighbors were peering over the now disassembled shed which was starting to get covered with even more ash, both of the men heard another crash. This was followed almost immediately by yet another one a little more of a distance away.

Robert turned to his neighbor. "Ash is really dense and the weight of it just destroyed your shed. This is bad."

The neighbor pointed his flashlight at the roof which had about six to seven inches of ash on it.

"If it's done that to the shed, what do you think it's gonna do to the house?" The neighbor said.

"Probably nothing good. The shed was weak aluminum though. Your house can take a lot more I am sure. I'm not going to take a chance though. I am going to get a shovel and get my roof cleared off." Robert said.

"No kidding. I am right with you." the neighbor replied.

Both men spent the next hour on their own roof shoveling the ash and dropping it to the ground. It seemed that as soon as the roof had been shoveled off on one part of the house the ash just accumulated again on the other side. Even erasing the foot prints sometimes in just minutes. It wasn't long before both men heard a huge crashing sound and a scream. It looked to be about two blocks away in a row of older homes. One of the homes had finally succumbed to all the weight of the Ash and a few minutes later sirens could be heard and blue and red flashing lights could be seen in the direction of the house through the ash falling down.

Robert could now see people following their lead a few houses away on neighbors were on top of their houses shoveling off their roofs. The message was starting to get around. He started to hear coughing coming from his next door neighbors and then Robert too started to feel like something was in his lungs. Robert got off the roof and opened up his first aid kit and put on one of his N95 surgical masks. He had a box of them and took them out and started handing them to the neighbors he could see outside or near his house.

As he was handing them out a police car with a loud speaker came through the neighborhood warning people to tune to the emergency broadcast system and to immediately evacuate their homes if they have not cleared the ash from their roofs. Robert went into his car and grabbed the portable battery powered shortwave radio he had and tuned it to the local news channel.

The Emergency Broadcast System was not activated but he listened to the radio personality talk about what you should be doing.

"Officials are telling us to stay off the roads as there are slick conditions being caused by the ash. Already we have heard about numerous crashes including one involving a fire truck in downtown Portland about an hour ago. Also officials are reminding all of us that ash is very dense and as little as four to five inches on your roof can cause a weak building or house to topple over. They also have reminded us that breathing ash is very bad for your lungs and you should wet a towel and put it over

your mouth and nose if you have to go out in this without proper breathing gear or face masks. If you are just listening to this broadcast and you have not checked your roof you should notify everyone and evacuate your home or office until it is deemed safe to go back inside..."

Just at that moment the radio host was cut off and the tones for the Emergency Broadcast System began to be heard. Robert hadn't realized it but there was a crowd forming around him to hear the emergency broadcast system.

His neighbor Jason who was just a newlywed and lived two doors down was there. Jason and his wife Sarah had gotten married about a year earlier and had moved into the neighborhood just before the wedding. Sydney and Robert had befriended both of them and had taken them out to dinner several times and they had come over for a game night once and for a barbeque on several occasions. Sydney and Sarah had really become good friends and they chatted daily though texts and shared things on Facebook, Instagram, and Pintrest.

Jason looked at Robert. "Looks like you're the info man now. The power went out a few minutes ago dude."

Since it was light outside Robert hadn't even noticed that the power was out. He was now noticing the crowd around him getting larger and moved under the protection of his garage. The crowd moved with him and he turned the radio up as loud as it would go.

"This is the emergency broadcast system with instructions and information you need to know. This is an actual emergency and is not a test. After this message please stay tuned to this station for updates and further information. There was a pause then a voice came on.

"This is the governor of the State of Oregon with a message of great importance to everyone. As most of you know Yellowstone erupted yesterday and it is a super volcano. We had some rocks fall from the huge blast it created and overnight the winds shifted and there is now an ash cloud extending from Oklahoma all the way to coast of Oregon. This is a danger to virtually everyone of us in Oregon and Washington as ash is very heavy as well as dangerous to breathe. In fact the weight of even ten inches can be enough to topple a building or a home. If you are in a home or building and you have not cleared the building's roof top of the ash build up please evacuate the dwelling now. Immediately. Do not wait for this message to end. If you must go outside, go to a car. You need to make sure if you turn on that car that you turn off the vent and turn the setting to recirculate only the inside air so you are not breathing the ash. If you must go outside to clear ash from a building or home, please take precautions such as using a breathing mask, respirator, or make your own breathing apparatus by wrapping a wet towel around your mouth and nose.

Many local jurisdictions are in the process of procuring masks to distribute to those who need them but these will be in limited quantities. We also need all citizens to stay off the roads. Ash is not only more dense but it blocks air filters and creates very hazardous driving conditions. It is both slick and hard to maneuver in. We expect the ash to continue to fall throughout the day. Good news is, the winds should shift later in the evening forcing the ash clouds to move towards the east overnight. Together we must be diligent and get through this today anticipating that we might get a few feet of ash in many parts of both states. This is going to be placing a huge burden on our emergency services and the National Guard which I have ordered in to service today. Please only call 911 only if you have true emergency. We expect many breathing issues and I am ordering all hospitals and trauma centers to begin to follow the states 'Mass Casualty Protocol' and begin setting up the triage centers as outlined in the protocol.

As we progress throughout the day we will continue to give further instruction and information through the Emergency Broadcast System. Thank you. This concludes this broadcast."

When the alert was over Robert realized that there was now over forty people in his garage including Sydney who had the baby in her hands. Immediately the noise level in the garage with everyone talking made it too loud to hear anything else on the radio. Robert remembered he had the box of N95 surgical masks under his arm and put the radio down and started handing them out. Jason put his ear next to the radio to see if he could hear anything else. Another neighbor which Robert had never met was on the opposite side as Jason trying to hear as well.

Sydney came up to Robert. "Guess this means we aren't leaving today then?"

Robert said nothing. Just shook his head no with a disappointed look and started to put on his face mask. He figured if he went back out and got on his ladder and started shoveling ash off the roof again people would leave his garage. It worked except for the neighbors who knew Sydney and Robert well and they stayed in the garage listening to the radio. They were at least the neighbors Sydney and Robert trusted to be in their garage.

From the roof Robert could see someone on virtually every roof as far as the eye could see including Thomas, Claire's son who was on his roof shoveling ash off for his mother. He stopped and waived when Robert looked over toward him.

Robert started to think about a rule he had learned after the Haiti earthquake and in Argentina after the economy crashed. Things were pretty normal and civil until the third day after the catastrophes. It was after the third day when things started to really go south and the looting, riots, murders and rapes started. The preppers had a saying for it. "Nine meals to anarchy" Meaning they should be somewhere safe by the third day. It was written in many of the articles and books for preppers.

We are on the second day Robert thought to himself. I should have left yesterday. But of course my house would have caved in he thought. Glad I stayed to save it was his own justification.

Chapter 4: Bug Out Time

Robert thought for a second about a saying that prepper author Sean Odom had said in one of his books about prepping called 'The Ultimate Preppers Resource Guide." The quote in the book was "For a prepper, when things are falling apart, they are actually falling into place." Such a great quote he thought.

Robert had actually replayed those words in his mind backwards and forwards. Over and over. It pushed him hard to prepare for most any disaster. He thought he had prepared for almost anything. Even preparing a bug out location and thinking of anything he and his family would need for three years if they had no access to anything. Now, he was getting worried that he had waited too long and he might never be able to get to his bug out location.

His tactics for protecting his family in an urban environment might have to change. He never wanted to be in this position and be forced to defend his house against intruders, theft, and protect his family in the city. He had planned to be out of the city and in a much more rural area and in a place more prepared to defend himself, his belongings, and protect his family. His house in the suburbs of Portland had too many windows and to many entry points to protect. His entire living room was plate glass windows overlooking the Redwood Trees on the church property behind his house. It would be almost impossible he thought to defend his house if things got really bad. Robert was scared.

Another loud explosion from outside awoke him out of his thinking with a jolt of adrenalin. He knew it was another shed or something with too much ash. He hoped it wasn't a house and prayed no one got hurt. It reminded him to get back on the ladder and shovel the ash off of his roof once again. This time however there was very little ash. Robert also felt the wind pick up and start blowing to the east. He came off the ladder and it started to sprinkle. Normally Robert hated rain but this was a blessing at this point as it cleared the air very quickly of ash. Robert looked up and put his hands out.

"Robert! The power is out!" Sydney yelled from the porch.

"I know." Robert murmured to himself as he walked up the porch and followed Sydney into the house. "The neighbors told me earlier."

He heard the wind and rain pick up as he started opening the bins he was packing to take to Bend.

"Robert." Sydney said from the doorway. "The water was working fine right after the power went out but now it is only coming out in a trickle."

Robert said nothing again and just shook his head up and down. He found several flashlights, a propane burner, and a couple of one pound canisters of propane.

As it started getting dark, Robert thought to himself that there was just one more day to nine meals. He had started making a pile of the items he was taking out of the bins to use at home instead of his retreat. He then turned to the pile and started putting everything back in the bins except for the flashlights.

"What are you doing?" Sydney asked.

"We're leaving! Get the baby in the car. I am going to get everything packed back up again." Robert said.

"I have a pot of soup on the stove." Sydney responded.

"Don't worry about it, I'll take care of it." Robert said with a smile.

Sydney picked up one of the flashlights and went off to collect Rylee and her things which had gotten unpacked due to the delay. As Sydney came out with the baby she saw Robert walking up the driveway.

"Where did you go Robert?" Sydney asked.

"I paid Thomas a hundred dollars to shovel off our roof if it needs to be shoveled. I have never seen a twelve year old kid so excited in my life. Claire told me she might go to Boise to live with her parents after they bury Greg. But that will be a little while." he said. "I didn't want to say anything about Boise. I think she is in denial."

"Well that's good for Thomas. I was worried what would happen to the house if the weather brought the ash back this way." Sydney told Robert as she was fastening Rylee in the car seat.

Rylee was sound asleep and even moving her little arms to put the straps around them didn't wake her up.

Robert ran back into the garage carrying box after box of blankets, pillows, and even silverware. He next grabbed the remaining box of toilet paper which he had gotten from Costco, the remaining paper towels, and all the towels in the hall closet. By the time he was done, Sydney had gotten everything she could contemplate needing or wanting in to her SUV and had been sitting in the Toyota's driver's seat with her head down on the steering wheel for quite some time.

Robert knocked on the car window and startling Sydney. She rolled it down window. "You have to go to the bathroom before we go?" he asked.

"Just went. Let's just get going" she responded.

Robert closed the garage door and locked it with the key from the outside. He paused for a moment just to scan the house in his mind thinking of anything he might have forgotten. A few moments later he had satisfied himself that he couldn't think of anything else that he might need.

Robert then looked at the trailer, stopped to check the hitch, and got in his SUV. As he got in to the Honda Pilot he grabbed his HAM radio from the pocket of the door. Sydney was staring at him from her car and he turned on the dome light and showed the HAM radio to Sydney through the window trying to get her to turn the HAM radio she had on as well. She leaned down and picked up hers and turned it on.

Through the radio Sydney's voice came on. "Okay. Let's go. I am tired."

Not the proper way to use a HAM radio because she didn't identify her call sign but Sydney was obviously tired and grumpy. Even though she was tired and grumpy she was still doing whatever Robert wanted her to do and being a good sport about it. She knew Robert had studied, prepared and had gotten all the family ready for this moment. Even though she hadn't spent the time to do much of any of the preparing other than take a HAM radio class and pass the test over a weekend because Robert had asked her to. She knew whole heartedly Robert would guide their family to safety. Her husband would provide for their needs even when the rest of the world couldn't. She had faith in that.

Robert had the music going from the local country station but with everything going on his nerves were shot and the music even down low started to give him a headache. He turned off the radio and just drove thinking about the bug out location in Sisters. He pondered how he would set up the beds, how he would camouflage the cars, and how he would get things situated in the mobile home he had parked on the property. He was thinking about how much work it was going to be to empty the trailer he was pulling when he heard a crackle come over the HAM radio.

"Robert, did you hear the news on the radio?" Sydney's voice said.

"Nope. I didn't even have it on" he replied.

"Riots in Los Angeles and Chicago." Sydney told him.

"You think it's bad now. Wait a week. It will be bad here to I am afraid." Robert said pessimistically.

"I used to not really believe you but after I saw what was happening at the gas stations and the stores just hours after the eruption, I am starting to believe everything you said and everything you prepared for might actually come true. I feel so bad that I teased you so much about it. I love you." Sydney said as it sounded like she was almost about to cry.

Robert was kind of taken back. They had been

married for six years and their relationship had gotten to the point where Sydney really never said she loved him much anymore. Robert leaned over, kissed her and told her he loved her every morning before he left for work. To Robert, doing that gave him good luck. One morning Sydney hadn't slept very well and he was leaving early. Robert decided not to kiss her before he left. He felt like he had missed doing something important all morning. Later in the morning he got a text from Sydney saying how sad she was that he hadn't kissed her before he had left.

A few minutes later Robert and Sydney made it to the freeway. There were only a few cars on the road all the way to the freeway but even though it was ten thirty at night, the freeway was stopped with traffic. All the two of of them saw was tail lights as far as they could see in both directions.

He saw a few state troopers pass on the side of the road and an ambulance passed on the other side of the road with its lights and sirens blaring as they tried to enter the freeway on ramp.

"What I wouldn't give to own and ambulance right now." Robert said to himself.

It took Robert and Sydney over fifteen minutes to actually merge on to the freeway from the on ramp. They had been completely stopped for about two minutes when a man in his forties came knocking on Robert's window scaring him starling him so bad he had to catch his breath before reacting.

Robert rolled down his window about two inches.

"Yes. What do you need?" Robert asked loudly.

"Sorry man, but I saw you had some gas on the back of your car. I'll give you a hundred bucks for one of those five gallon gas cans!" the man said putting a folded one hundred dollar bill in the window in front of Robert.

"Sorry man, I need the smaller cans, and the ones that are full are 14 gallon gas cans and the cans themselves are $150 plus the gas and I need it to get to where I am going." Robert replied.

The traffic started moving slowly and Robert started moving while the man walked next to the SUV keeping pace with Roberts driver's side window.

"I gotta go!" Robert explained to the man who was no stopping.

"I'll give you two hundred!" the man yelled as Robert slowly inched forward.

"It's not for sale. Sorry." Robert said as he pushed the button to roll up the window.

The man suddenly ran to the back of the SUV

between the trailer and the SUV and pulled on one of the gas canisters as hard as he could. Sydney was scared at what she was seeing, but then started laughing as hard as she could when the man got the gas tank out of the holder, started to run but bounced backwards flat on his back with the canister of gas hanging then dropping on the assailants head. Robert had not removed the bicycle locks he had put on the night before from around the canisters to keep them from being stolen.

Robert seeing what had happened stopped the car, and started opening the door. The man seeing that Robert was exiting the car and that there was no way to easily abscond with the gas got up and ran just as fast as he could to get away. Robert who had no real intention of combating the man gave chase until he got to the end of the trailer and the man was well past Sydney's SUV behind him.

Robert then walked back, put the gas can back on the rack and got back in his car. As he turned to get back in the car Robert noticed the one hundred dollar bill the man had on the road and picked it up. By now traffic had moved about two hundred yards but traffic from all the other lanes was taking advantage of the open road and by the time Robert had gotten in his car and released the brake he actually couldn't move ahead because cars had moved into his lane and one car was actually half way in his lane and the lanes to the right he had moved from.

"Robert! The man is back he's coming up the right side of my car with a big knife!" Sydney screamed in a panic.

Robert started to think maybe he was back for his money, then saw the man in the rearview mirror on the passenger side. He was trying to cut the cable using the long knife as a saw. Robert reached into the backseat and pulled out his Glock handgun from the zippered leather pouch he kept it in. He had put all his guns under a black wool blanket on the back seat before he left.

The man with the knife was struggling to cut the cable but realized quickly it was useless. The cable was only a quarter inch thick but the steel cable was twisted pair wire and was no match even for the large knife. As soon as man saw the driver's door fly open and Robert get out he had already turned to run even before Robert leveled his gun over the roof of the car. By the time Robert had used his car seat to move above the top of the SUV the assailant had run away again just as fast as he could.

Again Robert got back in his car and looked down the road and saw there was about fifty feet of space. He then looked again through the passenger side rearview mirror to make sure the man was not coming back. By the time he got the gun actually loaded in case he really needed to use it, Robert was only able to move up about two car lengths.

Sydney had said his name several times on the radio and also stated the man was not coming back. The coast was clear that they could move now. Robert finally picked up the HAM radio and pressed the 'SEND' button.

"Sorry, I was a little busy. Did you see where that guy went?" Robert said somewhat out of breath.

"I think he is a couple of cars back. What do you want to do?" Sydney asked.

"Well we need to hide these gas canisters that's for sure. As soon as we get to the next exit let's get to a safe spot and put the canisters in the trailer. Having these out in the open is just asking for trouble." he responded.

"Shouldn't we call 911?" Sydney said over the radio.

"We could but then we'd be here a long time answering questions and waiting for them to get here and they are too busy I am sure. Not only that but I don't want the officers to start looking at everything we have. I got my gun ready now. Let's just get moving. Keep an eye out for that guy though." Robert said though the HAM radio.

"Will do." Sydney said as she found an opening in the traffic to pull into the right lane so they could get off at the next exit.

She held up traffic so that Robert could get in front

of her as well and lead the way. A few moments later they heard a honk and In the far left lane they could see the guy who had tried to steal their gas pass everyone. He had pulled into the gravel on the shoulder of the road when traffic stopped again and pressed the gas to create a cloud of volcanic as he drove past. He had the dome light on in the cab of his truck and put up his middle finger up at Robert as his older white Ford truck passed his and Sydney's vehicles.

Robert felt a little relieved knowing that the man was now ahead of their cars and no longer a threat from behind them. He had been worrying about the man staging a third attempt and wondering if the man had his own gun and some bigger tool to get to the gas cans. He had been wishing the traffic would move ahead more quickly so he could get far up ahead of the man or at least keep a steady pace so the man couldn't just walk up and mount another attack on foot.

About twenty minutes later they pulled off the freeway and into an empty parking lot of a McDonalds. The McDonald's restaurant was dark but looked intact. The gas station next door did not look as though it had fared so well from the ash. The awning above the gas pumps must have been twenty feet high and no one must have removed the ash since it was so high. The awning had bent over and the two legs that had held it up looked like two giant twisted egg noodles and the steel awning had collapsed into the center of the small food mart attached to the gas station. This in turn had caused the roof to collapse from both the weight of the awning and the ash which was on the roof and on the awning itself. The front sliding automatic door was stuck open and the ash pile on top of all the shelves was coming out of the building's front doors.

Robert was still assessing the situation when a teenager exited through the food marts door carrying a milk crate filled with items. A moment later a second person came wobbling out with an oversized carton of beer in cans. The weight of the beer was obviously more than the man could run with steadily. Both teens ran to the far side of the food mart and then ran down the road in the opposite direction.

It took Robert and Sydney only seconds to realize what was happening. The teens were looting the store. Seconds later a dark colored truck pulled up and two woman and two men jumped out and ran into the gas station.

Robert quickly went to work undoing the cable around the gas cans. He quickly opened the back of the trailer and shoved in two of the fourteen gallon gas containers. He tried to place the gas containers so they stood straight up and wouldn't leak any of their valuable liquids. A few moments later Robert heard glass breaking at the food mart.

Robert had no idea what was going on in the store so he ran to the front seat of his car, reached in to grab the gun off the front seat. He placed the Glock in the waist band of his jeans then went to grab another gas can. Robert then placed one of the other two five gas cans in the back of Sydney's SUV. There was no room for another one in her SUV. Since there was no room anywhere else, Robert grabbed a black plastic tarp from one of the plastic buckets in the back of his car and wrapped the tarp around the remaining red fourteen gallon gas can. He then placed it on the rack laying down and then locked it with the bicycle lock. You could no longer tell it was a gas can at all. In fact in the dark it looked like an empty metal rack on the back of the car. Robert thought to himself that the next time they stopped he would just use the gas in that canister to fill up the cars and toss it. He would have done it now but there was no way they had used fourteen gallons of gas to make it thirty miles. When they left the house both of the cars fuel tanks were full.

The gas cans on the back of Sydney SUV were already covered but as much as Robert wanted to place them inside as well, there just wasn't any room left.

Robert got back in his SUV and saw that Sydney's SUV was already turned around and waiting for him to go. He started inching forward and saw Sydney start to move behind him. Both of them had to hit the brakes as the truck with the four that had gone into the gas station food mart came peeling out in front of them and on to the wet pavement. He could see beer and soda boxes being held down by the man in the back. He could also see the man had at least five cartons of cigarettes underneath his other arm and a lit cigarette in the man's mouth as the truck sped away.

"This is getting crazy!" Robert heard Sydney yell over the HAM radio.

Roberts smiled. "Yes it is."

A few minutes later they were back on the road. Traffic was no longer stopped now but was only moving about ten miles per hour. For the next hour there was only a few times traffic came to a complete stop. Robert had always used his GPS to find the bug out location and had never traveled there without it. He played with the map application on his IPhone but Siri's reply kept saying, "I'm sorry but I cannot complete that request right now. Please try again later."

He looked and saw that he had one bar for phone but no '4G' icon was showing indicating he had Internet. Robert imagined that it must be because the power is out. As he approached Salem on I-5 it was completely dark. Other than the occasional blue and red flashing lights in the distance off the freeway there was no lights except for the lights from cars on the road around him. You couldn't even tell the capital city was there.

Just before Salem he saw the signs for the exit to Bend Oregon and Mount Bachelor and took the exit. It was the first time Robert and Sydney were able to travel the actual speed limit the entire trip. Robert thought to himself that at the rate he should be to the bug out location just outside of Bend in about two hours. A few minutes later he was following an empty flatbed cargo hauler and had to slow down.

Suddenly Robert saw the truck in front him slam on his breaks. Completely locking up the wheels to the trailer of the large truck. Robert did the same but Sydney who had been trying to cover the baby didn't notice right away and by the time she hit the brakes it was too late. She swerved to not hit Robert but couldn't avoid hitting the guard rail.

The truck came to an instant stop after hitting the guard rail and Robert heart the car scrape the wall and then come to a sudden stop with a crashing sound. When the Sequoia stopped the back wheels came off the ground and back on from the impact. Robert got out of the Pilot and ran to Sydney. He tried to open Sydney's door but the door was locked. Sydney sat covering her face and unlocked the door.

"Sorry, Sorry, Sorry!" Sydney yelled as she was crying.

"It's okay!" Robert said.

He let the door go and ran around to the other side of the Toyota, jumped up on the guard rail and then down to the ground to open Rylee's door. He checked the baby but she had not even woken up from the accident. Robert felt her head just to make sure the baby was doing alright. As Robert touched her head he could see her start to suck on her pacifier still sound asleep.

Robert closed the door and looked at the front tire which was obviously bent on to its side and rendering the vehicle unusable.

At that moment the truck driver walked up. "Everything okay guys?"

"We are ok but the car is wrecked." Robert told him.

"There is an accident up ahead blocking the road. No one knows what to do because there is no phone signal. Even at the house over here they said the landlines are dead." the truck driver explained.

Sydney got out and surveyed the damage holding her right hand to her forehead.

"Oh, crap. I am so sorry. So sorry Robert." Sydney kept repeating.

Robert put his arm around her. " I need you to get Rylee out and start packing her stuff. We are going to need to move as much as we can to the other car and do it as fast as we can." Robert said in a stern voice as the truck driver just stood there.

"Anything I can help with?" the truck driver asked.

Robert thought for a moment. "Yes you can. Can you grab one of the fuel cans from the back of the wrecked car and fill up my SUV as much as possible? I will let you have the rest when you are done."

The truck driver got a smile on his face, shook his head yes and went to the back of Sydney's SUV and started unloading the fuel cans. He was soon working on getting the funnel installed on the gas can as Robert opened the back of the trailer which had only about a foot of space on top of all of the items in the trailer.

Trip after trip Robert started loading as much as he could of the baby's things at the very top of the available trailer space. Then he started moving around items in the back of his SUV, stacking them higher to the point he couldn't see out the back window of the SUV but he had made enough space to put the baby's car seat in. Soon he was carrying the car seat and then strapping Rylee in the car seat. While he was strapping Rylee in the car Sydney installed the seatbelt from Roberts backseat through the back of the car seat.

Robert looked at what he couldn't pack from Sydney's SUV and started to wish he had brought some kind of storage compartment for the top of his car for more storage space. There was food, water jugs, fuel cans, clothes and much more that he just couldn't fit and might have to abandon. He decided the best idea was to get out a shovel from the trailer and bury it for later. Just as he was about to close the back of the trailer holding a shovel, a man walked up to Robert.

He was a scruffy man in his late seventies and limped when he walked. "Son, I know you probably need the gas your savin there but couldja part with some of it?" he asked Robert.

Normally Robert would have scoffed at the offer but now he had three gas cans that he couldn't take with him. "What are you offering?" Robert asked.

"What do you want for a few gallons?" the old man queried.

"Is three hundred dollars for twenty eight gallons of gas asking too much?" Robert asked.

The old man's eyes widened, and he stood there for a moment like he couldn't believe his ears. Not saying a word he opened his wallet and handed Robert three brand new one hundred dollar bills. Robert took the money and started pulling one of the fourteen gallon gas cans he was going to have to abandon over to the man. The man had waved his grandson over and the grandson took the first gas can and started to make his way to the man's truck.

As he started walking Robert felt sick to his stomach that he had to part with such a valuable item. But then thought about how he had just made three hundred dollars on what he was about to have to lose completely. He walked to the second gas can and started rolling it over to the old man.

The old man spoke up. "I don't know if you are an angel but you are the answer to a prayer. I know that you are sacrificing this. Here is another one hundred dollars. I'd of given you a thousand for ten gallons at this moment."

Robert picked up the last five gallon gas can that the truck driver had emptied into Roberts car. It contained about two more gallons. He looked around but didn't see where the truck driver had gone or why he hadn't taken the remaining gas.

Robert handed the gas can to the old man. "Well here, you can have this too then." Robert said.

"I am doctor Raymond Sinclair" the old man said. "I don't know where you are going but I am trying to make it to my vacation home in Sisters, Oregon. Everyone knows me there. If you ever need anything in this world come find me. I owe you one." the doctor said to Robert.

Robert's eyes lit up. "Well I am going to Sisters as well where I have property up on Cedar Road. I do need a favor!" Robert exclaimed.

"My vacation house is pretty darn near to ya then. What do you need?" the doctor replied as his grandson was coming back to get the second fourteen gallon gas can.

"My wife wrecked our car and the reason I am selling you the gas is because I have no where to put it. Do you by chance have any spare room in your truck that and think you could take some of the things we would really not want to abandon? Maybe we could and get it from you tomorrow? It would really help me out." Robert stated.

The doctor shook his head yes. "We actually have a little space. Not much but we can probably take some things for you."

"Thanks!" Robert said as his grandson was pulling up in a silver Ford F150 Super Cab truck right by where Robert and the doctor talking because the traffic had started to move. Through the window he could see an older lady in front and a younger one in the back. He assumed it was the doctor and the grandson's wives.

Robert moved to the back of Sydney's wrecked SUV and started getting the duffle bags with clothes. As he carried them and walked to the back of the doctors truck he saw the grandson filling the gas tank with one of the last fourteen gallon gas can. He noticed the doctor in the back of the truck moving items around and stacking other items to make more room Robert things.

Robert was amazed to see that there was almost a third of the back of the truck available when the doctor was done. As he handed each item to the doctor, the doctor stacked them in the back as he went for another load. Sydney noticed what Robert was doing and started to carry things over as well.

After they had unloaded about 50% of the items in Sydney's SUV, the doctor walked up "That's about all we can take. Hopefully that will get you by. My wife wrote down our address on this piece of paper and you can come get it anytime day or night." he said as he handed Sydney the piece of paper.

Robert put down the box in his hand and extended it to shake the doctors hand. "You've been more than helpful. I can't tell you enough. If I was your angel you certainly turned out to be mine." Robert told the doctor.

The old man smiled. "You're so welcome! Safe travels my friend."

"You too!" Robert replied.

The old man started to walk away and Robert turned to figure out what to do with the rest of the stuff in Sydney's car. There was still food, cleaning supplies, pillows, a box of toilet paper, sodas and Robert's guitar. All things he wished he had room for but would have to sacrifice.

Sydney walked up as Robert was surveying the content that were left. "What are we going to do with all that stuff?"

Robert shook his head no. "Nothing, we are going to have to leave it."

Sydney opened the driver's door, looked in the glove box, emptied out the coin holder, and locked the door to the car. She looked back at Rob who had already locked the trailer, and started the Honda Pilot. He started to inch closer as Sydney walked with a handful of items she didn't want to leave behind.

A few minutes later they were again on the road driving.

About ten minutes down the road Sydney Sidney sat up in her seat. "We've gotta go back! I left the keys in the ignition and I left my wedding ring in the door."

Robert had just passed the accident scene and had no traffic in front of him and just smiled. He shook his head and turned into the next gravel road to the left. Then he backed up and started on his way back. It took another twenty minutes to get back past the accident scene again. As he passed the accident scene he noticed someone had just pushed the cars involved in the accident down the ravine and left them. As he rounded the bend, Sydney's wrecked SUV came into view.

Robert and Sydney both could not believe what they were seeing. All the side windows of her wrecked SUV were broken and the contents of the SUV were completely gone. Including the rack on the back of the SUV and the driver's door which was wide open. There were at least ten people rummaging through the SUV. Parked next to the SUV were several older pickups and two motorcycles. In the back of the furthest pickup was a man standing, smoking a cigarette and holding a rifle looking around slowly.

Robert just continued on and drove by as the man with the rifle stared right at them.

"What are you going to do?" Sidney asked.

"Nothing." he replied and just kept going. A few miles down the road Robert made a u-turn behind an ambulance and followed it past the bikers and the trucks on the side of the road. They men were no longer rummaging through the SUV but were sitting on it talking amongst themselves and smoking cigarettes.

Robert and Sydney said nothing for the next hour of driving which was uneventful other than the occasional slow down of traffic. Sydney sat staring out the passenger side window. Occasionally Robert heard her sniffing and thought she might be crying but couldn't tell for sure.

A little while later as Robert was driving he started thinking about all the skills he had gained to prepare for this. He honed these different skill sets based on his own research and not out of anything he had read. When crap hit the fan he felt he would need good physical condition, self-defense training, be an expert at bartering, know gardening, be a good teacher, know expert medical skills, and most of all be able to adapt to any situation. This last one he was in the midst of using right now. It seems that already he had to adapt to what had been thrown at him and he wasn't even half way to the safety of his bug out location.

Robert looked to his left and saw Sydney sleeping with her leg up on the dashboard and wrapped in a blanket she had brought with her. He looked in the back seat and saw Rylee in her car seat. She was sound asleep but her neck was leaning over in what looked like a very uncomfortable position.

At this point Robert had traveled about forty-five miles from the accident scene in a little over two hours. Traffic had been moving at a steady twenty to twenty five miles per hour and had started to pick up again. Robert looked at the clock in the car which read 1:47 AM and started thinking to himself that he was starting to feel tired and he wished he had an energy drink.

A few more miles down the road he started seeing people standing next to a few cars on the both sides of the road. After he had passed a few more cars, a man in a ski jacket and hat was standing in the back of a truck with a cardboard sign that read, "Need Gas. Have $$$" written with a black marker.

Robert had seen a few cars on the side of the road throughout the trip but now he was seeing car after car. He also noticed several wrecked cars pushed off the road. He passed several people who were in the back of their cars or standing on the side of the road holding up empty gas cans. Some were pointing at them as cars passed. He had noticed that all the gas stations he had passed were closed or had signs posted saying, "No Gas!" or "No Gas Delivery Today."

As he came up to the next town he saw an older man with two card board signs which read, "1 Gallon of Gas $100. Going fast." and another one that read, "Menthol Lights Pack Only $40.00."

As Robert passed he saw the man holding the first sign with three one gallon red gas cans below his feet. He said to himself, "You don't see that every day. And not at 2AM."

As he passed the man with the gas cans and cigarettes traffic came to a stop.

As he stopped Sydney's eyes opened and she slowly came to. "Where are we?"

Robert looked at her. "About a hundred miles away."

Sydney put her arms out to stretch as Robert heard two distinct gun shots. He looked in his rearview mirror and saw the man holding the sign and selling the gas behind him fall backwards. He only saw shadows because of the headlights behind him but quickly gathered what was going on. A few seconds later a man ran by Sydney's car window carrying two of the red gas cans the man had been selling just moments before. Robert also saw a revolver sticking out of the man's pants.

Just a few seconds after that, another man ran by Sydney's window pointing a handgun at the man yelling at him to stop. The thief took cover in front of a vehicle pulled over on the side of the road several car lengths ahead of Roberts SUV.

Suddenly there was a flash from a gun muzzle coming from the thief who was taking cover behind the car. A younger couple who appeared to be the owners of the car ran for their lives ducking to avoid getting shot. They ran away from the car up the hill toward some trees.

"Get down!" Robert ordered Sydney as they

crouched below the dashboard.

The man chasing the thief fired back continuously as he ran up the hill and took cover behind a tree. Robert looked in the rearview mirror and saw another man approaching with a rifle and a scope. The man took cover on the passenger side behind Roberts trailer.

Traffic on both sides of the street was at a dead stop and there was a car to the left of the disabled car that the thief was taking cover behind. Robert noticed the man with the rifle behind his trailer get in to a shooters position on one knee and start to take aim with his scope at the thief who had just taken another shot up into the tree line.

The man with the rifle took a shot and the back window of the car the thief was hiding behind exploded. A second later the thief let go a barrage of gun fire in the rifleman's direction. Robert crouched down as one round hit the far right edge of his passenger side mirror, then another hit his front light, then another hit the front windshield near the top on the passenger side.

Robert heard two more shots but they sounded like a different caliber of gun. Robert and Sydney stayed ducked behind the dashboard for a few more seconds until they heard yelling outside the cab of the truck and the man with the rifle came walking by the cab of the SUV no longer leveling his weapon.

Robert and Sydney looked over the dashboard and saw the man who had been chasing the thief motioning to the rifleman to come. He was about five feet from the thief but the man who gave chase was putting his gun away in the holster on his jeans. As he did this Robert could see that the man had a badge on his belt that had been concealed by his jacket.

As the man with the rifle approached the now neutralized gunman, Robert could see he was also most likely a police officer and also had a radio and a handgun attached to his belt.

Robert got up out of the SUV with a flashlight and slowly walked up to the front of the car on the driver's side where the thief was laying prone, face up and lifeless. He slowly summed up the dark skinned man who appeared to be to be about 45-50 with graying hair. His head leaned over to the left and blood was slowly coming out on the street below his head. The blood really stood out because of the undisturbed white and light colored grey ash that was on the street below the assailants head.

Bullet casing littered the area around him and some even had smoke still billowing from them. The gun he was using was about three feet away from the body and almost an equal distance between the police officer who had given chase. Robert noticed the distinct smell of gasoline and noticed one of the gas cans was leaking and had most likely been shot.

As Robert leaned over to get a better the look the police officer who had given chase yelled at Robert to step back as he kept his eye on Robert and picked up the hand gun the assailant had used.

Robert shook his head up and down. "No problem."

As he turned to walk back to the SUV he noticed another SUV on the road with an older woman in the front passenger seat and two kids in the back seat trying to see what had happened out their windows. Robert looked around and saw people all over the road walking over to the shooting scene or toward the man who had originally been shot.

Traffic still had not moved yet so Robert passed Sydney still inside the SUV to go see the condition of the man who had been selling the gasoline and cigarettes. The man's box of cigarettes and the last gas can were being taken away by a teenager and his dad. Several other men were in pursuit offering money and other items to trade for the gasoline can the man had just acquired. An older woman was tending to the injured man who had been selling the gasoline while a younger woman was sitting on her knees next to her. Robert overheard the older woman say to the younger one that she was a nurse as she was trying to comfort the man who had been shot at least two times in the chest.

The dark blood coming out from the shirt on to the pavement coupled by the gurgling sound coming from the bullet holes in the man's chest were too much for Robert to digest. He started to feel flush and sick to his stomach and never said a word to any of them before going back to his SUV. He heard the sound of Sydney unlocking the doors and got back in to the SUV. Sydney immediately locked the doors again even before Robert had closed his door.

"Are they dead?" she asked.

"The bad guy is for sure. The other guy is not doing so well. He got shot twice in the chest where his right lung is. But he is still alive."

Sydney said nothing more and snuggled up in her blanket with her head on Robert's shoulder. Robert sat back thinking about what had just happened and suddenly reminded himself that his SUV had taken several rounds during the ordeal. He got back out of the SUV and walking around slowly looking at every inch of the car with his flashlight. He noticed his front headlight was shot but amazingly still worked. The very edge of his passenger side mirror was cracked and he noticed places on the trailers front side that had gotten hit but because of the low caliber of the hand gun, none of the bullets had pierced the trailer itself.

Robert got back in the driver seat of the SUV.

"Is everything ok?" Sydney asked.

"Everything's okay."

As the traffic started to move again a few minutes later Robert started to feel tired. Normally when he drove long distances he drank a Red Bull and listened to music on the radio. This trip he had done neither. He was now many miles from his normal radio channels he listened to in Portland and many mountains blocked any chance of getting a radio signal from Portland. He looked over at Sydney who was now snoring and turned on the radio quietly. He started scanning down the AM dial for any channel with the latest news.

The radio automatically scanned through the entire dial without stopping. Robert started turning the dial manually knowing that if any station had static the radio would bypass it. He first found a channel in Spanish and kept going. Next he found a station that was coming in pretty well. He listened for a few minutes before the announcer started speaking and finally said this station is dedicated to music for Jesus.

Flicking through one more time he stopped at 1340 AM. It was a news station but he couldn't tell where it was from. It was in the middle of announcing the day's top stories. In between the static he made out that the clouds of ash had made it to Washington DC and was continuing to move east. He then listened intently as the announcer said the Chinese had closed all their embassies worldwide unexpectedly. This included those in San Francisco and Washington DC. Smoke could be seen rising from both embassies chimney stacks.

Robert didn't think anything of it until the announcer stated that it is rumored that the Chinese government has severed all diplomatic relations with United States.

"In other developments, Hong Kong has asked for the assistance from the United States as ships believed to be Chinese have surrounded the island nation of Taiwan. Martial Law has been declared in the following East Coast cities because of looting and..." said the radio announcer.

Robert thought to himself. The Chinese are taking advantage of the fact we are in the middle of a natural disaster.

"...Chicago, New York, Oklahoma City, and a curfew is ordered for Boston this evening. The press room at the Whitehouse has been ordered to be evacuated and there is no word on where the President will be running the country from or how the president is traveling as Air Force One crashed in Idaho." the radio announcer continued.

Sydney woke up and started to adjust her eyes.

"What's the latest news?" she asked.

"The Chinese government cut ties with the U.S. and they are surrounding Taiwan. Probably since we are paralyzed from the volcano. And a bunch of east coast cities are either under curfew or Martial Law. That's all I have made out so far." Robert responded.

"The static is starting to give me a headache though Robert." Sydney told him in a groggy voice as she stretched.

"Okay." Robert said as he turned the radio off.

"I didn't say you had to turn it off. Just put on something else." She said as she sat back up and looked at Rylee.

Robert smiled and put his hand on her leg. "Unless you want to listen to gospel music or learn Spanish really quickly there really aren't any other options right now."

"How much farther?" she asked.

"About thirty miles to Sisters."

"Good." she replied as she started putting blankets she used to cover herself on the back seat floor and started putting trash from the front floor and center console in to a bag by her feet. She then turned to check on Rylee. She saw the way Rylee was sleeping and undid her seatbelt and turned around. After adjusting

Rylee's head and picking up her sipee cup off the floor and a few toys she had next to her she turned back around and put her seatbelt on.

As they passed into Sisters the first thing both of them saw was the local Shell station on the right. It was littered with cars including two Sheriff's Ford Explorers with their lights on and one of the Sheriff deputies directing traffic. Robert saw a sign next to the road that said, "DO NOT BLOCK THE INTERSECTION YOU WILL BE CITED." As he drove a little farther he saw another sign that said, "GAS, 5 GALLON LIMIT. NO CANS! CARS ONLY." He was surprised to see lights on and a generator running in the parking lot.

There were cars lined up on the street running on the side of the gas station but the police officer was doing a good job at keeping traffic clear and from blocking the roadway. As he drove farther there were cars everywhere and people stopped on both sides of the road. As Robert approached he saw another sign, "$10 PER GALLON, CASH ONLY".

"You going to stop?" Sydney asked.

"No, we can get more gas in the morning."

"Okay." she said.

Robert passed the gas station. About ten minutes later he was pulling up to his single acre piece of property. He had bought this property because it was right next to the Whychus Creek which was more like a river that ran right by the property. He had thought this would make a great water source if there was ever a situation where the power went out and the water stopped.

The property in Sisters was mainly secluded from the road with a wooden fence and a tree line hiding virtually everything on the property from being seen from the road. Robert had installed a locking gate to keep people from driving on to the property.

Robert's plan was to eventually bury a couple of shipping containers and make an underground bug out retreat. He had never made it that far though and had only gotten a mobile home with a wooden triangle frame built around it so the weight of the snow wouldn't cave the roof in. He had also installed a 120 pound propane tank and had two generators. One that used gas as fuel. The second used propane. He had originally bought the gas generator but learned that storing gasoline was not a good idea as even with gas additive called Sta-bil, the gas only stayed good for two years or so. Whereas propane, diesel, and Kerosene lasted for ten years or longer.

Robert had started his underground shelter with a small underground 10x15 root cellar which he made a sign "RC" and actually named it "Root Cellar". Sydney had joked with him about how original of a name he had come up with the first time they came to the property together and started stocking it with supplies.

In case he needed it, he had started digging out another secret room behind the 10x15 room which he wanted make at least eight feet by ten feet in size. Even before Sydney and Robert had arrived with more food, they had already stocked the root cellar with about six months of food and almost everything they needed to survive with the exception of water. All these were already in the hidden room even though it was still only the size of a small closet.

Sydney and Robert had taken a trip to Bend to either go skiing or spend time together a couple times a year. Normally Sydney would go shopping or take Rylee to go play while Robert stayed and worked on the property, work on the mobile home, or unloaded the new items they had brought with them. Sydney had made up beds in the mobile home but they had never actually slept in them or stayed overnight on the property. They had always stayed in a hotel nearby in Bend Oregon. Sydney liked the comforts of home and the Starbucks next door to the hotel. She had always joked that she only camped with a shower.

As they approached the gate Robert stopped and got out of the SUV. It took him a moment to find the right key and get the gate unlocked in the dark. He was careful to make sure that after he had pulled the trailer and SUV inside, that the gate was relocked. Before getting back in the SUV he threw a sign over the gate which then hung from a chain on the front side of the gate. The sign had a figure of a man with a shot gun and a dog and the sign read, "THIS GATE IS LOCKED FOR YOUR PROTECTION NOT MINE." Robert had always laughed every time he read that sign. It humorously got the point across.

Robert drove up to the mobile home and took out his flashlight to look around. The mobile home was a medium sized forty-five footer with a sliding glass door on the back side which exited on to a burgundy colored wooden deck that Robert had built. Another door exited out of the back bedroom on to the back deck as well. The front of the trailer had one small window above the sink in the kitchen and one large window in front of the living room.

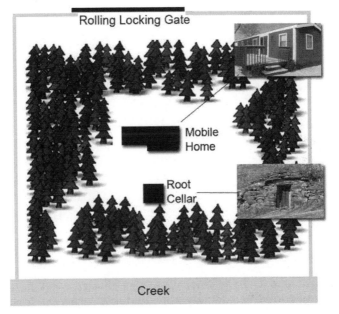

Robert and Sydney's Property

As you walked in to the mobile home from the sliding glass door there was a living room area to the right. The living room had a couch, a love seat and a rocking chair. To the left if you walked through the sliding glass door there was a small kitchen table large enough to fit four people. A small kitchen was against the wall and the hallway started between the table and the small kitchen. The small kitchen was complete with a gas stove, sink and a microwave. As you continued on past the kitchen going down the hall there was a bathroom to the right with a toilet, sink, and a very small three foot by three foot tub and shower. The bath tub was the perfect size for a baby but not for an adult to take a bath. On the left side going past the kitchen down the hall there was a small closet and shelves for towels. In the back of the mobile home there was a master bedroom with one twin sized bed and the back wall was lined with cabinets and drawers.

As Robert scanned the area from the cab of his SUV with a flashlight nothing seemed out of place and Sydney waited in the passenger seat for Robert to go down the other side of the mobile home, open the root cellar and get out the propane generator. It took him several minutes to find the propane gas connectors and hook it to the propane tank already installed behind the mobile home. Next he had to plug in the main electrical connector from the mobile home in to the generator. As the small 3,500 Watt generator sputtered to life a light from inside the living room could dimly be seen, then got brighter as the generator got going. It took a minute or two but the generator started running normally and the light inside the mobile home turned to a normal brightness.

"Robert, can you unlock the door?" Sydney yelled so he could hear over the generator.

Robert turned and could see Sydney cold and holding Rylee against her chest trying to get in the mobile home. Robert ran to the door. He had left his flashlight somewhere down by the generator and reached down to his pocket to get his keys but realized he had left them in the SUV that was still running.

"Left your keys didn't you?" she asked.

Robert smiled as he jumped up and reached behind a wooden beam several times but retrieved a spare key hanging on a nail. He unlocked the door and let both Sydney and Rylee in the cold mobile home.

"Is there any heat?" Sydney asked.

Robert turned on a small space heater in the window sill next to the kitchen table. When the heater clicked on he could hear the generator get louder and the lights dim slightly.

"That's it?" Sydney asked.

"They are not big generators. There is a propane heater in the trailer but I it will use up our fuel up too fast. Between the tanks we probably only have about 200 pounds of propane. I can run that little generator for two days with probably five pounds of fuel. The one in the trailer would probably burn that much in three hours. The little heater should work just fine. We have plenty of blankets and if we keep it going it should warm the place up."

Robert went out to shut off the car, lock it and bring in his guns and the suitcases they had for Rylee and themselves. He decided to leave the rest for in the morning after they got some sleep. He was exhausted but still decided he needed to go back outside and get the ice chest and put the food items in the refrigerator so they didn't go bad. He ran back outside quickly not putting on a jacket or shoes.

He tried to be quiet but the pain from his feet made him whisper loudly to himself. "Ouch, ouch, ouch" he said every time he stepped on a rock or twig until he got to the back of the SUV.

It took a minute to shuffle things around and grab the ice chest and run back into the house hurting his feet again.

He opened the refrigerator and the light came on. It was cold inside and there was a musty smell but Robert wasn't sure if the cold air inside the refrigerator was because of the trailer being so cold or the generator it was hooked up to causing it to start getting cold. Quickly he grabbed item after item from the cooler and put them into the refrigerator. He had to hold each item over the cooler for a few seconds to let all the melted water drip off each item before he placed them in the refrigerator. He didn't take the time to organize any of it as he was too tired and just wanted to get them in to the refrigerator.

When he was done he closed the refrigerator door and locked the front door of the mobile home. He walked back into the back bedroom to see Rylee on one side of the bed and Sydney on the other side of the bed sound asleep. He noticed Sydney had plugged in an electric blanket and placed it over both of them. The controller light was the only light in the room other than the little light coming in from the hallway.

Robert walked back out, opened the hallway closet and took out a blanket and pillow. He turned off the hallway light and walked out to the living room and laid down on the couch. He was cold for a few minutes as he kicked off his shoes and spread out the blanket. He closed his eyes and thought to himself how nice it felt to go to sleep.

Chapter 5: Things Just Got Worse

Thinking to himself how nice it was to be going to sleep was the last thing Robert remembered before being tapped on the face by Rylee. It was now light outside and Rylee was next to him in a pink onesee and her favorite blanket.

"Daddyyy, I'm hungwy. I'm gonna to stob to def."

Robert slightly laughed at the comment.

"Hold on Rylee, give me a second."

It took Robert a few minutes to wake up and realize where he was. He noticed how cold it was in the room and couldn't hear the generator anymore. Robert didn't know what to think since he thought the generator was connected to a full one hundred and twenty pound tank of propane. He got up and put on his shoes. He picked up Rylee and put her underneath his blanket to get warm. He then walked over to the diaper bag and got out a bag of graham crackers and Rylee's sippee cup with water.

The cup was still about a quarter full from the night before. Robert took off the top to make sure it was water and not stale milk. After verifying it was water he put the top back on as Ryee stared at him watching to make sure it was food he was getting for her and not doing anything else. As Robert approached her she stuck out her hand and took the two items. She didn't say a word just took a drink, opened the bag of crackers and seemed satisfied for the moment.

Robert got up and walked to the back bedroom and found the bed empty. As he walk back out of the bedroom Sydney opened the door and looked at Robert.

"I think we have a problem." Sydney said.

"What's that?" Robert said.

"My period should have started today. I have a sick stomach and my breasts are so tender I can't even put on a bra."

"Oh, wow." Robert responded.

"We need to find a pregnancy test?" he asked.

"You can if you want to but I know when I am pregnant." she blurted out as she passed Rob and fell backwards on the bed laying on her back.

Robert didn't know what to say.

"I gotta go outside and check the generator. Hold on."

Sydney waved him off in a way that told Robert she didn't want to be pregnant right now. He got his coat on and went outside. Robert checked the tank and saw the gauge on the side still showing that the tank was completely full. After checking all the connections he turned the choke back on and pressed the electric start button. Nothing happened.

Robert stood there for a minute and noticed that there was a pull string. He pulled the string about fifteen times until his arm started getting sore but couldn't get the generator to start. Frustrated he walked toward his truck thinking to himself he would try again later. He reached in his pocket and pressed the button to unlock the SUV. He pulled the handle but it was still locked. He pressed the button again and nothing happened.

"What is going on?" he thought to himself.

Finally he took the actual key and unlocked the driver's door and opened it. He tried the key in the ignition and not a single light illuminated. Thinking he must of left a light on, he pulled the lever to open the front hood and went to the back of the car and got the battery jump starter. This was a 12 volt battery that you could jump start a car with. He pulled it out of the back of the SUV and hooked it up to the batteries positive and negative terminals. He walked back to the driver's seat and turned the key. Nothing happened.

At that moment Robert was startled by Sydney holding her cell phone.

"Hey didn't you charge my cell phone all the way here?" she asked.

"Yes. Both of ours." Robert replied.

Sydney handed the phone to Robert and walked away. The screen was black and the power button did nothing. Robert picked up his phone from the center console of the SUV and tried to turn his on as well. Nothing happened when he hit the power button.

This was starting to get Robert concerned because it usually took two days for his phone to go dead and he had checked the phone several times to see what time it was and to make sure it was fully charged the night before.

"What is going on?" Robert thought to himself.

He started thinking about a TV show he had watched called 'Revolution' where an EMP had stopped all the electronics. An EMP can be caused by a nuclear explosion high up in the atmosphere or from a solar flare from the sun. In the 1960's the U.S. did a nuclear test in the Pacific Ocean and inadvertently knocked out all the street lights on the north side of the Hawaiian Islands because of the EMP it created. They later learned that if a nuclear weapon was detonated high up in the atmosphere the effect was compounded.

In 1859 the sun sent a solar flare that had the same effect and crippled the wiring for the early Telegraph system. Today the electronics from everything from cars to game systems to computers are all much more susceptible to an EMP because the electronics are so small and delicate.

Robert went to his backpack in the back of the SUV, opened it up, took out his laptop and tried to turn it on. It was dead. He then opened up the battery powered portable DVD player they had brought for Rylee to watch her cartoons. It was fully charged and he had a spare battery for it. He dug it out of his backpack. He tried to power it on. Nothing happened. He took out the battery that was in the player and installed the spare battery. Again he pushed the power button. Nothing happened.

He thought to himself, "What else can I check?" He wanted to believe this was all coincidence and then thought to himself, there is a handheld HAM radio under his front car seat which he took off the charger before he left. He and Sydney had each gone to a HAM radio class for a weekend to get their licenses and Robert had bought both of them handheld HAM radios for Christmas. He pulled it out from under the driver's seat. Turned it on. He heard nothing. Not even static. The display didn't even light up.

A scared feeling came over Robert. He had heard the reports the night before of China breaking ties with the United States and surrounding Taiwan. The U.S. is already crippled by the volcano. Perfect time to fire two or three nukes into the atmosphere and cripple us a little more. They probably sent a few more nukes at our air force bases, the Pentagon, Washington DC, and other strategic places to really hurt us too he thought. He wasn't sure it was China but the coincidences were too much.

"They probably had this planned out years ago and were just waiting for the perfect time to strike!" Robert thought to himself.

He grabbed an armload of things from the car and carried them into the mobile home.

"Couldn't get the generator started could you?"

"It's a little bit worse than that I am afraid."

"Worse?" Sydney asked with a look on her face that said, "What are you talking about?"

"Last night, China stopped all diplomatic relations with us. They just up and said that they weren't our friends anymore. "

"So what does that have to do with the generator?" she said in a more disturbed voice. "Or my cell phone?"

"I think China let off some nuclear weapons in the atmosphere." Robert said loudly.

"What?" Sydney said even louder. "Are you crazy? That wouldn't break a generator!"

"Sydney, it would. If a nuclear weapon goes off in the atmosphere it creates what is called an electromagnetic pulse which is known as an EMP."

Sydney interrupted. "And that can kill a generator?"

"Yes. In fact it has fried all of our electronics. Nothing electronic works. The car won't start, my computer won't turn on, Rylee's DVD player doesn't work, my HAM radio doesn't work, our cell phones don't work." Robert had to take a break so he could breath.

Sydney opened her purse and took out her calculator and tried to turn it on. It didn't come on. She took out Rylee's Sony DS which she played the game Frozen on, it too wouldn't power up. She looked around the house for anything that was electronic trying to disprove Roberts theory.

She finally picked up the flashlight and turned it on. "See the flashlight works!"

Robert laughed at the way she was scrambling. "The flashlight doesn't have any electronics. Just wires and a battery. It's only things that have computers in them which is about everything we use now to survive. Except that flashlight."

Sydney sat back on the couch with her arms out. Rylee who had been following her mom around the house jumped up on the couch and laid her head on Sydney's shoulder. Her blanket in one hand and her cup in the other.

"So what do we do Robert?" Sydney asked.

"Luckily I had known about EMP's when I was planning for doomsday and at the bottom of the trailer is a faraday cage with another set of HAM radios, and a bunch of other electronics. It's going to take me a while to get it emptied and find it but we will have some electronics soon."

Robert walked out the door. As he got to the trailers back door and began to unlock it, he thought to himself that he did have another gas generator in the root cellar and that was underground. He wondered if everything in the root cellar had been protected because it was at least two underground. The excitement was too much and he ran to the root cellar. He struggled to carry the gas generator up to the back of the mobile home. This generator had never been used and wasn't even out of the box. He opened the box and started removing the contents.

As he pulled out the pieces he noticed a sticker that

said, "DO NOT START WITHOUT OIL." Quickly he opened the bag containing the instruction manual. Oil is something he had not planned on needing. He scrolled through the pages until he came to page where it stated it needed one quart of 30 SAE oil. Robert ran to the back of the SUV and pulled out the spare quart of oil from the back. It was 10w-50 oil. It's all he had and he hoped it would work. As he walked back to the generator he was kicking himself for not planning and stocking oil.

He plugged in the trailer, filled the tank with gas, and then opened the quart of oil. It was at this point he realized that he needed a funnel. This he had put somewhere in the back of the trailer. He attempted to pour the oil in once but the steep angle and the location of the little hole for oil made it impossible.

He ran to the back of the trailer and started taking things out so he could get to his plastic bin of tools. It took him twenty minutes to move enough things and lift out the plastic bin full of tools out. He removed the cover and spent several minutes going through the bin but couldn't find any of the funnels. He paused for a moment to think of what he would have put the funnels under.

As he sat there thinking about it and standing inside the trailer he focused his eyes in front of him. There stood a shelf with three shelves. On the top shelf was toilet paper, the middle shelf contained sleeping bags, and the bottom shelf contained propane stoves and heaters. In between two of the sleeping bags on the middle shelf was a yellow pipe sticking out. It was the end of one of the long funnels and he had placed it between the sleeping bags.

Robert grabbed the funnel and ran back to the generator. It only took about two minutes to empty the oil into the hole and screw the oil cover back on. The oil cover had a measuring stick attached to it and Robert opened it back up to see the oil level was exactly at full.

The magic moment was here. This generator though was a little more primitive than his first one and didn't have an electric starter. Only a pull string. He pulled the string several times as hard as he could but nothing happened. He opened the instructions and noticed on the instructions that there was a power button.

"Dah!" he said to himself as he turn the switch to on.

He pulled the string again but nothing happened. He pulled it again and he thought he heard a sputter. He opened the instructions again. He noticed that on the front page there was a choke switch. Looking at the generator he found the switch and moved the lever all the way to the left. One more pull of the string and the generator roared to life.

Sydney ran out of the mobile home after hearing the sound, ran up to Robert and hugged him. It was a great feeling. They had power. At least until they ran out of gas. A minute later he turned off the choke. He then unplugged the propane connector from the generator and plugged it into the line connected to the mobile home so that they could get gas to the stove for cooking.

"Sydney, you better cook us some breakfast while you can. I think we are only going to run the generator during the evenings and when we need to cook. I will get some ice going in the freezer so we can keep the refrigerator cold during the day and refreeze the ice at nights." Robert told her.

She walked into the house picking up Rylee on the way in. Rylee had come through the open door outside and stopped to watch her parents.

Robert started to unload everything from the trailer. He first started with things that they needed right away or were the most valuable inside of the mobile home. He brought all of the long term storage and food items down to the root cellar. About halfway through unloading the trailer he was starting to feel exhausted and there was still close to fifty buckets, two hundred gallons of kerosene, five boxes of toilet paper, coolers, plastic bins, suitcases, sleeping bags, blankets, and much more to go.

Halfway finished unloading the bug out trailer.

When the enclosed trailer was finally unloaded it was light enough to be unhooked from the SUV and rolled over to an area by the trees. This is when first he noticed a man and his twelve year old son approaching. Robert suddenly realized he didn't have his gun.

"This is private property!" Robert yelled.

The man obviously was under dressed and wearing only shorts and the temperature outside was only about fifty degrees. The boy was wearing pants but only a tank top and rubbing his arms. Robert summed them up quickly and realized that these two were absolutely no threat and didn't even think twice about walking up to them.

"Our car died down the road and we need to use a phone. We need help really bad." the twelve year old said. "I am so cold."

The father spoke. "Hi I am Brian Tandino and I have a cabin about five miles from here. We went to go get gas this morning and on our way back the car just died. If you wouldn't mind giving us a ride or letting us use your phone I will pay you."

"Well we have no phone and our car is dead too."

The man got a confused look on his face. "Your car died too? This morning?"

"Yes! Do you know what an EMP is?" Robert asked.

"I have heard of it. I watched a few episodes of Doomsday Preppers on the satellite a while back. But Yellowstone erupted. It's not an EMP."

"That was three days ago." Robert said to the man. "Last night on the radio they said that China had stopped diplomatic relations with us and that they had closed all of their embassies worldwide. Then they surrounded Taiwan with ships threatening invasion. Then this morning I woke up and every electronic device we own won't power up including our car."

Sydney walked up with a plate of eggs and bacon.

"Who's this?" Sydney asked.

"This is our neighbors from a few down the road and this is his son. Apparently their car died this morning and they need a little help. Do we have more bacon and eggs?" Robert asked.

"We will in about ten minutes." Sydney replied.

Robert invited the two cold strangers into the house. It was cold in the house still but Robert handed each of them a blanket from the couch. The little boy went over to the space heater which Sydney had moved to the kitchen table and sat on a chair in front of it. Sydney placed a plate of eggs and bacon in front of the boy. Robert picked up some of the things in the living room to clean up including two of his guns and moved them to the back room. After he got in the back room out of view he took his Glock 9MM hand gun and put it in his pants and put his shirt over it to conceal it. He then grabbed a pair of sweat pants and a sweatshirt.

By the time he got back the entire plate of food given to both guests were already gone. Both were drinking water that Sydney had given to them and the little boy was teaching Rylee how to give high fives.

"I don't have any warm clothes that will fit your son but I do have warmer clothes that will fit you sir. We don't mind watching your son if you need. If you want to walk back home and then come back with some clothes for him I am fine with that. We'll take care of him." Robert said to his father.

The man paused for a minute thinking about it and realized that there wasn't too many other choices.

"Five miles is pretty far to walk. I probably won't be back until later tonight. I will probably ride my bike back and bring his bike back with me." the man said. "Trevor are you alright with staying here?"

Trevor looked at his dad and shook his head yes and put his chin on the table and his hands toward the heater on the back of the table.

Sydney handed the man a water bottle full of water and the man put on the sweat pants and sweat shirt Robert had given him and opened the door to leave.

"Good luck. He'll be fine here." Robert said as he handed the man two granola bars for the trip.

"I can't thank you guys enough!" Brian said to everyone. "Trevor you be good I will be back as quick as I can."

Brian slowly walked out the door to get back to his

house and slowly jogged up the dirt road to the front gate. Robert and Sydney didn't know it right then, but they would never see this man ever again.

Robert finished eating and found a bag of Jolly Rancher candies and gave them to Trevor. He was happy to take them. Robert also noticed he was pretty bored and gave the boy some computer paper and pens to draw with.

Then Robert went out to finish sorting all the items in the root cellar. At first it was somewhat overwhelming because Robert had so much more items than he had shelves for. He realized that they only had about one hundred and fifty rolls of toilet paper. He slowly took the rags he had brought and started cutting them into 5x3 inch strips.

He then took two empty buckets to the creek and filled them up with water and carried them back into the mobile home and placed them in the bathroom. He then went back outside and brought in the bucket of cut up strips. He explained to Sydney how they needed to save toilet paper and to only use toilet paper when they had to go number 2. If she just had to wipe after going pee then to use the little strips and save them. He would wash them in the creek every week.

Sydney surprisingly understood and thought it was a good idea. She was glad Robert had brought in water so they could flush the toilet as well. She dreaded having to go outside to use the outhouse to go to the bathroom. She was exceptionally worried now to because she had already had to go to the bathroom three times this morning and it was only going to get worse.

Sydney looked out the window and yelled for Robert.

"Robert! Someone is out front!"

Robert ran to the side of the house to see who was out front. It was a man and woman with backpacks.

"This is private property. What do you want?" Robert yelled to the two.

These were not like the other two from early. They were clearly wearing warm clothes and the woman was taking cover behind a tree.

"Robert, the girl has a gun!" she yelled to Robert.
Robert turned and could see Sydney in the window holding the .22 rifle. She had used this gun several times when they had visited.

"Drop the gun! We see you with the gun!" Robert said.

Robert had his Glock in his hand and was taking cover behind the side of the trailer.

The man with the woman yelled, "We are not here to cause any trouble. Just looking for something to eat."

"Drop the gun and we'll talk." Robert yelled back.

Sydney startled him when she came up behind him carrying the rifle.

A few seconds later the rifle the two were carrying was thrown in front of them.

"Don't come any further!" Robert yelled. I will get you some food.

Robert ran in to the mobile home quickly and grabbed two MRE's from one of the bins and a couple of granola bars. He placed them in a gallon zip lock bag and came back out.

"I am throwing you a bag of food." Robert yelled. At this point he couldn't see the man or the woman. He threw the bag and the woman came out to pick it up. "This is it? have anymore we need go another twenty miles!"

A second later the man spoke from behind Robert and Sydney holding a handgun out. Sydney was scared turned around quickly and without thinking and fired her rifle. The bullet struck the man in the chest just below his right collar bone. The gun the man was holding dropped to the ground. He stumbled out to the front of the trailer toward the woman holding his wound.

The woman ran toward him then changed directions toward the gun. Robert yelled, "If you grab that gun your getting shot!". The woman changed course again holding her hands up, she ran in a complete circle and then into the tree line. The man who was shot followed the woman until they were out of view.

Sydney was in shock and couldn't believe what she had just done. Robert ran out ducking down and picked up the rifle the woman had thrown down as he ran to a tree for cover. He leveled the rifle looking to see if he could see either of the two. He didn't see either one.

He quickly changed positions and ran to another tree, then another until he was through the tree line. He watched as the woman helped push the man over the gate and on to the street. There was a shopping cart out front and the woman lifted the man and held his head as he laid down in the cart with his front legs sticking out the front. She took off her backpack hang it from the shopping carts handle and then started running down the road toward town.

Robert walked back to the mobile home with both guns in his hands. He stopped to pick up the bag of food and carried it back in to the mobile home. When he walked into the living room Sydney was crying on the couch. To the left of her was Trevor patting her back and Rylee was on the other side mimicking Trevor and patting her mom's back and smiling.

Robert scooped up Rylee and put her on his lap. He put his arm around Sydney.

"It's O.K. you did good. They are gone and had you not shot him who knows what he would have done to us. They were definitely up to no good and wanted to rob us and maybe even kill us!"

Sydney didn't say anything. She just sat there crying with her hands over her face. Robert stayed there for a few minutes hugging her. After a while Robert decided to give her some space and kissed her and went outside.

Robert went to the root cellar and opened the bucket he had for safety items. He took out the four bear bells he had inside of the bucket. He needed to make an early warning system and bear bells are good for just that purpose. He opened two more bins looking for the personal items. He found two rolls of dental floss. He then took a box of nails and a hammer out to the end of the tree line. He started hammering in nails in each of the trees about four inches from the ground. After he hammered each nail in about an inch he bent the other side over to make a ring.

There was about thirty trees to nail. He then ran dental floss from the fence and through the first tree's nail, through the first ring, then the next until he reached the mobile home with the string. He then made a small hole in the window screen and ran the dental floss through. He then hammered in another nail and made another ring inside. After running the dental floss though that ring he tied a bear bell to it.

Next he went outside and did the same thing around the back side of the trees near the creek running the dental floss to another bear bell next to the other one. He then ran a third set of lines about 6 inches high inside the tree line and connected a third bell inside the window. Robert then tied a line around the three lines and tied them to another bell outside the trailer in case he was outside and couldn't hear the bells inside.

He next had Trevor go out and test the lines. They worked but weren't very loud. Robert laid them on a cookie jar so if they were moved they would fall off and make more noise. Trevor went out and tested and Robert heard the inside bells from outside. It had worked but now meant the bells would have to be reset every time they were triggered.

Sydney started making lunch and Robert went out to see what else he could do for security. He walked down the road. He thought the sign out front might be letting people know they were there and inviting trouble. He walked out to the gate and looked over. He saw people walking up and down the street.

Robert grabbed the chain with the sign and pulled it over the gate so it was not able to be seen from the outside. Next he took super glue and started placing sharp one inch nails to the fence with the head down about every inch. This took him almost an hour to get done. He was pretty proud of his handy work. Not too many people will try and go over the gate now he thought.

He thought about what he could do for the fence which was about a six foot high fence with lined with one half inch thick five inch long boards. They were strong enough to hammer nails in going up or sideways.

Robert got an idea and ran to the root cellar which had kind of become his makeshift work shop. He took out a one inch by one inch piece of wood and took a little saw and cut them into five inch pieces. After he had made about ten pieces he was interrupted by Sydney yelling that lunch was ready.

Robert walked up the small hill to the mobile home and turned off the generator to save fuel. He walked in the sliding glass door and saw Trevor and Rylee eating a peanut butter sandwich on paper plates. Sydney had made a Cheese sandwich and Top Ramen soup for Robert and herself. She handed him a glass of soda and it actually had ice.

Sydney asked, "Did you hear that?"

Robert paused for a moment and heard someone yelling in pain from a far off distance in the direction of the street. Robert grabbed the rifle they had gotten from the woman earlier and ran outside up to the gate. He noticed blood on two of the small nails sticking up and heard a man behind the gate cussing and in pain. Robert kind of chuckled. The gate had two no trespassing signs on it so Robert had no sympathy for the man who had hurt himself.

Robert chose a tree to stand behind and watch. A few minutes later the man's hand grabbed one of the slats of the fence next to the gate and then another leaving a red stain on one of them.

"That's far enough! No trespassing!" Robert yelled.

The man's hands disappeared without a word. After hearing nothing for about five minutes Robert ran to the gate and carefully looked over. There was no sign of the man and the street was completely empty in both directions.

Robert walked back to the house. When he got there he saw Sydney hiding next to the side of the house holding the .22 rifle.

"Robert is that you?"

"Yup!"

"The bells went off."

Robert realized he had forgotten about the bells and must have walked on one of the lines.

"Everything is O.K. It was just me."

A little while later Robert found himself back in his root cellar sorting boxes. He came to a plastic tub that he had almost completely forgotten about. This was what he considered his most valuable tub. Not because it held gold, silver or food. It held some of the dearest things in life. He opened the lid and the first thing on top was an identical blanket to Rylee's favorite pink blanket with a little Koala Bear emblem. Robert had foreseen in his bug out plans that had crap hit the fan and they had to go, Rylee might not have been able to grab her favorite blanket and Robert was trying to cover all the bases.

He took the blanket off to reveal a treasure trove of things in his life. He took out an Altoid mints metal container which held a pair of thumb drives which Robert had spent time scanning in and collecting every picture he and Sydney had as a backup. He wondered what had happened to them since the EMP hit and if they were still on the drives. He thought maybe since they were in a metal container that they might have survived. He would have to wait and see.

He took the thumb drives and placed them on the

shelf in the pile he was going to take in the mobile home with him. Next he took out an IPAD mini box. This was a box he knew he would need but had completely forgotten about. This was definitely his personal box. Inside was a box of condoms, personal lubricants, and a small personal item that Sydney liked and nick named buzz. It was an exact duplicate of her favorite one at the house in Portland. This box definitely went into the pile next to the thumb drives.

Next he took out a smaller clear plastic bin full of the old 35mm pictures of Sydney and himself throughout high school, their wedding, and other fun trips they had taken. These were the ones they had early in their marriage before they got smart phones and digital cameras.

The bottom layer contained survival books, medical books, copies of some of his favorite reading books, books on how to dehydrate, canning, and smoking meats. The last book was one he kept as a young child all the way until he got into high school. He spent the next 20 minutes scrolling through the pages reminiscing and wondering where many of the people who had been mentioned in it were today. He read on until he heard Sydney yelling that she had dinner ready and Robert carefully placed it in the pile of things to go into the house.

As Robert walked outside he noticed it had started

to get dark and he stopped at the generator to pour in a full tank of gasoline and start it. He wondered if the lights from inside the mobile home could be seen from the street and decided he would check after dinner when it was darker outside.

As he looked around he noticed toward the back of the property he noticed a campfire burning on the other side of the creek through the trees. He studied it for a minute or so but only could see the glow. No people.

Soda in the back of the Honda Pilot.

He opened the back of the Honda Pilot to see what else needed to be brought in. All he saw left in the back of the SUV was about twenty cases of soda and a brand new chain saw. "This can be brought in later" he thought to himself as he closed the SUV's back door and continued on into the mobile home to eat.

As he walked next to the kitchen table he found Sydney with her arm around Trevor and stroking his hair with her other hand. Trevor was sitting at the kitchen table crying and saying he wanted his dad over and over again. Robert thought this was surprising coming from the twelve year old that seemed to have tons of confidence all day and up to this moment.

Sydney continued to try and comfort him and tell him his dad would be back soon. Robert watched as Rylee got off her chair and walked over to Trevor and started to slowly pat his arm. It was such a touching sight.

Robert looked and saw that Sydney had made Spaghetti which even had real cooked hamburger in it. He thought to himself that he better savor the fresh meat because in a week or so they wouldn't be eating fresh cooked meat. As he sat down to eat he started thinking how taking down the sign must have really helped in keeping people out. Other than the man who tried to scale the fence he hadn't really had any trespassers since the sign came down. He thought to himself that the sign must have been more of an invitation to come or a signal that people were behind the fence.

He next started thinking that he hadn't found the ammunition box which he had been using as a faraday cage yet. Inside that box contained his night vision goggles, two hand held HAM radios, a much larger High Frequency HAM base station, a tablet computer, and a shortwave radio. All those electronics should have survived the EMP with no problem he thought. He wasn't finished eating but left the table to go find the box. He took a flashlight and looked all over the root cellar but nothing seem to match the ammunition box in his field of view. He next went to the back of the SUV and started shuffling all the many items still in the very back of the SUV. He moved several bow and arrows on the floor in the backseat and finally found the green metal box.

He carried the box into the house to find that his plate of food was gone. Sydney had already cleaned up his place at the table but she noticed he was back and sitting down.

"Were you not done?"

"Nope." Robert smiled.

Sydney grabbed Roberts plate from the counter and placed it back in front of him.

"Where's Trevor?" Robert asked Sydney.

"He wouldn't eat. I think he is home sick. I told him to go lay down on our bed and see if it made him feel better."

Robert opened up the ammunition box and started pulling out its contents. Two HAM radios came out first which he paused to test. He didn't hear anything but static but the displays came on and lit up. He turned both of them on and did a test send. The other radio although receiving a lot of feedback because the radios were so close picked up each other's transmissions. Next he pulled out an envelope containing $2,000 in twenty dollar bills, then he pulled out a shortwave radio.

Robert had thought about getting these items out of the faraday cage earlier. He decided to wait in case the EMP that had effected them earlier in the day wasn't the last one. He turned on the shortwave radio and started turned the dial through the different frequencies. Normally it would take him about two seconds to scan to the first frequency with radio transmissions. Today was different though. He tried and tried to hear anything he could but went through all the frequencies several times without hearing anything but static.

He was about to give up trying to find a station when he finally heard a voice come out of the speaker. He turned the volume up. It was a human voice but was speaking a language he couldn't understand maybe even Chinese he thought. He listened to the words pretty intently for a few minutes trying to make out anything. He continued looking for another station with a transmission but couldn't find one. After about ten more minutes he turned off the radio and placed it back in the box after removing his night vision goggles.

Prior to this whole event, Robert had read almost every book he could get his hands on related to prepping and in a few things he read about survival there were several military items you could buy that were considered force multipliers for defense. The biggest multiplier was night vision. Robert had bought an earlier "Generation One" night scope that was just a single scope that projected a red infrared light. He had now upgraded to the "Generation Three" binocular type with hands free head gear to hold up the goggles to his eyes. It had a built in Infrared but with starlight it didn't need to be turned on. These new night vision goggles were much more stealthy and could see perfectly in pitch black for over one hundred feet as opposed to the "Generation One" version which could only see about twenty five feet and had to use an ultraviolet light attached to the device.

Robert left the other handheld HAM radios and two CB's in the box and closed it. He then took his night vision glasses and inserted the CR123 battery. He immediately saw a green light illuminate from the viewing side of the goggles.

Robert looked around the room and saw Sydney with the two kids in the living room. She had a stack of computer paper and colored pencils and was showing the kids how to draw Snoopy the dog. Robert walked over to see their work. He looked at Trevor's drawing and saw he was doing a great job and seemed to have some real drawing skills. He noticed a few other pages next to him where Trevor had drawn boxes like he was going to draw his own comic strip.

"That's pretty good." Robert told Trevor.

Trevor looked up and smiled but put his head back down and started to draw again. Robert could tell he was trying to impress him with his drawing. Robert looked over at Rylee who was laying on her stomach and drawing as well. The drawings however looked more like different colored lines all over the page with sporadic holes where she had pushed the tips of the pencils through the paper.

Sydney was laying next to her with pencils and handed them to Rylee as she named a color she wanted. It was only a simple drawing but both of them drawing on the floor seemed to lend a sense of normalcy. As Robert was watching the kids the bear bells fell off the cookie jar and made noise. Sydney and Robert both instantly stood up and a look of fear came across both of their faces. Robert raced over to put on his night vision goggles. He started adjusting the head gear and put it on his head. Trevor got up and quickly started to put his papers together.

"My daddy's here! Finally!" Trevor announced.

Robert overhearing this somewhat felt a little less scared about the bear bell going off. He wasn't going to take any chances but he didn't have the adrenaline rush he had with the other visitors earlier in the day. He turned on the goggles and was immediately taken back by the bright white screen in his eyes. The room was already illuminated by a light. He walked to the sliding glass door and felt for the rifle propped up next it.

After walking outside he could see perfectly. He pushed the goggles up just to see what a difference they made. He could see the deck in front of the mobile home fine because the light illuminating from inside. He walked down the stairs of the deck to the ground and everything was pitch black. There wasn't even light from the moon through the trees.

Robert lowered the night vision goggles once more and started to look around. He looked through the trees and saw nothing. He went around to the front of the trailer because he couldn't hear anything but the sounds of the generator engine. He walked through the trees toward the front gate. He saw movement about twenty yards to his left. He made out that it was an animal of some kind. He had to adjust the focus of the goggles lenses and the determined quickly that it was a raccoon.

Robert walked the entire property and didn't see anything. He decided to make one more sweep around the mobile home just to make sure someone hadn't gotten past him. There was no one he could find. The raccoon had set off the bear bells. He walked up to the front gate no longer going slow as he had already checked the entire perimeter and found it was safe. When he got to the gate he took off the night vision goggles to see if he could see the mobile home's lights through the trees.

The trees had concealed both the noise from the generator and the mobile home's lights. That is perfect he thought to himself. Couldn't be better. As he was moving to different positions in front of the trees to see if he could see any lights he heard a squeaking noise coming from behind the fence. Not an animal but something mechanical. He put on his night vision goggles and looked over the fence next to the gate. Looking down the street he saw at least six different people and all were pushing shopping carts. He stood there and watched as several passed by the gate to his property. Only one of the passerby's had a flashlight. The rest were simply using the light from the moon to guide their way. Occasionally a cart would bump the fence or someone would stop to take a drink or adjust their load. At one point a man with two little kids in the cart stopped just below Robert. He looked in to the cart and saw one child which was maybe four or five sitting up and one that was one or two just laying down in the cart sleeping. All three never even knew Robert was there above their heads looking down.

Robert walked to the mobile home.

"Who was it?" Sydney asked.

"Actually I think it was a raccoon." Robert said. "I peaked over the fence and saw a lot of people walking up and down the street. Almost everyone was pushing a shopping cart. I think tomorrow I will ride a bike into town and see how things are going there."

"Is it safe you think?" Sydney said.

"I saw people pushing kids in carts and no one seemed to be distressed. I will call it by ear." He replied.

"The bear bells kept going off while you were out and again just as you walked in the door." Trevor said. "You didn't see my dad?"

Robert walked over to Trevor, "No but if he doesn't come tonight, tomorrow we can go see where you live and go there ourselves if you want."

"I don't know where it is. We are from Salem and

this is only our vacation house. We only come here once or twice a year." Trevor said.

"Well hopefully your dad will..." Robert was interrupted by the bear bells moving again. Robert picked up the .22 rifle of Sydney's. As he walked out the door he turned to the kids and Sydney. "Don't get scared if you hear a gun shot. That raccoons gotta go!" He lowered the night vision goggles and walked out the door closing it behind him.

Sydney gathered up the kids and sat on the couch holding both of them. A few minutes later they heard a gunshot from the rifle. Then another. Then all was quiet.

Chapter 6: It's Only Day 4

Robert had slept the entire night without waking up. He focused on the floor of the living room and saw Trevor sleeping in blankets and the sun coming in the sliding glass door. He heard a gunshot in the distance. Then another. Then two more in bursts. He got up and started to put on his shoes and it was also then that he realized that there was no sound coming from the generator.

As he opened the sliding glass door his nose caught the smell of burning wood. Either there was a fire nearby or there was a lot of wood stoves or fire places were burning he thought. He walked down the stairs to the generator. He no longer heard any gun shots as he opened the gas cap to see how much gas was left. The gas can connected to the generator was completely empty. Robert was glad that an empty fuel tank was the issue and not another EMP overnight.

He poured in more gas finishing the last of the gas in the first five gallon can he had used. He pulled the starter cord and the generator roared back to life after a couple of sputters.

Robert was startled by Trevor who was standing on the edge of the deck yelling something to him. However, because of the noise the generator made Robert couldn't hear him. He turned off the generator so he could hear Trevor.

"Did my dad come yet?" Trevor asked.

"No. I am going to go into town to see what I can find. What's your last name?" Robert inquired.

"Um. My mom's last name is Rodgers and my step dads last name is Tandino, and my real dad's last name is Johnston." the boy rattled off.

Robert paused for a second trying to piece together everything Trevor had just said and justifying in his mind how it could be possible. "Alright. So what is your last name?"

"It used to be Johnston but my mom got married last year and now it's Tandino."

"So your Trevor Tandino? Does your mom go by Tandino?"

"I think so." Trevor responded.

"Alright. When I go into town I will see if I can figure out where you live and see if I can find your parents."

"What's your moms name?"

"Mom." he was laughing.

Trevor laughing was a good sign Robert thought, "Do you know what your mom's real name is?"

"Jolene Lynn Tandino." Trevor replied.

"So I am looking for Brian and Jolene Tandino?"

"Yup. Find them please!" Trevor said. He paused for a moment. "I wonder if my dad couldn't find me because he forgot where he left me?"

"Maybe." Robert replied. He thought to himself that maybe Trevor's dad was looking for the sign that he had taken down as a marker for the property and couldn't find it again. Then he thought again and realized that the gate for the property really stood out and not like any others around the area. He looked up to the deck in front of the mobile home expecting to see Trevor again but he was not there. Instead Sydney was standing in almost the same spot holding Rylee who had a pacifier in her mouth and again had her favorite pink blanket in hand. Robert could tell she had just woken up and was still a vegetable in her mother's arms.

Robert and Sydney both turned their heads in the direction of the creek. Somewhere over on the other side was a woman screaming for help. Then they heard yelling from a man's voice but could make it out because of the distance. The yelling was silenced by three quick gun blasts. Then another barrage of gun fire and then another.

Robert had no idea what was going on over there but was glad it wasn't on his side of the creek. He knew Sydney was going to tell him something but he ran down the hill to the root cellar and found a pair of binoculars. He went outside and hid behind a tree trying to see if he could see anything on the other side of the creek. He could see nothing. There were too many trees in the way.

As he went back up to the house he heard gun shots again in the distance and then more throughout the morning. Nothing like he had ever heard from the creek. More gunshots came from even farther away. For the rest of the morning there wasn't ten minutes that went by that there wasn't another sound of gun shots.

A few times when the gunshots sounded close Robert ran to the fence and stuck his head over to see if he could see the source of the gun fire using binoculars. The first time he had seen a man with a shopping cart running down the street pushing it. But every other time he had not even seen a single person on the road.

After Robert had finished his breakfast he pulled out his bike from the inside of the enclosed trailer. He checked it to make sure it was working fine. He checked the chain and the tires. The front tire seemed low so Robert walked back to the root cellar and opened the bin with his tactical gear. He had read many prepper books about 'force multipliers' and along with his night vision goggles, Kevlar vests were highly recommended. So he had bought two. He had also purchased steel plates that weighted about 30 pounds to repel bigger rounds. He decided to wear the Kevlar vest underneath his shirt. He also grabbed all three clips for his Glock 9mm handgun a small little bicycle pump and key lock.

Next he grabbed a backpack and placed two water bottles and some money in it. He had wanted to bring a five gallon gas can to get more gas but settled with a two gallon smaller can because it would be easier to carry on a bike. A little bit of gas was better than nothing he had thought to himself and two gallons would be three nights of generator use.

Robert went in to the house to let everyone know he was going into town. Sydney walked up to him and gave him a long hug. As if it might be the last time she ever saw him again.

"You be so careful Robert! I can't do this without you, you know." Sydney said with a tear coming down one eye.

"I will. I promise."

Rylee walked up to her dad and started hugging her dads leg. Robert picked her up and hugged her to. Then gave her a kiss on the cheek. Robert then put her down and she stayed there holding on to her cup with her teeth and holding her arms out signaling to be picked up again.

Sydney came up behind her an scooped her up so Robert didn't have to tell her no.

As Robert walked away he saw Trevor sitting on the couch still drawing his comics. He just waved when Robert looked over.

Robert waved back and walked outside, then down to where his bike was leaning against the deck. He took the backpack off his back and got the bicycle pump out. It took him about two minutes to pump up the front tire of the mountain bike. Robert then walked the bike up to the large gate and unlocked it.

Before opening the gate he first looked over the fence to make sure there was no danger. He saw a man walking down the road. He was pulling everything he had in a blue tarp by dragging it on the ground. He seemed very tired and struggled to pull the load.

Robert decided it was safe enough and pushed the gate open. He then closed it and heard the latch close and lock on the other side before beginning his ride into town. As he reached the main road he could see people walking back and forth and several people on horses. As he passed person after person there were many others pushing shopping carts. He seemed to have a lot of stares from people who were walking. Maybe wanting his bike he thought.

As he was riding he got way ahead of the others walking toward town and saw a lonely woman pushing a small girl in a shopping cart. She was wearing the same type of clothes that a nurse would wear and had a name badge on. Robert thought this person might be safe to talk to and pulled up beside her. Robert could tell she was hesitant to speak and kept looking forward.

"Hi I'm Robert and I live up on Cedar Road. What's going on?"

The lady kept going. "What do you mean, what's going on? We are going into town to watch the execution and see if we can get some food!" she snapped back.

"Execution?" he asked.

"Yeah! Apparently the whole world is under Martial whatever and they are executing a bunch of thieves they caught. Apparently if you steal something now you just get shot at noon. I heard they are trying to make an example for these kids."

"So do you know of any news of what happened other than the volcano and the EMP?" Robert asked.

"I sure as hell don't know anything about no EMP but the volcano sure has messed with all the electrical stuff." she snapped back.

"Thanks for the info I appreciate it." Robert said as he rode up ahead.

As he pulled into the town of Sisters he saw the gas station which was now closed with signs saying, 'NO GAS TODAY!'. The station was dark and chains were blocking all the entrances. The police Bronco that Robert had seen several days earlier was still parked in the parking lot but the window on the passenger side was broken.

Robert rode up a few more blocks and saw the sign to turn left to city hall. Everyone seemed to be heading there so Robert followed and went that way. He heard four gun shots, then two single shots followed those. The crowd suddenly started dispersing all at once. Robert could see two police officers in front of the City Hall building uncuffing two people who were in metal chairs. Behind the metal chairs was the brick wall of the City Hall building. The two had obviously been shot several times. Another man was walking with two white body bags. One in each hand. He was trying to lay them out but the wind kept pushing them away.

Robert stopped a teenage boy walking away from the crowd.

"What did those guys do?" Robert asked the teen.

"I heard they got caught breaking into McCann's Pharmacy last night. They shot like four people today. They got another guy they said robbed and killed a dude last night. He's gonna get shot later today they said. The town doctor said that they couldn't execute him until he wakes up from his coma. Sounds like the cops beat him up real bad." the teenage said.

"Yeah, that makes sense. Fix him up so he can get shot up again." Robert chuckled as he thanked the kid and started walking his bike up to the City Hall building. As the police officers passed him carrying the body of one of the executed criminals, Robert asked where he could report a missing person. One officer let his hand go of the bag and pointed to the front entrance.

"Go to the front desk and they can help you." the officer said.

Robert walked up to the entrance and parked his bike in the bike parking area. There was about twenty bikes trying to lock up on a bike rack made for five bikes. As he locked his bike to a tree nearby Robert noticed there was a huge line of about twenty people waiting for the front desk. He was nervous knowing that he was carrying a loaded gun in his backpack. Occasionally a police officer walked through the waiting room with a shotgun in hand but never stopped to talk to anyone.

Robert had waited in line listening to every problem other complained about from someone had stolen their gas all the way to they couldn't find their wife or girlfriend. As he stood in line there was a commotion and the double doors opened inside the waiting area opened up. A man handcuffed in front, came through the doors with a bandage on one of his hands and another on his neck. He was being lead out of the doors with a blind fold on face with an officer on each side of him guiding him. Robert immediately recognized the man as the one with the woman from the day before that Sydney had shot in the process of stopping the two from robbing them. The chaplain was following all three of them outside to the City Hall open area where the two other men had just gotten executed thirty minutes before.

There was a girl in front of Robert who spoke up. "That's another one they are going to execute. Guess his trial didn't go so well."

"What did he do?" Robert asked.

"I have no idea. But if you go out and listen they will tell you what he was found guilty of before they shoot him."

A few moments later the doors opened again. This time it was the woman from the day that had been with the man screaming her lungs out. "I want an attorney! I don't even know him! Please, please, please! Just stop. I didn't do it!"

Robert had been thinking while he stood in line about reporting that he had shot someone on his property yesterday. He decided now that there was no need and he probably didn't want to get involved in any police investigations.

He finally reached the counter where a very overweight woman asked him how she could help him.

Robert summed her up and could see she was tired

and looked like she hadn't slept recently. Her hair was uncombed and the buttons on her city uniform were buttoned down three buttons.

"My name is Robert Ralston and yesterday I helped a man who came on to my property. He left his twelve year old son with me and said he would be back by yesterday afternoon to get him. I need to find out if there is a way to find out where he lives." Robert spit out quickly.

The woman looked at him and pointed to a wall on the other side of the room. "There is a list we have of missing persons but we have no computers, no radios, and really no way of finding anyone. The Registrar's Office is not open to look up properties either. What's the boys name? Maybe I know his parents."

"He says his name is Trevor Tandino but it used to be Trevor Johnston."

The lady behind the counter picked up a clipboard from the desk. "Tandino is not a very common name and we happen to have a Tandino in our morgue. The funny thing is that those people just led out to get shot, they say killed Mr. Tandino while they robbed him. Those two apparently ran away but bystanders caught them a little while later after they hid their guns and one of them shot him so he couldn't get away. At least that 's what I hear anyway. Do you want to see the body to see if it's the guy you're looking for?"

Robert reluctantly shook his head yes.

"Just so you know." the lady behind the counter

added. "A lady identified the body yesterday and told detectives he had a kid with him. The detectives thought that maybe they killed the kid. They assumed the two got rid of the kid when they disappeared for a while."

"Was he wearing black sweat pants and a BYU sweatshirt?" Robert asked.

"Hold on, let me check." she said as she walked in to the back. A few moments later she returned.

"That is exactly what he was wearing. A detective will be out shortly to talk to you. You can wait over there." she said as she pointed at a group of chairs that were filled with people.

Robert stepped aside and waited. It was over forty minutes before a police officer came out.

"Hi. You're the one with information on the Tandino murder?" the officer said.

"Yes." Robert replied.

"That case is all wrapped up and the perpetrator was executed already by Martial Law."

"I have the man's twelve year old son and I need to get him back to his parents."

"Oh, that's interesting." the officer said. "Guess you can take him home then." The officer said as he started to walk away.

"Hey wait. I don't know where he lives." Robert yelled.

The officer stopped and opened the manila folder in his hand. He wrote down an address on a notepad, tore off the piece of paper and handed it to Robert.

Robert looked down on the paper but it was an address in Salem. "Hey wait. Do you have the address to their cabin here?"

The officer turned back slightly shook his head no and completely ignored everything else Robert tried to say and walked into the double doors. An officer guarding the door put his hand put stopping him from going any further. Robert had no choice but to leave and walked out and unlocked his bike. As he got on the bike he noticed someone with a bucket of water washing off the wall where the executions had taken place.

He started riding his bike again, looking at everyone walking or riding bikes that went by. As he rode he passed business after business with broken windows or busted glass doors. Some were even missing the whole door and even a wall was smashed in on the hardware store. As he pulled in to the parking lot of the Food Place Market he rode up to the front and noticed all the carts were gone. He looked in to the broken front doors and saw that all the shelves were empty. The place looked as though a tornado had destroyed the whole inside of the store.

Robert got off his bike and started to approach the front door when a police officer came from the side of the building. "That's far enough! What are you doing here?"

Robert yelled at the approaching officer. "Was coming to get food."

"There's no food here and unless you want to get shot you better keep moving!" the officer yelled with his left hand clutching his service revolver.

Robert immediately got back on his bike and started riding back downtown away from the officer. He thought to himself that he had over a thousand dollars on him but nothing in town was for sale. He noticed a handwritten sign that showed an arrow on it. It said, "Emergency Shelter. High School."

Robert tried to stop and talk to a few people as he rode in the direction of the high school but they all seemed scared to talk to him or pretended he was not even there. He rode up a few more streets and again noticed the same nurse he had talked to earlier with the little girl sitting on a park bench alone. He rode his bike up to next to her.

"Are you stalking me?" she blurted out. "Because

ifyou are this really is the worst day of my life."

"What's happened?" Robert inquired.

"Well my apartment burned down last night. My car is dead, my credit cards don't work. I literally have nothing." she started to cry uncontrollably.

"This is your daughter? Where is the father?" Robert asked.

"Her father left a year or so ago for a newer better model. He is a doctor and he went for the prettier newer nurse. Being thirty five apparently I didn't hold a candle to the twenty something year old skinny brunette that went gaga over him." she said looking down trying to find a napkin in her purse to replace the tear soaked on in her hand.

"Do you have any family nearby that can help you?" Robert asked.

"The closest family I have is in Caldwell, Idaho which is just outside of Boise. That's where I am from. I don't know for sure who I have left anymore."

"What about the shelter?" Robert asked.

"I went there and now there a waiting list like three pages long. The maximum capacity is 2,500. And they have more than they can hold already. They suggested I needed to find a way to get to Salem of all places. I guess there are more shelters there."

Robert thought for a moment. "What's your name?"

"Oh, I am so sorry. My name is Allison Turner and this little girl is Addison."

"Well Ms. Allison my name is Robert. You and Addison can stay with us."

She wiped her eyes and thought for a moment. "Who is us?" Allison inquired.

"Well my wife Sydney, our two year old Rylee, and a now temporarily adopted twelve year old boy Trevor."

"How do I know you're not a psychotically deranged killer or something?" she said smiling.

"I'm not. Just a normal now formal computer geek trying to survive. We have three or four years of food and we will get through this fine." Robert said.

"Three of four years of food?" her jaw dropped after she said it.

"Well maybe not now if your coming. We will have to stretch it. Maybe grow some more?"

"I am a pretty good judge of character and I can see you have a good heart. Okay, so where do we go?"

Robert handed Allison the bike and Robert started

pushing the cart. He noticed there was only her purse and Addison in the cart.

"Is there anything else you are bringing?" Robert asked.

"What you see if what we have. Literally only the shirts on our backs. Well...and pants." she said as she smiled.

Robert shook his head and rolled his eyes while wondering how Sydney was going to take this. It took a little over two hours to walk the distance it took Robert twenty five minutes to ride earlier. As they walked several people looked at the bike Allison was riding but no one probably cared about robbing them of a purse or what looked like an empty backpack. Robert was sweating and exhausted when they arrived at the front gate. Robert opened the fence and pushed the cart inside. They walked in and went through the trees and again, Sydney was there holding her .22 rifle. One of two of them must have triggered the bear bells and Sydney was ready for a fight. She first saw Allison.

"Hold it right there or your gonna get shot!" Sydney yelled.

Robert quickly ran up front carrying Addison. "Sydney, Sydney it's okay. It's me!"

Allison looked relieved when Sydney lowered the

gun.

"Where have you been all day?" Sydney yelled at Robert. "I have been crazy worried that you got shot or something."

Robert looked around to make sure Trevor wasn't listening. "Long story, but Trevor's dad is dead."

"What?" Sydney exclaimed.

"Yes, from what I gathered from the police that couple that tried to get in here yesterday murdered him. They robbed and killed him before they went over our fence to get away. After we disarmed them and chased them out of here, bystanders who saw them murder Trevor's dad caught them and brought them to the police. They have the fathers body in the morgue and they actually thought the couple had killed Trevor and buried the body during the time they were on our property."

"Wow." Sydney said as they all started walking back to the mobile home.

"Not only that. They declared Martial Law. They executed the couple right in front of the Town Hall while I was there by firing squad." Robert reiterated. "While I was there! In fact they executed four other people just during the time I was there too. The Food Place...completely cleaned out and most of the town is pretty much looted and trashed too. Nothing is left in any store."

Sydney fell back and sat on the steps leading up to the deck of the mobile home. "It's really happening then. Just like you always said it would. Who is this?"

"Oh, I am sorry. This is a nurse named Allison and her daughter Addison. Someone burned down her apartment last night, the shelter at the high school is full and she literally had nothing to eat or any place for her and her daughter to go other than a bus bench." Robert responded.

"Oh, my." Sydney responded trying to take everything in and trying to process everything she had just learned.

Allison extended her hand to shake Sydney's as her three year old daughter Addison noticed Rylee and took off up the steps. "Nice to meet you ma'am."

Robert interjected, "I think it will be good to have some help for you since your pregnant and it sure won't hurt to have a nurse here if there are no hospitals either."

Sydney looked up as her and extended her hand to shake Allison's. "It's nice to meet you. We need to get dinner started. Robert is it alright to start the generator again?" Sydney asked.

"Sure."

"Did you find my dad?" Trevor yelled in a growling voice as he walked up behind the adults.

"Get the generator started, I will handle this." Sydney told Robert.

Robert got the generator started and a few minutes later Trevor ran out of the house crying. Robert watched as he ran down to the creek and almost fell in but stopped when his right foot sank in the mud. Robert could see him pull his foot out and start flinging mud all over the ground. A few kicks later and Trevor's shoe went flying about eight feet from him. He didn't go after the shoe. Just sat where he was Indian Style on the ground. He grabbed a stick and yanked it. Robert realized that wasn't just a stick. It was a poison oak branch and quickly ran out to Trevor.

"You gotta drop that stick little man!" Robert yelled loudly.

"What?" Trevor asked as Robert ran up to him.

"It's poison oak and that will give you a rash and make you itch."

Trevor threw the stick down like it was radioactive. Robert picked up his shoe and had Trevor follow him to the root cellar. After Robert opened the door Trevor's eyes lit up.

"Wow mister." Trevor said loudly. "That's a lot of food!"

Robert smiled and grabbed a bottle of water, took off the cap and poured while Trevor rubbed his hands together. Robert then picked up a bottle of hand sanitizer and had Trevor rub his hands together again several times.

"You know that we will take care of you until we can find your mom." Robert told Trevor.

"It's alright. I am sad but he is not my real dad. I think I know where I live from here. Can we walk there tomorrow?"

"Sure." Robert said while holding his hand on Trevor's head. "Let's see what we can do to get dinner going."

As they were walking up the stairs, Robert paused after hearing more gun shots even with the generator going. They were a distance away but he wondered why. He looked over toward the creek and again saw a fire burning on the other side just as he had seen the night before.

Robert walked in and saw Sydney and Allison serving mashed potatoes, gravy and smoked pork. He thought about all the people who had no food and how he was eating like it was a week ago. As he was handed his plate he went to the couch and sat down. The three kids ate at the table while the adults took their plates to eat in the living room.

Allison said a prayer and thanked the lord for being in a house that had heat, electricity, good food, protection, and great people. She asked the lord to bless those who were less fortunate and to keep the righteous in the world safe from the wicked. As soon as she said "Amen." everyone started eating.

It seemed like things were returning to normal at least for the moment. Robert and Sydney had been on odd schedules and they had forgotten to say a prayer and bless the food since they had left Portland.

As they were eating the bear bells fell and made a ringing noise. Robert set down his food and ran to the door. Put on his night vision goggles and grabbed the rifle next to the door. He overheard Sydney explaining to Allison what the bells meant while Sydney reached behind the couch to get her rifle.

Robert opened the sliding glass door and surveyed the area from the deck before he went out. He didn't see anything but he overheard the bells fall down again. Quickly he made his way around the deck so he could see the tree line. He made his way through the tree line and didn't see anyone or anything. From the other side of the tree line Robert could see that two fence slats had been kicked in and that there was a ten inch hole in the fence.

This scared Robert. He knew his perimeter had been violated for sure. Where were they? He made his way back around the other side of the trailer and still didn't see anyone. He walked around the backside by the generator. He saw a flash in his goggles. It was a flashlight beam that had shined in to his night vision goggles. Whoever it was, was down below the deck area near the root cellar. He was scared and he could feel the adrenaline kick in.

Quickly he made his way down to the root cellar. In his night vision he noticed the door open then someone lunge at him from below his view. He fell backwards hitting his head on soft dirt. The fall caused the night vision goggles he was wearing to come off his head. He could see a shadow of a figure grabbing the knife he had on his belt. As the assailant tried to get his grip on the handle he also pulled Robert rifle as hard. Robert immediately reached behind his back and pulling out his Glock handgun.

The man finally had the rifle but was too close to Robert to aim and took a step back so he could get in to a firing position. The man started to level the rifle as Robert pointed his Glock at the figures direction and pulled the trigger as fast as he could. Several of the shots missed the chest area where he was aiming but the man was injured. He saw the man stumble down to the hill towards the creek. Robert was now out of bullets in his Glock and stood up and realized there was something wrong. He had a pain in his pelvis right around where his Appendix should be. He felt warm liquid going down his pants leg. He had thought maybe he had been stabbed by his own knife but realized it was still on his belt.

Robert ran as fast as he could to the sliding glass door and grabbed the .22 rifle from Sydney and stopped. He readjusted the night vision goggles that had been flopping on his head. He saw Sydney on top of the couch getting another gun down from the shelf where they were hidden on above the couch.

He returned to the open sliding glass door and scanned the area before running down the decks stairs as quietly as possible and taking cover on the side of the trailer scanning the area for the man. Using the night vision goggles he saw the man standing behind a fallen tree holding his left shoulder but proned out with a hand gun in a firing position pointing toward the mobile home.

The intruder not noticing Robert aproaching from behind.

The intruder moved the gun toward every sound. In the pitch black Robert could see the man clearly. The man could not see Robert but the man's figure stood out in bright white against the cold backdrop in his night vision goggles. Robert moved to another tree trying to get behind the man and watched him move to another tree closer to the mobile home. Robert moved closer to the man taking cover behind another tree while closing the distance. A twig snapped and the man took aim in Roberts direction. A few moments later the man ran to a tree only twelve feet from Robert who was now behind the assailant.

The assailant had moved closer and was now in view of the sliding glass door where he realized Allison was standing in front of. As the assailant leveled the rifle toward the direction of the mobile home Robert pulled the trigger of the rifle he had. Nothing happened. The trigger didn't even move. Robert realized Sydney had the 'Safety' on the rifle. Robert clicked the Safety Pin out and started firing at the man. Through his night vision he saw the man's light colored shirt fill with black dots and then the shirt turn a mostly white color as the man fell straight back and stopped moving. As Robert approached he continued to fire until he had no bullets left.

Robert grabbed the rifle and made his way back to the mobile home to check his wound. He walked in to the living room and fell on the couch.

"Get Allison." Robert yelled to Sydney.

Allison had heard him and came running out to the living room.

"What happened?" she asked.

"A bad guy broke our fence and snuck in. He tackled me by the root cellar and I think he stabbed me." Robert quickly explained.

"Where is he now?" Sydney asked.

"I think he's dead." Robert said as he unzipped his pants to reveal a large incision in his gut.

"You think he's dead?" Sydney said.

"I got him at least once with the 9mm and at least ten times with the .22 all in the upper body. If he's not dead yet he will be soon."

"Where are the medical supplies?" Allison asked.

"In the root cellar still. There is a complete trauma kit and first aid supplies on the top shelf behind the door when you first walk in." Robert explained.

Sydney started reloading the .22 rifle and then put on the night vision goggles. "How do you turn these on?"

"They are already on, just go outside. It's too bright in here for them to work. They auto shut off in the light."

The bear bells fell down again making noise. Sydney went out the sliding glass door. A few minutes later Robert and Allison looked at each other when they heard four shots come from the front of the trailer. Robert quickly grabbed the other two clips for the 9mm and buttoned up his pants. He took out the empty clip, inserted a new one and rounded one in the chamber just in case.

He looked out the window but without the night vision goggles he was helpless. He told the kids to go run to the back bedroom and hide under the bed until they were told to come out. Trevor grabbed both girls by their hands and they all ran to the room. Robert heard Trevor say they were going to play hide-and-seek.

Robert then turned off all the lights in the mobile home and both Allison and Robert looked out the windows to see what they could see.

A minute later the sliding glass door opened and Sydney asked, "Why are the lights off?"

Robert flicked the lights back on.

"Two bad guys are now dead." Sydney said as she dropped the blue reflective trauma bag on to the floor.

"I think we need to check them but I got the one out front with four shots perfectly in the chest. I found the knife the guy stabbed you with." as Sydney held out a small green handled steak knife with blood on the blade. She placed it on the kitchen table.

"Lay down!" Allison told Robert as he was about to get back off the couch. He did as he was told and Allison started to unbutton his pants. She pulled them down just enough to reveal the now heavily bleeding injury. She started going through the trauma bag to see what medical supplies she had to work with.

"Pretty good bag." Allison said as she pulled out

Rubbing Alcohol, Neosporin, the medical stable gun and SteriStrips. She took the rubbing alcohol up to the sink and poured it on her hands to sterilize them. She then walked back and stuck her finger in the wound to see how deep it was as Robert closed his eyes in pain.

"This is going to hurt" she said as she took the alcohol and poured it in the open wound."

Robert let out a scream of pain and then grimaced for a few seconds.

"Can we come out now?" Trevor asked from the back bedroom.

"Yes! It's alright." Sydney yelled back.

All at once the kids came running out but stopped when they saw the work being done by Allison in the living room.

"Go ahead and sit at the table for now kids." Allison told them. She had started to take control.

Allison looked at Sydney, "Do you have a stick or anything?"

"I have a chop stick."

"Well let's see if it works." Allison replied. She took the chopstick and placed it between Roberts teeth. Right after that she stapled the wound with a medical staple. Robert jumped as he was not anticipating the pain. She did another and another. Robert was now tolerating the pain and Allison continued until she had placed eight staples and successfully closing the wound.

She then started applying SteriStrips between the staples. "If it doesn't get infected you will live. But you gotta take it easy and not reopen the wound. It should be a little more tolerant to movement than stitches." she said as she took out medical tape and a gauze and covered her handy work.

Robert looked at Sydney. " We need to fix the fence right away or it will invite others and give them an easy way in."

Sydney looked at him with a glaring look. "I don't know how to fix a fence Robert."

Allison looked up. "I do. Tell me what needs to be done and I'll do it."

"You need to go to the root cellar and get the hammer and the box of four inch nails from the tub labeled tools. Then you need to get two new fence slats from the lumber pile behind the trailer, pull off the two broken slats and replace them." Robert said. "Sydney you should go out there with the night vision goggles and make sure it's safe and guard them while they fix the fence. Maybe Trevor can go and help hold the flashlight for Allison."

Trevor went to get his shoes on even without being asked. He was eager to help. A few minutes later all three were outside going to fix the fence. Robert looked out the window and saw flashlights outside moving here and there over the next twenty minutes. The first one to return was Trevor who was carrying a blue tub full of dried food packets.

"Where did you get that?" Robert asked.

"We found three of them outside of the fence we were fixing." Trevor stated.

Trevor ran back out the door again with a flashlight in hand. Robert moaned but got up. The staples poking in his stomach really hurt as he got up. He looked at the blue plastic tub labeled with one of his labels. The men had actually gone in to the root cellar and made several trips before triggered the bear bells and Robert had just realized it.

Robert knew he needed to conceal the root cellar better, reinforce the fence somehow, perfect his early warning system, and get the nails sticking up on the fence on the whole top of the entire fence line, and not just the gate. Not to mention he now had two bodies to deal with in the morning.

Sydney, Allison and Trevor all came back in at the same time. Sydney had two bags of things she had found on the men who had been shot and in a shopping cart parked next to the hole in the fence which obviously belonged to the two men. She placed the bags on the table. Trevor and Allison each had blue tubs they placed on the floor by the sliding glass door.

Sydney dumped out the contents of the smaller of the two bags which contained two prison identification cards for Shutter Creek Correctional Institution. Both men appeared to have been inmates before the crisis. Allison explained that Shutter Creek was an old Air National Guard base converted to a prison and was on the outskirts of Bend. How the prisoners got here Robert wondered. Then an even more horrendous thought entered his mind. How many other inmates were let go or escaped?

He and Sydney mentally inventoried the contents on the table. There were three gold watches, eight gold rings, two rolls of Indian Head dimes, three 1884 and 1885 silver dollars, a silver necklace, a flashlight, two packs of AA batteries, a can of SPAM, an unopened water bottle, checks with an address and a girl's name from two streets away, a can opener, and two unopened packs of cigarettes.

"If they are from the prison it's all going to be stolen." Robert said. "What's in the other bag?"

Sydney looked in the bag which was actually a white pillow case and very heavy. "It's all canned food, soups, gravy, and a smashed loaf of bread."

She dragged the bag over to the cupboard with all the canned goods and started sorting them on to shelves. As she was working she asked, "What are we going to do with the two guys out there?"

Allison perked up. "I'll take care of them in the morning. I don't want Rob digging with a shovel in his condition."

"Can I walk?" Robert asked.

"As long as you don't overdo it." she said.

"Good. Let's get to sleep. Trevor and I will take the floor. Sydney and Rylee can take the bed, Allison can take the couch and Addison can take the love seat." Robert announced.

"That's not fair it's your house." Allison retorted.

"Robert sleeps on the floor even when there's a bed. He thinks it helps his back. So don't worry about it." Sydney Interjected and ended the conversation as she picked up all the items on the table and started put them back in the bag.

Robert sat on the couch and slowly reloaded the 9mm clip he had emptied earlier while Sydney handed two pillows and blankets to Allison for them to make their beds. She also handed Allison one of her night gowns to use. Luckily Allison was about Sydney's size and Addison was small for age and it looked like Rylee's clothes were for the most part going to fit Addison just fine.

Sydney explained to Trevor that she was going to strip him naked tomorrow, give him a bath, and put him in a towel while she washed his clothes. He was able to wear Roberts socks but they had no other clothes for a twelve year old boy. He smiled and said as long as the little girls didn't see him naked he was alright with that.

Tonight for some reason was colder than the other nights had been and the small space heater was not keeping up. Robert took the flashlight outside to the root cellar and came back with a much larger Kerosene heater. He lit the heater which already had a full tank of Kerosene. After a few minutes he turned the heat down to as low as it would go and opened the window behind it about an inch to let fresh air in. The heater was on the kitchen table but even on low you could feel the heat all the way in the living room.

"Anyone need a flashlight?" Robert asked.

No one said anything.

"OK. I am turning off the generator for the night to save gas since we have the Kerosene heater."

Robert walked outside and turned off the generator

and the house went dark. As he walked back up the steps he saw at least three flashlights that were turned on through the sliding glass door. He went in the sliding glass door, locked it and laid down in the bed Sydney had made for him on the floor.

About two in the morning he woke up because the mobile home was so hot. He got up and opened the window in the kitchen to let some more air in. He turned to quickly go to the bathroom and found Sydney in the bathroom leaning over the toilet.

"Morning sickness sucks." she said quietly.

Robert could only scratch her back and hold her long hair back as she heaved in to the toilet. When she was done he poured the last of the water in the bucket down the toilet and went to the bathroom. He mentally noted that he needed to go to the creek and get some more water for the toilet in the morning. He walked back down the hall and laid in his bed. He then realized that Allison snored and he laid there for quite some time trying to sleep through her snoring. Eventually he did get to sleep and woke up with Rylee and Addison leaning over him.

"Daddy, we... are...hungry." Rylee said.

Robert smiled and opened his eyes as Allison was picking up both Rylee and Addison. She placed them both on chairs in the kitchen and looked in the cabinet for snacks to give them. She found Froot Loops and placed a pile of them on paper plates in front of the two kids.

Robert looked at the gold watch in his pocket that he had gotten from the pile of items from one of the men shot the night before. It was already 9:17AM in the morning. They had really slept in. He went outside and started the generator. He walked down to get a better look at the two men who had invaded their space that night. He first went to the man who he had shot first. He was dead. Robert rechecked his pockets to make sure there was nothing missed. He found a picture in the back pocket of the man and two credit cards with the same name as the checks back on the table in the mobile home.

He then walked out front of the mobile home. He saw blood on the ground but no body. He looked all up and down the property but found no body. As he walked down the fence line he saw a three foot section of the top of the fence stained red by blood. He got up on the fence and looked over. He saw more blood on the side of the fence and on the weeds all the way up to the street. But no one could be seen. He looked up and down the street and saw no one. The shopping cart was also gone. He asked himself. "Did the guy live and run or was there at least one more guy who came and got him?"

He looked on the dirt below the fence and only saw one set of foot prints. No dragging marks. It seems the man who was shot walked away on his own power. He lost more blood than robert thought anyone could between the place he was shot and the road.

Robert got off the fence and walked over to the trailer. He picked up the enclosed trailer which had two doors that opened up in the back and a smaller door on the left side. He slowly walked the nearly empty trailer down the hill backing it in with the back doors wide opened completely and pushed the back end right in front of the entrance to the root cellar. He then stepped back and took a look at the trailer. He realized the enclosed trailer completely hid the root cellar. It looked like there was simply a hill behind where the trailer was parked.

He next opened the SUV's back door and took out the trailer tire locks he had stored in there. He placed the locks on the tires so the trailer couldn't be moved. He then placed another lock on the hitch so it couldn't easily be towed out. In order to get in the root cellar now without moving the trailer you would now have to unlock the side door of the trailer and walk through the empty trailer to the open door of the root cellar which opened inwards.

This now added another layer of protection and another layer of difficulty to steal anything out of the root cellar. Not only that they could now use the root cellar as a safe house and it would be very hard to get anything through the trailer that could ram the root cellar's door open.

He walked out of the enclosed trailer and locked the side door behind him. He was about to go get the buckets to get water from the creek for the bathroom when he heard Sydney yelling out that breakfast was now ready. He dreaded telling Sydney her assailant from the night before got away and he wasn't dead.

Chapter 7: Day 10

Trevor was back begging Robert to take the route he believed would get him to his house to get back to his mother. Robert had relented acting on his requests because of his injury and the need to improve security around the property. Things had been quiet for the past six days and Robert had taken the opportunity to improve the security around the property. He had hammered in three inch nails in to two inch by one foot boards. He then ran the wood with nail sticking up along the entire length of the fence line of the property. He had made a one in groove down the center of the boards so they sat on top of the fence slats. He the nailed the sides of the wood to keep them from coming off the top of the fence slats. This prevented anyone from reaching up and grabbing the fence to pull themselves over without doing significant damage to their hands even if they wore gloves..

Next, he had reinforced the fence by placing 2x4's at top of each support beam so they diagonally supporting each beam. This was done so the support beams could not be rammed or kicked in as easily. He had wished he had the foresight to buy razor wire for the inside or top of the fence.

Lastly, he had spent about two hours each day digging out another room below the secret room in the root cellar. Robert wasn't sure yet what he would use this room for or how big he would eventually make the room but wanted to get started on the project. He had enlisted Trevor to use a small bucket and slowly take the dirt he was digging out in the root cellar and dump the contents on the bottom of the fence line to add additional reinforcement.

Robert had started to see how much help a twelve year old boy could be for the first day he was working. However Trevor began to help less and less because his hands had grown itchy and swollen from the Poison Oak stick he had grabbed. Still even though his hands were infected and had to be treated hourly by Allison with Calamine lotion, Trevor not only tried to help but never complained about any job he was ever given. If Trevor ever left Robert thought to himself, he was going to miss having him around.

"So can we go to my house today? You kind of promised" Trevor insinuated.

Robert shook his head up and down. "Let's get some food and water packed and let me get my gun."

Robert went in to the house and after announcing his plans he really had to sell the idea to Sydney who was completely against it for safety reasons. Eventually Robert won over and asked Sydney if she wanted to go. Sydney quickly declined but wanted Robert to get the HAM radios out of the faraday cage so they could be in constant contact. Robert had already been trying to get someone on the HAM radios but had no success throughout the week.

He was using a handheld HAM radio which only had about a ten to twenty mile range. Robert had a High Frequency HAM radio that would receive transmissions from all over the world but the antenna would have to be up above the tree line and might give their position away and advertise that there were nice expensive things on the property to be had. Robert thought about creating something to put up after dark and could be taken down during the day but he hadn't gotten to it yet.

Robert got on his bike after lowering the seat on Sydney's Mountain Bike so that Trevor could use it. Slowly both of them made their way riding the bikes up to the gate. Robert stepped up on the lowest gate hinge to look over the fence to see that it was safe outside. He hadn't actually looked over the fence periodically over the last several days which he normally had done. He was surprised at the number of people he saw. Those walking toward town were all walking with their head down. All of them looked very unhealthy and sickly. Almost all looked like couples or families with kids. Each group carried a bucket or pushed a cart with water jugs.

Those coming back seemed to be out of breath and carried at least one full water jug. They carried them slowly in their arms, pushed them in a cart, and one father carried one on his head. Everyone seemed to be out of energy.

As a family passed down his fence line Robert heard a little boy asking his mother. "When are they going to have something more than soup mom?"

She replied to him. "Just be thankful we are getting some food right now."

Robert walked the fence line on the other side of the family just listening to their conversation.

"Well how come we can't get back in line and get two bowl's mom? I'm still hungry."

"Because Jacob, the food cards only allow us two punches a day." she replied.

The conversation continued with the little boy and his mother and Robert felt so bad that the little boy who couldn't be more than four was crying as he talked because he was hungry. Robert looked in his back pack he had packed for the trip and took out a box of peanut butter granola bars and opened the gate. He quickly pulled the bikes through the open gate one by one and locked the gate from the outside.

Robert turned and saw the young family about three hundred yards away and got on his bike. Without even waiting for Trevor he got on the bike and rode up to the family. At first it startled the father who seemed to not know what to do to defend himself or his family. He was relieved when he saw that all Robert had in hand was a box of granola bars.

He stopped next to the little boy who had been slowly lagging behind his parents.

"Here you go Jacob." Robert said to the little boy as he rode on.

He looked back and saw the father opening the box and waving at Robert. Trevor already passed the family and was riding up to Robert.

A man from across the street yelled. "Do you have any more?"

"No, Sorry." Robert yelled back.

The man was obviously disappointed but continued walking in the opposite direction.

"So how do you get to your house?" Robert asked as he changed gears on his bike to a lower gear to go up the hill.

"I think it's this way." Trevor replied.

"You think it's that way?" Robert said.

"Well I recognize that house." Trevor said as he was pointing at a house that ten days earlier had windows and a garage door. The house now had several bullet holes, broken windows and looked like a truck had driven through the white tin garage door.

"You recognize it from that?" Robert said sarcastically.

"Well, the mailbox I mean."

Robert chuckled as he looked and saw the mailbox was surrounded by bricks all the way to the ground and a little green roof.

"Definitely not another one of those mailboxes around." Robert said to himself.

Robert and Trevor continued down the road about a mile until Trevor yelled. "This is definitely the road!"

"Are you sure?"

"Yep! But it's still a long way." he said with a smile.

"Well let's get going. Your dad said it was about five miles away and we have gone maybe gone a mile."

As Robert turned down the street he noticed a name on a mailbox that caught his attention. The name sounded familiar. "Mr. and Mrs. Raymond Sinclair" the sign read.   He looked up and saw the charred remains of what used to be a very large dark wooden vacation home. He noticed in the garage that there was a truck and he recognized the truck from the trip from Portland to Sisters.

Robert yelled at Trevor to stop and steered his bike in to the long driveway of the charred home. As he walked the bike up to the house he noticed his gas cans on the side of the home which laid empty. Their lids and the small clear plastic funnels were scattered on the ground nearby. As he walked around the side of the home he parked his bike next to the house and put down his backpack. He saw some of his boxes and bins that the doctor had brought back for him scattered around the side of the house. He stopped and looked inside each of the different boxes and bins. He realized that everything of value had been picked clean. Even the packaging materials were gone. There was absolutely nothing left of what he had given to the doctor to bring back for him.

As he went around to the backyard he found the body of the doctors son. He laid face down and it was obvious he had been shot several times and may have been there at least a week. The smell was excruciating even ten feet away from the body. He didn't come any closer and could see fly's and other insects littered the body.

He walked over to the back door of the burned out home. The back door was a broken sliding glass door which the door itself had been taken off the rollers and placed leaning against the wall. Robert stuck just his head inside the house and looked inside. He slowly scanned what looked like it used to be the living room and he saw several other dark piles of black in shapes which were recognizable only as bodies. There was no way to tell who they were or even if they were a man or woman.

As Robert took several steps in to the home Trevor came up behind him. "What happened here? Did you see the dead guy in the yard?"

"I don't know, but I did know these people. He was a doctor from Salem I think. This was a vacation home for him. All those boxes and bins out there. They were mine." Trevor got a dismayed look on his face. "They were yours? How?"

"Yeah. We had two cars when we driving up here. One got wrecked and we gave the doctor gas and he was helping us bring things from the wrecked car."

"Oh."

"Okay. Let's go." Robert said.

When they walked out front to get their bikes and Roberts backpack they were gone. Both looked around but there wasn't anyone around anywhere.

Robert quickly ran up the street to see if he could see who took the bikes but they were gone and so was his backpack. He didn't care about the knife, the food or the water in the backpack but the three extra clips of bullets for his 9mm, and the HAM radio being lost was a major setback. Robert was upset with himself for not paying closer attention to his bike when he should have known better.

Trevor had caught up to Robert and he ran his hand down Trevor hair. "Sorry little man but we are going to have to go back."

Trevor looked at Robert. "It's alright. I understand." He reached up and grabbed Roberts hand.

Robert looked down at Trevor. It was the first time he wanted to cry but since Trevor was there he didn't but as they walked down the road going back home a tear came to his eye. He wiped it away without Trevor seeing. They had only traveled about a mile and a half before they had gotten their bikes stolen and he had lost three of the clips for his gun and a HAM radio. He just couldn't believe how they had taken his bikes and backpack without even being seen or heard.

It was compounded by the fact that he had lost everything he had given to the doctor to bring back for Sydney and himself. One of the things that he had mentally put on his to do list was to find out where the doctor lived and get his things back. Now he knew he wasn't going to get those things.

He was sad and it was the first time that he mentally felt like he had been pushed down. The thoughts of wanting to just give up came to his mind.

A few minutes later he was telling himself, "It was just bikes and a few bullets. Why am I so stressed out about it?"

Trevor said nothing as he walked. The streets were virtually barren but as they got closer to the gate two kids on skateboards came up to them.

Robert yelled to them. "Hey!"

One of the skateboarders a teenager looked to be sixteen who was about five foot high and had red hair jumped off his skateboard while the other passed and then circled back. Both were carrying machetes on their belts.

"What's up dude?" the red haired skateboarder asked.

"Where is everyone?" Robert asked him.

"Dude, if you want grub for your food card. You gotta get in line way before four man. Everyone's down at the school dude."

Robert looked at both the boys who were definitely standoffish. "The city is issuing food cards?"

The other skateboarder who was a little more scruffy and had long blonde hair and was a little shorter than his friend spoke up. "Yeah man. But the food sucks. Crackers, Bread and flavored water...I mean soup."

"How do you get the food cards?"

The red haired kid spoke up. "Juss take your I.D. and go to Town Hall during the day and they will give you one if you live around here. If not your screwed. It's for town residents only dude."

The blond haired kid pulled his buddy as he was speaking and they jumped on their skateboards and rode away without saying anything else. Robert thought about the conversation Jacob had earlier about the bad soup that left him hungry. Sisters has four thousand or so residents and only a few stores. Not much food.

He thought to himself that most people go to Bend about twenty five miles away for big shopping. Bend has a population of about ninety thousand and that doesn't include the thousands who were vacationing at Mount Bachelor and the other mountains around the city. It must be a mad house down there. It's amazing how bad it already was just ten days from the eruption.

He finished walking to the gate in front of his property. He quickly looked around but didn't see anything as he and Trevor quickly ran in the small opening and closed and locked it.

As he walked down the trail to the mobile home he saw Sydney with a rifle walking up to them.

"Back already?" she asked.

Robert just shook his head and all three of them walked back up to the mobile home while Trevor explained to Sydney what they had seen and what happened to their bikes and bags. Upon learning her bike was gone, Sydney got upset and slugged Robert in the arm.

"I loved that bike Robert! And we were probably going to need that." she complained.

"I know but there isn't much we can do about it now. I am so upset too. We still have my old Mountain Bike and we'll have to make the best of it."

"Robert!" Sydney yelled very loudly.

"Hey, I am upset about it too but what can I do? I learned a lesson."

"Uh, huh."

Robert went to the root cellar and started looking through the bins looking for a fourth clip he had for his 9mm. He had stopped using it because he had taken it to California and it was illegal to have a clip that took more than ten bullets. It was a thirteen shot clip and his brother whom he was visiting at the time punch a rivet in the clip to keep it from taking more than nine bullets at a time.

A few minutes later he had found the clip and loaded it with 9mm hollow point rounds. He wanted to sit down but looked around the root cellar and realized other than the dirt and gravel on the floor there was no place to really sit down. He spent the next forty-five minutes organizing things out of bins until the door opened. It was Trevor with his five gallon bucket coming in to get another load of dirt out of the secret room. He didn't say a word, just smiled as he passed Robert and went to work. Such as good kid Robert thought to himself.

A little while later Robert grew tired of sorting things in the root cellar and walked outside. He could smell the delicious smell of homemade bread and he followed it in to the mobile home. It was a bread mix from one of the large #10 cans Sydney had opened and had cooking in the oven. Sydney handed him a piece smothered in honey. It was the best tasting food he had tasted in over a week and it seemed like it had been ages since he had fresh homemade bread.

He thought about how they were eating like kings as he watched Allison opening a can of beef chunks and pouring them in a pan to put on the instant mashed potatoes they were cooking on the stove.

"We were going to surprise you when you got back with a great dinner but you came back to quick." Sydney said as Robert took another bite.

"Wow. It really looks great!" Robert said excitedly as he saw Trevor come in the sliding glass door. His face covered in muddy streaks.

Allison cut a piece of bread, put honey on it and handed it to Trevor. He took one bite and his eyes lit up. "This is good!"

Dinner was served just about the time the generator ran out of fuel and they all ate dinner by candlelight. It was tough to imagine that the world was falling apart as everyone sat around talking, laughing, and eating good food. It got really quiet and everyone listened as Robert and Trevor told the group what they had seen at Doctor Sinclair's vacation house and what had happened to many of the houses just within a mile or so of their property.

"We have to be more diligent." Sydney said. "We really need to go in to town tomorrow and see what is actually going on."

Robert sat down on the couch closing his eyes. He laid his head back on the head rest. He had prepared as much as possible and had been a pillar of strength. Now, his strength was faltering. He was scared. Things were starting to look like they were going to turn really bad. He started to ponder giving up.

He started thinking of all the reasons he bought the property and all the things he had prepared for. He could think of about fifteen reasons why he had prepared and what he had prepared for. He first started prepping in case of an earthquake. Then prepping in case there was an epidemic. He learned early on that the government was prepping itself for something big too.

This became evident when every part of the government including enforcement, governing, and administration agencies started arming themselves to the teeth. Then every police force started becoming like its own militia with its own military grade weapons. This scared him and he started prepping in case of a collapse of the monetary system. Everything he prepped for required different types of preparedness items and usually anticipating being without help or supplies for a greater and greater amount of time.

Robert thought that the most probable event was the money system going downhill. Especially when the debt ceiling hit twenty trillion dollars. If you watched the news about any elected official, not a single one had any semblance of a comprehensive plan to solve any of the country's financial issues.

Even when there was ordered cut backs in the military and other agencies by the president, they were met with special spending bills in congress that actually spent more money than the cost cutting saved. If there was a spending bill to spend ten million dollars for something, then there was a billion dollars in pork added to it to get enough of congress to vote for the spending bill that was actually needed. Every election made life more and more comfortable for those on welfare, assistance, social security, disability, and food stamps.

More and more of the population started not working because they made more by not working.

Robert could see that everything life-sustaining, electrical delivery, water delivery, shipping of goods, had developed one large off switch...The Internet. After a while everything became susceptible to a hacker attack. Power distribution, fuel distribution, and water distribution, as well as the water treatment system was all on the Internet.

He really felt like prepping was the right thing to do when he watched a TV show that said the earth had eight billion people on board. If you placed all the available food in a great big pile in the Grand Canyon and then distributed the food equally because of a global event there would only be about three weeks of food for everyone. If there was no way to grow more food then the world would starve to death. The world was teeter tottering on destruction.

On top of that he learned from experience that the grocery stores which have only been around for a little over seventy years, in an emergency, they would have bare shelves in less than one day. Robert now knew this was true from his own experiences. But he corrected the show's speaker in his mind to eight hours or less.

He then started prepping with additional supplies to last a longer period after an earthquake, a drought, volcano eruption or flood. Then he prepped a little for an EMP because he learned about them from a prepping TV show he had watched. That caused him to buy a Faraday Cage and to put some electronics in a steel box to shield them from an electronic pulse. Never did he ever imagine a scenario where there would be three events all at once. First a volcanic eruption, an earthquake, and then an EMP.

If people in the world were violent and crazy before all this, things will only be worse now that the lights are out, the waters not pumping, there is Martial Law and the food supply is interrupted.

Robert had apparently fallen asleep thinking about all of this because when he woke up it was still somewhat dark outside. He was in the same position but someone had put a blanket around him. It seemed colder than before and he got up, and quietly found a flashlight. Robert knew he needed to restart the generator so the freezer could make new ice to keep the refrigerator stuff cold when the generator was off. As he got up from the couch he took the watch from his pocket that he used to keep the time. The watch said it was 8:22. This was impossible he thought to himself. He turned the dial on the side to wind the watch but it didn't take as many turns as normal to wind it up. He usually only had to do this once per week but he remembered doing it just a few days ago.

"What is going on?" he thought to himself.

Robert went out the sliding glass door on to the porch and looked up to the sky. The sky was a yellowish brown color. It reminded him of when there was a large forest fire burning nearby only this time much more light from the sun was being drowned out.

Robert felt a touch on his back near his kidney. Then warm hands come around his stomach.

"Why don't you come back to bed?" Sydney said.

"It's not early. It's about eight-thirty in the morning." Robert stated.

"What? But its dark right now." Sydney said sounding concerned.

Allison spoke up from behind both of them. "It's the ash from Yellowstone. I know from history that in 1815 or 1816 Mount Tambora erupted. It was a year without a summer and thousands froze to death or starved to death because the ash in the sky blocked out the sun."

Robert and Sydney just looked at her stunned. After staring at Allison for a few seconds all three looked up to the sky. As they stared the amount of light showing through the clouds got better and then faded. It reminded Robert of the little dial for a light which allowed you to fade a light bulb darker or lighter. This time however it was not controlled and at times it seemed that it was midnight but it was early morning. Then sporadically every few minutes you would be able to see everyone around you and at times even the creek.

Robert walked over to the generator and refilled the gas tank with the five gallon jug he had on the porch. He restarted the generator and all the lights in the mobile home illuminated. This in turn woke the kids who came out asking why everyone was up so early.

Allison turned the kids around and walked them in to the living room. She then gave each of the kids a quick tutorial on how ash can block out the sun. This new event troubled Robert even more. He would now be using more fuel, flashlights, and more than likely his portable solar panels he had to help recharge batteries and radios would no longer work and help to save fuel.

Robert took a bag from the kitchen and started going around the house collecting batteries and removing used ones from the flashlights. He had two battery chargers in the root cellar and he plugged both of them in to the running generator. This allowed him to charge eight batteries at a time between both chargers.

He also became concerned about his supply of CR123 batteries. These are the ones he used for his night vision goggles and his night vision scope. He went back in to the root cellar with a flashlight. He opened the Faraday Cage and took out his batteries for the night vision equipment. He had eight batteries in a new package, three left over in the other opened package and one good one in the goggles themselves. He had used four of the batteries in just eleven days. He would have to conserve the use of his night vision. If he used them the same way he was now he had only two months of batteries left.

The last few days had been pretty quiet and he hadn't had to use the night vision gear at all. No one had tried to enter the property in the past five days either but he didn't know how long that would hold out. Things might be better with no light and they might get worse if people thought they could move around more stealthily.

Robert grabbed the night vision goggles and turned them on. He wanted to see what was happening on the other side of the fence out on the street. As he approached the fence he saw flashlights shining through the fence slats. He stuck his head over the fence enough to see the people. What he saw was insurmountable. He put on his night vision goggles and saw almost everyone moving very slowly. Most men looked like they had not shaved in at least a two weeks. Their clothes were all dirty and grungy.

Robert could smell the sweat and bad body odor from a couple of people that passed by the fence near where he was looking over. He watched the people slowly making their way toward town for a few minutes until a woman with a baby came by. The smell of the babies messy pants was excruciating. The mother obviously had no new diapers and no way of cleaning the ones she was using. If she had any diapers at all.

Robert got off the fence after the smells seemed to linger and he started getting sick to his stomach. In the short time he was out there it had seemed the temperature had dropped ten degrees as well and his fingers were starting to feel numb.

Chapter 8: A Town In Crisis

Robert and Sydney both started the day off early and with a goal. They had both planned to go in to town the day before and had never made it. They had both spent a better part of the previous day inventorying, moving fuel up to the house, finishing the back fence in front of the creek and allowing Trevor to pack out more dirt from the secret room in the back of the root cellar. After the weather had turned colder they needed to find the bins with their cold weather clothing and both Sydney and Robert felt going in to town could wait another day.

This morning Sydney and Robert stood in the root cellar putting on a Kevlar vest. Each of them strapped on a knife, and steel toed boots. They were both wearing black jeans and if they were going out right now they looked more like law enforcement serving a warrant on a drug house then normal every day people. Robert opened another bin which had been filled with hoodies and other cold weather clothing. He took out two sweatshirts with hoods that said "Sun River" on the front and had the Sun River logo on the back. Robert thought this would help them fit in better and it would conceal the body armor under their clothes.

Sun River was a high-end vacation destination just outside of Bend which Sydney liked to go and shop when they were in town visiting. Many times Robert and Sydney had taken Rylee and sometimes her cousins there to ice skate or eat ice cream. It was also where Sydney and Robert had taken Rylee to see Santa the past two years.

Robert took a small back pack out and placed some food and water inside as well as a couple of flashlights and batteries. He did not want to risk taking the night vision gear out in the open and he had learned a lesson from the bike theft not take anything with you that you didn't want to lose or was valuable.

As they opened the door to the root cellar Robert tucked his 9mm Glock handgun under his shirt and handed Sydney a .22 six shot revolver. Both placed them in their waistbands and headed out the door and through the trailer parked out front. It was a very cold morning and Robert could hear birds chirping. He couldn't remember hearing them for a long time and even though it was dark outside he heard them this morning.

Sydney heard them to. "Allison said it was the birds mating season and they have little baby birds now in their nests."

"Hopefully they can find food." Robert said.

As they walked up the hill to the gate they passed the deck to the mobile home. The porch light was on and illuminated the deck area where the kids were waving good goodbye. Allison was right behind the kids watching over them and waving too.

"Good luck!" Allison yelled as they walked by the deck heading to the front gate.

"We may need it." Sydney yelled back with a smile.

It was now completely black outside and not a star or light peered through the sky. It was now 8:15AM in the morning and the only light showing their way was the flashlights they were carrying which illuminated the area in front of them as they walked. As they approached the gate they heard a woman screaming and pleading to another person on the other side of the fence.

"You can have it just don't hurt my kids..." the woman screamed.

"Robert looked over the fence but in the dark he could only see the flashlight that the assailant had on the woman's face. She slowly turned and started to hand the man her backpack. Robert wasn't sure what to do and stood there until he heard Sydney tell the man to drop it or he was dead. The man suddenly jerked toward Sydney and a shot was fired. It seemed like slow motion. He heard the noise of the assailants knife hitting the ground. He watched as the assailants flashlight stayed still for a few seconds then fell to the ground. Then the noise of a person crumbling to the ground came next.

Robert got off the fence and ran out the gate to see the assailants flashlight on the ground and shining right back at the man who was now lifeless on the ground. The bullet had entered above the man's right ear on the right side of his head. He was laying on his left side and in the dark you could see a gush of black liquid come out of the hole with every heart beat. He started moaning and it was obvious the man was not dead.

The woman whom he had just tried to rob grabbed her kids and started running down the street away from town leaving the backpack she had just had stolen from her by the man with the knife. Several other people just walked by as if nothing had happened but looked at the dying man as they passed. Robert and Sydney discussed what to do and it started to turn in to an argument. Should they shoot him again? Should they let him die? Take him to town to get help?

A man dressed in a police uniform and a flashlight suddenly approached from behind them and startled Robert and Sydney as they were talking about what to do.

"This is how we take care of thieves here!" the officer yelled. Suddenly the police officer leveled a handgun and fired several times in to the man. Immediately he stopped moaning.

Robert and Sydney just stood there stunned as the officer put his gun back on his belt and pulled the dead man by his collar and dragged him in to the ditch on the other side of the street.

The officer turned back toward Robert and Sydney while wiping his hands on his pants. "A couple of people stopped me and told me what the man did." the officer said. "Thank you for intervening."

It took Robert a few seconds to reply to the officer. "Do you need to take a report? Need my ID?" Robert inquired.

"Not during Martial Law. If you want to be a thief right now you just become a dead one. You two going to get food in town?" the officer asked.

"We were on our way when this man tried to rob a woman and her kids of their backpacks."

"Well you did a good thing then." the officer responded.

Robert put the woman's backpack on his back without telling the officer it belonged to the woman.

Sydney spoke up. "How do you get food in town?"

"You guys are new?" the officer inquired.

"No we live actually right here." she said as she pointed to the fence. "We just haven't gone out of our house in a week or so."

"Probably smart if you don't have to come out. You have to get a food card from the Town Hall but it will only get you food for maybe today and tomorrow."

"The town is out of food?" Sydney asked.

"Oh my...we had enough food to last until the end of the year for all of our residents and we were doing a great job of slowly dishing it out. Then the....okay I won't cuss here. FEMA came in two nights ago and said the president gave them control of the food and the right to confiscate all of it and control the distribution. So they took most of it. We thought they were going to use it at the high school shelter we were setting up. Instead it sounds like they took it all to Salem seventy miles away and now we are down to two days of food and it was really only about a day of food but they made it in to enough soup to last for two days. The basic thing is tomorrow when we run out I bet its gonna get real ugly here!"

"Wow. So what is the town going to do about the food situation? Send them to Salem?"

"Not a chance. You want food you're going to have to hike to Salem and who knows if you will get any when you get there. The roads all have check points setup now in and out of Salem. I heard they are only letting residents get in and out as of yesterday. Hopefully FEMA will send us some food to the shelter. They know about it. When things get bad I wouldn't doubt those government guys start going house to house looking for food."

"You really think they would do that?" Sydney spoke. Her voice trembling.

"After what I have seen the last two days ago I wouldn't put anything past our government. I think perhaps higher ups in the government want to take what they can get to get through this whole thing and who cares about who it belongs to or who dies because of it. I really feel that way. I probably told you guys too much. Go eat! Eat well it might be your last meal from this city."

Sydney and Robert tried to shake hands with the officer but he put his hand up and refused the gesture Robert was not so sure why. Maybe germs? Maybe he didn't want to be too friendly? Sydney grabbed Roberts hand and put her head on his shoulder as they walked away. As soon as the officer was out of site Robert pulled Sydney back toward the gate, unlocked it and went in.

"Oh, my gosh. Can you believe that?" Robert said to Sydney.

Sydney's eyes widened. "We gotta hide our food quickly! If it takes every minute for the next few days we gotta hide it Robert."

"Yeah. Go get Allison and Trevor and let's get that secret room finished today. Let's dig another hole and put a backup supply of food in there too just in case the food we hide in the cellar's back room gets found. Any food that is expired or gone bad let's leave on the shelves in the front room of the root cellar. That way if anyone comes to take the food, we have something to give them and can say that's all we have. Don't tell Allison or the kids about the backup supply of food in case they are forced to tell someone about the secret room. I will estimate about a year of freeze dried buckets and bury them after everyone is asleep under the mobile home tonight."

Robert headed straight to the root cellar while Sydney went to get everyone and tell them what was going on. Robert unlocked the trailer hitch and removed the tire locks from the trailer so he could move the trailer out of the way to stop blocking the door. It would take too long to move the dirt from the secret room if they had to walk through the trailer with every bucket of dirt.

Robert got a shovel and started digging the hole below the secret room. He was soon joined by Trevor, Allison and Sydney. Together they started moving dirt out and food in. The process was moving very quickly. Allison soon went to work disassembling some of the shelves from the root cellar and reassembling them in the new secret room.

The women put the kids in the car with a flashlight and games to keep them busy. By eight in the evening the secret room had been finished and the food, buckets, and bins had all been moved in. Virtually everything from the root cellar had been moved in to the secret room except for the shelves in root cellar which had been built in to the walls. The built in shelves were stocked with all of the out of date or questionable food as well as broken flashlights and other items that didn't work anymore. Robert then placed a few boxes of bullets and tools on the shelves to make it look like it wasn't staged. Sydney then raked the dirt on the floor to disguise any movement and foot prints to the secret room and left the rake next to the door so anyone who came in could rake the ground before they left.

Everyone was exhausted and Sydney opened a large can of beef stew to heat up for everyone. It was simple and quick to warm up and feed everyone and give them some fresh needed protein and calories. They had all worked harder than they had since the whole ordeal began. The adults sat on the couch in the mobile home's living room and could barely move. Each complained about how sore they were and how they hadn't worked this hard since they could remember. The two little kids were laying on the adults trying to get attention since they had been virtually ignored all day. Sydney walked slowly and passed out bowls with food in them when the bear bells fell to the side and made a noise. Robert was completely unprepared for this and the timing he thought couldn't be worse.

A burst of adrenaline sent Robert looking for his gun and night vision goggles. Sydney ran down the hall and grabbed her rifle and handed it to Robert as he was trying to get the power to come on the night vision goggles while simultaneously putting extra magazines of bullets in his pockets. The bells moved again. Robert turned off all the lights in the trailer and opened the sliding glass door and quietly slipped out.

As Robert peered in to the darkness he realized his night vision goggles didn't work well at all. He couldn't see more than fifteen feet in front of him. He realized that the night vision goggles used starlight or infrared light. There was neither due to the cloud and ash cover. He had a built in infrared light on his night vision goggles but that meant he was no longer stealthy and people could see the red dot illuminating his position if they stared hard enough. The red dot stood out in the pitch black darkness. He had read about getting infrared flood lights for property and now he wished he had gotten them. He had no choice but to turn on the infrared light and illuminate the yard. He saw a dark figure come out from the trees.

"Halt!" Robert yelled loudly.

The figure turned around and ran. Robert started to give chase and soon heard the man run in to the fence with the sound of a crash, then scream in pain as his hands met the nails coming up out of the fence as he tried to quickly jump over.

By the time Robert found where the man had gone over the fence he was gone. After investigating the fence he realized that the nails had not only done their damage to his hands but his mid section as well as remnants of blood could be seen on the nails and dripping down the fence top a few feet from where the intruders hands had been pierced as well. Pieces of clothing were caught in the nails as well. Robert turned on his flashlight and saw ripped pieces of a white shirt, blue jeans and something with leather. Maybe the man's gloves he thought?

Robert walked the entire length of the fence line but could not see where the man had entered. Every so often he occasionally looked over the fence and didn't see anything or anyone. He was about to give up and go back in when he noticed the top of a ladder propped up to the fence on the side of the property just before the tree line near the creek. Robert ran to the fence, climbed it and held his night vision goggles while looking over the fence and again saw a tall dark figure approaching the ladder.

"You come any closer and I am going to shoot!" Robert yelled.

Again the figure ran away in to the trees on the opposite side of the fence. For a few minutes Robert could hear the sounds of someone moving in the brush and twigs snapping. The sounds got fainter as the intruder ran farther away. Robert quickly slipped out the gate. Ran to the ladder and lifted it over the fence. It landed on the other side of the fence with a crash. Before he headed back to the gate he carefully scanned the area with his night vision to make sure that no one was around. There was no sign of the intruder. There was several people walking down the road with flashlights however. Robert estimated them to be a half mile away.

Robert started to walk the entire fence line scanning all of it with his night vision goggles. As he got to the street the people he had seen up the road with flashlights were passing. They were walking very slowly and turned around to look behind them every minute or so. As they got closer Robert turned off the infrared light so he wouldn't be seen and hid behind the far corner of the fence. He could see that it was two women. One was carrying a shotgun and the other was carrying a machete. Both were spinning quickly with their flashlights every few minutes as if they were paranoid someone was around them or following them. They appeared to be very scared.

Robert considered saying something to the women but kept quiet as they passed. Once they had gone past his position, he waited for a few minutes, turned his infrared light back on and continued past the front gate and down the other side of the fence line. As he walked he looked at all the fence slats and the ground but nothing seemed out of place.

When he got to the end of the fence just before the creek he started walking back. This time paying a little more attention to the ground farther out. He noticed something move in his goggles and it was warm because it showed bright white. It was too small to be a person but Robert wasn't expecting an animal to be there. He leveled his rifle towards the animal.

He started walking toward the animal slowly, tip-toeing, trying to quietly get closer to get a more accurate shot. As he walked up about twenty feet from the animal a twig snapped and the animal turned to look and then began to run. Robert raised his gun, aimed and fired. The animal kept going but was limping and moving much slower. Robert started following the animal to a fallen tree that was only about fifty feet from where his back fence ended and the creek began. It started to go under the tree where a small hole had been dug. Robert quickly aimed and fired once more. It took two more steps on the other side of the tree and then came to a stop. Robert could see the animal from over the tree with his night vision but couldn't get to it because of the brush and thick blackberry bushes were blocking his way. He realized that without getting a chainsaw and cutting the tree limbs or digging a whole under the large fallen tree, there was no way he was going to get whatever he shot.

Robert didn't know what the animal was but it had four legs and would make a nice meal and he started making the hike to the street to go in the gate. He thought to himself it would be quieter to get a shovel and see if he could dig the hole underneath big enough to slip through and grab the animal.

Before he opened the gate he took time to scan his surroundings with his night vision. He saw no one but his night vision only worked to see about thirty feet now even with the infrared light on to see. Unless they had flashlights on it was hard to see someone coming from a long distance. As he put the key in the lock to open the gate he heard screaming from a ways down the road going in to town. He paused and looked around. He could see nothing. As soon as he got tired of waiting for another sound and started to open the gate again, he heard another scream. Then the sounds of rumbling like an engine.

The engine sound reminded him of a motorcycle engine without a good exhaust. After hearing another scream and then several gunshots Robert decided to stealthily go investigate what was going on. Instead of walking on the road he slowly started walking toward the sound through the trees next to the road. As he moved closer he heard more screaming and the screaming was getting louder and the terrain had slowly pushed him farther in to the woods. He had been cautiously walking from tree to tree for about ten minutes when the trees ended just above a cabin.

He took his night vision goggles off because the woman who was wearing a ripped shirt and a long skirt had her hands tied behind her back. There was a man on the ground that he assumed had been shot. A child about four or five years old was clinging to the woman's leg and both were obviously cold. On top of being cold the woman was obviously distraught and crying while the child stood motionless. Robert could see them well because of the light from the front of three motorcycles was shining on the woman and the child. Next to the motorcycles was a dark figure with a rifle taunting the woman. Robert could see flashlights moving in the cabin's windows periodically.

As he watched every few minutes a figure with a flashlight would leave the house and place an armful of items from the house in a long trailer attached to one of the motorcycles. After watching for about fifteen minutes Robert had summed up that there was three men that were ransacking the house. They had tied up the woman and her husband. A fourth person was watching over the woman and child while the others looted the house. The man on the ground had not moved the entire time Robert had been watching and he assumed he was dead and probably the husband or boyfriend. Robert only saw one of the motorcycle members with any type of weapon and that was the man was standing guard with the rifle trained on the woman.

Robert was conflicted as what to do. He had a rifle with a scope and a hand gun and a height advantage. He wasn't sure whether he should get involved or not. He felt his heart pounding in his chest. He thought of his pregnant wife and the kids who needed him. If he got killed trying to help this woman he didn't even know what would happen to them. He made a decision to just watch and not get involved. It would be safer.

A few minutes later the man with the rifle came over to the woman and backhanded her so hard she flew backwards. The child started screaming and Robert could tell it was a young girl. The man yelled something Robert couldn't understand at the little girl and she immediately became silent. The man then grabbed the woman's long hair and threw her violently to the ground face down outside of the light from the motorcycles. The man had thrown the woman down on the ground just outside of the light and Robert couldn't see anything but every few seconds a shadow moving on top of the woman.

Robert started watching through the scope on his gun and could see the man's rifle on the ground in the light from the motorcycles. He could see the man's shadow when he sat up every few seconds and Robert had the sites right on his head every time it came up in to the light. Robert's heart started pounding because he knew the man was most likely forcing the woman to lay there while he had his way with her and it made Robert angry. He heard the little girl scream again and the man picked up the rifle from the ground. He started to get up and Robert instinctively without thinking pulled the trigger and the man with the gun fell to the ground.

The woman got up and ran toward the woods with her daughter following behind. Her hands still bound behind her back. Robert realizing he needed an advantage and not knowing what to do started shooting out the lights on the motorcycles knowing that darkness would be an advantage for him. A shot must have gone through the light on one of motorcycles and punctured a gas tank because a second shot created a huge fireball that lit up the entire front of the house. As the other men came out of the house running toward the explosion Robert shot the first two he saw and they immediately dropped. They were easy to see with the light from the burning motorcycle. The last man was a little more stealthy and must have come from the back of the house. He was able to maneuver around behind the fire and got the rifle the first motorcyclist had dropped.

The fourth assailant picked the rifle up and aimed it at the fleeing woman and fired several shots before

Robert was able to reload a new magazine and shoot the man three times. The assailant dropped to the ground face first on top of the rifle. Robert ran down the hill while carefully watching to make sure there were no more intruders.

When he reached the woman he could see she had been shot at least twice in the back. She looked up at him with wide eyes barely able to breathe. Robert had a good sense and could tell she wasn't going to last very much longer. She tried her best to push Robert away.

"I'm not one of them! I am here to help you! I shot them!" Robert yelled furiously to the woman.

The woman took a look at him in sheer terror. "My baby!"

"I got her right here. She's okay! The bad guys are dead."

"Not that one." Were the last words she said before she closed her eyes.

Robert looked down at the little girl.

"What's your mommy talking about?" He asked rather abruptly.

The girl was paralyzed in fear and didn't say anything. Robert ran to the front door of the house, put on his night vision goggles and slowly entered. He wasn't sure there didn't happen to be more bikers and so he cleared the house as if he was a police officer. Slowly checking down the hall and checking rooms one by one. As he was checking the first room he saw the little four year old girl run down the hall past the room he was in. He ran to catch up with her and saw she went in to the last room of the house at the end of the hall. Robert quickly walked up to the room and saw the little girl climbing in to a crib with a little baby boy who was sleeping. The girl was startled when Robert spoke.

"I am not here to hurt you. Those bad guys were. They won't hurt you anymore." Robert said gently.

"What is your name?" he asked the little girl.

It took a minute or so but the girl finally spoke.

"My name is Hallie." she said. "I can't see you."

"I know my glasses let me see you though."

"You can see me just fine?" she asked.

"Yes. Just like it is daytime."

"Really?" she said astonished. "How many fingers am I holding up?"

Robert chuckled. "Two."

"How many now?" she said quizzing Robert.

"Three."

"Okay. You wins." Hallie said.

Robert was suddenly struck by sorrow and couldn't help but blame himself for her mother's death. He certainly wanted to help the girl's mother and never imagined it would turn out the way it did. He wanted to be the woman's hero and save the day.

"You and your little brother are going to need to come with me." Robert told the little girl gently.

"Are you going to hurt me or my widdle bwodder?"

"No. I am going to help you and your little brother. What is his name?"

"Steven." she said.

"We need to take your food and diapers. Where are they?" Robert asked Hallie.

She paused for a second. "We don't have any food."

"When is the last time you ate something?" Robert asked.

The girl started to cry. "We had yucky soup when we walked yesterday but they ran out and said we needed to wait. Mommy said food would be coming soon. My mommy made us hot chocolate with water cause she said we don't want to gets behyberated."

"You and your brother haven't eaten since yesterday?"

"Well my brother has eated. My mommy feeded him with her boobies. She feeded me that way too when I woked up from my nap and tode her I was hungry. I think it hurt her cause she was crying when she feeded me."

"Ok. Is there diapers for the baby?"

"Nope. Mommy's been using washing rags cause there's none at the store she said."

Robert put his head down and paused for a second to think of what to do.

"He put the safety on the rifle and let it hang off of his shoulder and picked up Steven out of the crib who was still sleeping. He grabbed his blankets out of the crib and put them around him. He looked down and saw that Hallie had no shoes on her feet.

"Do you have shoes Hallie?"

"On the floor somewhere." she said.

Robert looked around the floor with his night vision goggles. There were toys and clothes all over the floor. He finally found the tennis shoes under the crib. He struggled to lean over and pick up the shoes with the baby in his arms. He balanced the baby on his chest while grabbing one of Hallie's legs at a time and putting the shoes on one by one.

"How about a jacket or a coat?"

"Front closet." she said.

Robert picked up Hallie out of the crib and put her on the floor so she could walk.

"Follow me Hallie." Robert said in more of a stern voice.

She followed him and every time she got a few feet away he waited for her. When they got to the closet he used the night vision to get a coat for the baby and one for Hallie.

"Go ahead and put this on Hallie." Robert said as he pushed the coat against her so she could feel it.

Robert opened the front door which was next to the closet and walked outside holding Hallie's hand with one arm and holding Stephen with the other. The fire from the motorcycle had now burned out and all Robert could see glowing metal. Robert was thinking to himself how hard it was going to be to carry a baby all the way back to his property when he heard the rumbling of the motorcycle with the trailer. He walked over to it and survey it. The trailer was half full and he moved things around with one hand to make a place to lay the baby down between boxes.

Robert picked up Hallie and placed her in the motorcycle. As he tried to put her down next to the baby in the trailer Hallie wouldn't let go.

"I..I'm, scared. " Hallie screamed.

"It's okay. You're safe with me." Robert said gently.

Hallie still would not let go of Roberts arm and he had to lift her down and hold her hand while he walked out to see if her father or any of the other men were alive still. He walked to the girl's father who without even touching him he could see he was dead and no point in checking. Luckily Hallie wasn't able to see what Robert was able to see in his night vision goggles what he was doing in the pitch black darkness. He went to each biker and found each man was also dead.

"Okay Hallie, we are going for a motorcycle ride. I will hold on to you."

Hallie said nothing as Robert got on the motorcycle. He placed Hallie on his lap and slowly kicked the kickstand up and used his body weight to pull the motorcycle backwards on the paved driveway. When he was far enough away from the other bikes he pulled in the clutch and took a minute or so to figure out the controls, gear shift, and brakes. Luckily he had his night vision goggles on because it was pitch black and he had shot out the front headlight. He noticed the back tail lights did not illuminate and had duct tape all over them. He slowly sped up to the gate which had been forced open. Before he got on the road he stopped and looked back at Steven in the trailer. He had been placed between boxes and it was keeping him laying down and safely in place. Robert could tell that Stephen was awake because he saw a hand move up. He would soon be home anyway. If Stephen were crying Robert couldn't hear it over the loud motorcycle engine.

When he pulled up a little further up the street he noticed that a light from a motorcycle was coming in the distance from town at least a mile down the road. Robert pulled out and started driving quickly toward his gate and Robert thought that the motorcycle might pass him so he quickly pulled off the road and hid behind a tree and turned off the motorcycle to eliminate the sound. He watched as the motorcycle pulled in to the driveway to the house he had just left.

Robert quickly started the motorcycle and drove down the road. He sped up faster hoping the person on the motorcycle wasn't already looking for him. He got to the gate, quickly unlocked it and drove in. He turned off the motorcycle to eliminate the sound, closed the gate and locked it just in time to hear the sound of a loud motorcycle come flying by the front gate at a very high speed but continue down the road.

Robert pushed the motorcycle up to the mobile home and yelled for Sydney and Allison. Sydney came from the opposite side of the house armed with a rifle.

"Robert, where in the world have you been? Where did you get a motorcycle? And it runs?" Robert could tell she was obviously mad and shining a flashlight on Roberts face.

"We need to talk about this later! Right now I need you to come take this little girl her name is Hallie. There is a baby boy in the back of the trailer named Steven."

Sydney got snotty. "What are you collecting kids now? Don't the kids have parents?"

"They're dead!" Robert yelled spontaneously.

Allison walked up with a flashlight.

Robert spoke sternly to her. "Allison can you get the baby."

"What baby?" Allison asked.

"The one in the back of the trailer on this motorcycle."

Allison moved the flashlight she was holding on to the back of the trailer. "Oh, how cute. It's a little boy." Her face cringed. "It's a very stinky little boy."

"We need to clean the baby up and get him in some real diapers. I will have to get some from the root cellar." Robert said out loud.

Robert went to the root cellar. It took him a few minutes to find the tub full of baby supplies. He got a baby bottle, a tub of baby formula, baby wipes, and a package of number four sized diapers. He also grabbed a flashlight and brought them inside the mobile home. Once inside he found a naked baby being held by its legs while Alison was cleaning it with a wet wash rag. Robert handed Alison the baby items and she went to work putting the diaper on. Allison handed the baby a Ninja Turtle figurine that was on the floor to keep him occupied. He started chewing on the toy while she got him dressed.

Sydney had Hallie sit at the kitchen table with a package of Cheez-Its and a piece of homemade bread. Sydney turned to Robert, raised her eye browse and held out her hand wide open toward Hallie. Robert knew she was wanting answers.

"Our neighbors down the road got attacked by a gang of bikers. They tried to take their stuff and rape the mother." Robert said.

"So we adopted them? We are going to give them back right?" Sydney asked sounding upset.

"We can't!" Robert replied.

"Why not?"

"Because the bikers killed their parents." Robert said. Sydney got a concerned look on her face. "So what if they come here?"

"They won't."

"How do you know?" Sydney inquired.

"Because I shot them."

Sydney paused. "Oh wow." She started putting a pan full of water on the stove and turned on the burner. "We really don't even have enough baby things for our own baby coming. What are we going to do Robert?"

Robert shook his head. "I don't know. I will go back to their house tomorrow and see what I can get from it to help us out."

Hallie came up and held Sydney's hand. "Can you show me the bathroom?"

Hallie and Sydney walked down the hall to the bathroom while Robert took the flashlight and went out to the motorcycle to see what was in the back trailer.

The trailer was about five feet long, four feet wide and about four feet deep. Robert couldn't help but think of all the uses he had for the trailer and the motorcycle. When he shined the flashlight in to the trailer the first thing he noticed was a five gallon steel gas can. He lifted it and it was nearly full. He took it out and placed it on the ground beside the trailer. He then opened the top box and shined the flashlight in on its contents. It was full of old coins, silver bars, jewelry, watches, and about twenty five packages of unopened AA and AAA batteries.

He took that box out and placed it on the ground. Next he opened another box. Inside had twenty eight stainless steel bottles of unopened KRU Vodka. He took this box out and looked at the next box. It was an unopened box of twenty-four MRE's. All were spaghetti with meat sauce with assorted deserts and made for two people. Robert thought that he had hit the jackpot right there. After taking this box out he found another one with the same contents. He was amazed that he could see there were four more boxes to open and the trailer was much deeper than he had first realized. Between the boxes he could also see that there was an AR-15 rifle with a scope.

He opened the next box and inside found over thirty cans of Camp's Beef and Barley Soup, honey baked beans, and SPAM meat. The next box contained a can opener, eight lighters, two cartons of cigarettes, a twenty-two handgun, ten boxes of fifty count twenty-two rounds, a machete, and an axe.

After he had removed those two boxes he was excited about opening the last two boxes. It was almost like Christmas he thought to himself. He opened the next box and it contained candy, granola bars, small bags of chips, five bags of sunflower seeds, three boxes of hot chocolate packets, and four pounds of teriyaki flavored beef jerky.

Robert was getting cold and he hurried to open the last box. Inside was six canisters of one pound bottles of propane and over five hundred rounds of AR-15 shells. Underneath the canisters was a box of empty shells, a box of gun powder, bullet tips, and a bullet press. Everything you needed to make your own bullets. Robert couldn't help but feel like he had just won the Prepper's Lottery. He started grabbing boxes and hiking them down to the root cellar. One by one he carried them down and sorted them in to bins. When he walked back in to the mobile home the lights were out and everyone was asleep. Hallie was sleeping in Robert's normal spot and Steven was asleep with a bottle in his mouth on Allison's chest. She was sleeping in the sitting position with her head laid back on the couch.

Robert sat down on the other end of the couch. He slowly reminisced of everything that had happened that day. He suddenly remembered he had shot an animal earlier in the day but he was too tired to move. He figured it was too late and another animal most likely had already gotten it.   He was so exhausted that he fell asleep sitting up on the couch.

Chapter 9: You Can't Plan For Everything

It was the morning after Robert had killed the four bikers assaulting the man and woman. Robert found himself again using his night vision and approaching the house stealthily. This time he had come to collect things for the kids and scout a little. He had brought a duffle bag and a backpack to carry things back. He had to approach cautiously because he knew that there was at least one other biker who hadn't been killed.

When he got to the hill overlooking the house it seemed exactly as he had left it. He saw the bodies of the woman and the biker he had first shot laying in the exact same positions he had left them in the night before. Robert saw nothing of any heat sources whatsoever in his night vision scope. He scanned the area three times just to make sure it was clear before slowly walking down the embankment toward the house. He stopped next to the woman and turned on his flashlight.

She was a blonde haired woman with a very nice figure and Robert turned her over to look at her face. He started to get tears in his eyes thinking about how he could have done things differently and she might still be alive. He noticed a card in her bra and he picked it up and read it. It was a driver license for the woman and it read Cynthia Marie Wesley. He felt somewhat uncomfortable doing it but he ran his finger inside of the full length of the top and bottom of her bra to see if there was anything else. There wasn't.

He took her license and placed it in his pocket and then moved to the man who had shot her. He started to clear the man's pockets where he found a pocket knife, a lighter, and the man's wallet. He opened the wallet which was a about an inch thick because of the contents it held. As the wallet opened the dead biker's license and several credit cards fell out.

The dead biker was Walter Simmons according to his driver's license. Robert shined the flashlight on the man's face to match it to the picture to make sure the wallet wasn't stolen. The man was indeed Walter Simmons. There was three business cards in the front pocket of the wallet as well and they all had the man's name on it. He pulled a business card out to reveal something astonishing.

He read the business card. "Walter M. Simmons, Assistant Deputy Prosecutor for Clark County Oregon."

He found a family picture and looked at it. It was a picture of the man with a wife and four kids. All appeared to be under the age of eight. Robert had studied how people react to the loss of food and stability. He had read how normal law abiding citizens will turn to crime and do just about anything to feed themselves and their family. This man though had really turned Robert thought to himself.

Robert went closer to the house to find the other two bikers but couldn't find either of them. As he shined the flashlight on the ground he saw bear tracks all over the lawn and marks where a bear had dragged something in to the woods behind the house. Robert didn't know for sure but he decided to assume that a bear or two had just made the two dead men a meal. Then he remembered the husband. He scanned his surroundings and couldn't find him either.

Robert turned off his flashlight and put his night vision goggles on and cautiously entered the house. It took him about ten minutes to check the entire house for anyone who might be inside. Some of it was made easier because any body heat showed up brightly in his night vision goggles and it was so cold in the house that he most likely would have seen any body heat in the house through a wall.

Robert started grabbing items he had on a list from Allison. Written very large and underlined several times was to find a spotted dog named "FETCH". Apparently Hallie had woken up several times in the night crying for her stuffed dog. Robert found a pink plastic bed and sitting on a pillow was a small big eyed spotted white dog. He placed this in the duffle bag and started going through the kids drawers collecting shirts, one sees, pants, socks, coats, shoes, baby blankets, baby toys, and pacifiers. He had filled up the entire duffle bag with just those items.

Robert scanned the kitchen for any food but there was not a scrap to be found other than several bags of egg noodles which he packed as well. Robert next headed to the master bedroom where he found a black notebook of phone numbers and addresses and in the back of a closet he found a twenty gauge shotgun. Robert set the shotgun by the front door to take with him along with two boxes of ammunition he found on the top shelf of the closet above the gun. Robert also found a five gallon gas can half full in the garage and he put that by the front door as well.

Robert was trying to collect anything he thought might be useful to survive, provide sustenance or things he might be able to barter with later. He focused on the garage where he found a portable crib, a case of bottled water, a box of paper towels, a somewhat used box of toilet paper, and four sleeping bags which he brought in the house and placed next to the front door one by one.

One of the things he noticed in the garage was a whole wall of different types of lumber stacked up and in order of various sizes from small to longer. Robert didn't have any need now for the wood and really no time to carry all of it back to his property but he made a mental note on where he could get wood if he needed it later.

He next opened the hall closet where he found a Battleship game, Monopoly game, Clue game, guitar, a violin, sewing supplies, and snow gear for both the kids and for two adults. In the backyard he collected a hand saw, large axe, wood splitter, two spindles of rope, and a mostly full propane tank from the backyard grill.

Robert was about to leave when he noticed four large boxes next to the couch in the living room. He took out the knife he had gotten from the biker and used it to open the tops of the boxes. Inside the first box was over twenty large candles. It turned out that Cynthia was a candle dealer and she had plenty of samples and product for sale. Between all four boxes there were over one hundred large and small candles. He placed all four boxes next to the door.

Robert knew all of the items he had collected were too much to haul in one load walking and he would probably need ten or more trips unless he brought the motorcycle and the trailer. Robert grabbed the full backpack and duffle bag and headed back for his property through the woods. Within an hour Robert had made the trip back, gotten the motorcycle, loaded it up at the Wesley's house and made it back to his property all without seeing another single human being on the road. When Robert got back he pulled up to the mobile home and opened the sliding glass door.

As soon as he opened the door Sydney came up to him before he even set foot inside. "Did you see that?" Sydney asked pointing backwards toward the creek.

Robert took off his night vision glasses and looked between the trees where he could see a very faint orange glow above the horizon.

"Someone has a fire going?" Robert asked.

"No it's something way bigger!" Sydney said anxiously.

Robert stepped off the deck and started walking toward the creek. He stepped up on one of the dirt mounds they had made against the back fence bordering the creek. The dirt mound was a result of digging out the secret room in the root cellar. Even though he was on the mound Robert could barely see over the fence but noticed that in the distance there was a line of fire going up the hill on the other side of the creek. The ground was wet, the trees were green and there was a creek making a wide fire line but Robert immediately decided not to take any chances. He knew how fires can jump across streets and even rivers very easily.

Robert ran up to the house as fast as he could and started shouting orders. "Grab all the blankets, food, pillows and clothes and start boxing them up! We need to get them in the root cellar as quickly as possible. If the fire burns the mobile home down we need all our stuff to be safe. The root cellar should be safe!" he shouted. "Trevor I need you to grab all the buckets and let's get them filled with water from the creek as quickly as we can!"

Robert then ran outside and shut off the generator. He picked up the generator and placed it on the back of the motorcycles trailer not realizing that he just turned off all the lights to the mobile home where everyone was packing thing up.

Sydney was suddenly there with a flashlight. "We are going to need lanterns really quickly if you need us to pack all this up Robert." she said in an annoying voice.

"I am so sorry. I didn't even think what would happen if I turned off the generator. I will be right back with light."

Robert grabbed the gas can and propane tank up on the deck and put them in the trailer and drove the short distance down to the root cellar. He quickly emptied everything out in to the cellar, grabbed the kerosene lanterns, and drove back up to the deck where he saw several boxes packed and ready to be taken to the root cellar. Robert brought in the lanterns, lit them and then started loading the boxes in to the trailer of the motorcycle. He noticed Trevor trying to lug a five gallon bucket of water up to the mobile home.

"You can leave the water buckets by root cellar. We just need to get to them if we need to fight a fire." Robert said to the boy.

Trevor seemed a little relieved that he didn't have to hike the buckets of water all the way up the hill and turned back to walk back down the hill. Trevor had been about five feet away from Robert when he spoke but Robert could smell the water he was carrying and it smelled like raw sewage. He realized that people upstream must be dumping their waste in to the creek instead of disposing it in the ground like they should be doing. It's returning to the wild west and those who don't have bleach or something to purify the water with are going to get sick and maybe even die he thought to himself. He knew this was really bad and he mentally noted that when they had to use the creek for drinking water that it had to be treated with the 'Cloudy Water Purification Process' and not just the regular cap full of bleach for a five gallon bucket. It would take much more time to make it suitable for drinking and it was going to taste terrible when he got done purifying it.

About an hour later the mobile home looked bare other than furniture and everyone had gathered outside of the root cellar. The smell of smoke was getting very stronger and with their flashlights they could see the smoke. Trevor started playing with a flashlight pretending he had a light saber from Star Wars as the beams of light the flashlight made were perfect beams.

The sky to the back of the property was now a glowing red and in the distance you could occasionally hear people yelling now. Everyone walked down to the root cellar and carrying folding chairs while Robert setup the portable crib in the first room of the root cellar. The kids were put on a blanket in the back corner of the room. All Robert, Sydney and Allison could do was just wait.

Robert could see the fire getting closer and he grabbed a bucket of water and ran down to the creek. He opened the gate he had made on the back fence to get to the creek and started making trips to the creek and dousing the fence with the water. When he was done with the back fence bordering the creek he started dousing as much of the trees nearby as he could at the bottom of the property.

He looked back and could see the fire was now only about a quarter of a mile away and he could feel the heat from the fire. He ran back up to the mobile home and grabbed the fire extinguisher from underneath the sink. He then ran to the Honda and grabbed another small one out of the back of it. Then he got an idea. He carried the fire extinguishers to the outside of the root cellar and placed them next to the buckets. He then ran in to the secret room and came out with the oxygen tank he used for diving and a box of N95 masks. If the fire over ran the property he thought it might use up all the oxygen in the root cellar and make it hard to breathe. He wanted to be prepared.

By the time he got out the door of the root cellar Allison and Sydney were watching the fire reach the bank on the other side of the creek. The winds had shifted pushing the fire away from town and pushing the fire down the creek but away from them. A large tree however caught fire and soon came crashing down over the creek and landed about twenty feet away from their fence. This in turn started a grass fire right next to the fallen tree where Robert had shot the animal the day before.

Robert immediately grabbed the two fire extinguishers and jumped on the motorcycle. By the time he got out of the gate and to the fire on the other side of the fence it had spread about twenty feet away from the tree and had started his back fence on fire. Robert started spraying the very edge of the fire with one of the fire extinguishers to try and contain it. He could hear Sydney, Allison and Trevor yelling at each other on the other side of the fence. Each was taking turns throwing water on the fence to quell the fire. Steam and white smoke rose every time water from one of the buckets hit the fence or the ground on the other side.

It took about ten minutes to get all the flames on the fence and the grass to go out. There were red embers from the tree, fence and grass but no longer were there visible flames. Robert felt he had just dodged a bullet and other than losing about ten feet of fence line they were safe and relatively unscathed. A few minutes later Trevor walked up with a bucket of water which Robert took and dumped little by little on edge of the fire line and everywhere he saw a glowing ember.

About thirty minutes after the tree had fallen there was no light except for those made by the flashlights and embers that were still hot on the other side of the creek. Robert remembered the lumber he had seen at the Wesley's house and now had a need for it. He would go get the wood in the morning with Trevor.

When he got back up to the root cellar he noticed two candles burning inside. Robert saw Allison on the floor playing with Hallie and doused both the candles.

Allison spoke in a stern voice. "Why did you do that? We can't see anything now."

"Even though it's all in the room next door, there is literally enough fuel in this root cellar to blow us all to kingdom come about five hundred times if any were to be leaking. It's better that we only use flashlights in here and have no open flames." he said in a commanding voice.

Allison didn't say anything else but started packing up all the kids things and began taking them up to the mobile home. Everyone was exhausted from the day's events and Robert could see the exhaustion on everyone's faces. The stress and exhaustion was making everyone irritable and the adults were all snapping at one another and not talking in friendly voices. Robert worried that there would soon be an argument or fight simply because of the stress. He could feel the tension brewing. Robert took Rylee's hand and they both walked up to the mobile home together. Allison had already made the beds for the kids and Robert tucked her in to bed. He was feeling hot. Suddenly he was dizzy.

Robert awoke and found himself in the bed in the back of the mobile home where Sydney usually slept. It was pitch black and he heard Allison yelling at the kids to be quiet.

Robert yelled "What's going on?"

Allison ran in to the room. Robert could hear her but not see her.

"You gotta be quiet right now Robert. Someone is outside. Sydney is out there taking care of it!"

Robert felt his arm and he could tell he had an IV attached to it and that he had no clothes on. He felt pain below his stomach where he had been stabbed and something thick and gooey all over it.

Allison had left the room and was shuffling the kids in to the bathroom. She had the night vision scope which Robert hadn't been using.

"What do you see Allison?"

"I don't see anything."

"How long has Sydney been out there?"

"About five minutes."

"I need to go help her." Robert demanded.

"Oh, no you're not! You're in no condition mister!" Allison said quietly.

A second later a gunshot was heard. Followed by a barrage of gunshots.

Both Allison and Robert heard Sydney yelling. "Drop that gun or I am going to kill you!"

Soon after that Robert heard the sound of his Glock firing. He knew it was his Glock because the sound it made had become very familiar.

Sydney screamed at the intruder. "Why didn't you just drop it! Why?"

Sydney came in the house making a lot of noise. She turned on the light, grabbed a box of .22 shells and started loading her gun. Robert stood in the hall holding the empty IV bag and watching Sydney reload the rifle.

"I had to shoot her...I had to shoot her..."

"Had to shoot who?" Allison inquired.

"That stupid lady with a kid. She wouldn't put down the stupid gun and she tried to shoot me!"

"Where's the kid at?" Allison asked her.

"I have no clue. Somewhere in the yard. I gotta go find it."

"How old is the kid?" Robert asked. Startling the two women.

Sydney looked over at Robert. "You're up? That's good. But I have a bone to pick with you! Not staying down when you had a stab wound and taking care of yourself. You almost died Robert!" she said in an irritated voice.

Allison spoke up. "It's a damn good thing you had all those antibiotics or you would be dead right now Robert! How the heck did you get all those antibiotics without a prescription anyway? You have Cipro, Penicillin, and tetracycline."

Robert chuckled. "I got them in case my fish get something they can't shake. Fish us the same antibiotics we do only they sell them over the counter at pet stores."

"Your fish must get sick quite often. Glad they we can share their medicine. Not even going to ask how you got a case of IV fluid, needles, and tubing. How old is the kid out there Sydney?" Allison asked again.

"I don't know, I think it is a girl, seven or eight maybe. She can't get out so I gotta go find her and make sure no one else was with them." Sydney put on the night vision goggles and went out the sliding glass door.

A few minutes later Robert and Allison could hear Sydney yelling at the little girl to come down. This was followed by the little girl saying she was too scared. Then Sydney started yelling for Allison to bring the ladder so she could get the girl down from a tree.

About twenty minutes later a little girl came in to the mobile home. Allison took her coat off to reveal a cute little eight year old wearing a tattered teal princess dress. She was crying and wanted her mommy.

Allison looked at Sydney. "Is her mommy dead?"

"I don't know. I suck at shooting. I shot her until she dropped the gun and then I took the gun away."

Allison grabbed the flashlight and ran out to the yard to check on the girl's mother. She quickly removed her coat and could see that she was breathing. She had been shot twice in the right arm, the left hand, her shoulder, and knee. Nothing that would kill her. At least not right away. But she was a mess. Allison could do nothing but drag her up to the porch of the mobile home where finally Sydney came out to help carry her in to the house.

They carried the woman in to the bedroom and kicked Robert out. Allison opened the Trauma bag and started going to work to repair the damage brought by the bullets and bandage the woman up.

Robert put some sweat pants on and slowly limped to the couch where he sat down. He looked at the little girl, "What is your name sweetheart?"

"My name is Ciara." she said.

"Why was your mommy trying to shoot us?"

"She wasn't. We were trying to find someone with some food. You gave my brother Granola bars about a week ago and my mommy was coming to say thank you and see if you could help us."

"You don't have any food where you live?" Robert inquired.

"Some bad men on motor bikes came and took all our food and robbed our house. We ran away when they were hurting my mommy's friends next door. We watched from a tree and they broke our door down and smashed our windows."

"Then why did she have her gun out?"

"The lady said she was gonna shoot us."

Sydney chimed in. "The lady was me and your mom wouldn't drop the gun."

"You shot my mommy before you even said to put the gun down." Ciara said as she started to cry. "Is my mommy going to die?"

"I don't know. I am truly sorry for shooting your mommy but she was trespassing on our property. Your mommy is in with a nurse right now. Let me go and check on her for you." Sydney left the room and went in to the back bedroom and closed the door.

"How old are you Ciara?" Robert asked.

"Eight."

"What grade are you in?"

"Third grade. How do you have light? Mommy said no one has light anymore."

"We make our own power." Robert said. "Are you hungry?"

Ciara shook her head up and down and Robert got up to open the refrigerator. To his surprise the refrigerator was empty. Sydney walked out as Robert was opening the cabinet and noticed the shelves with cereal were bare.

"Are you hungry Robert?" Sydney asked.

"A little but I was going to get cereal or some eggs for the little girl. Did they all go bad?"

"Robert, I don't think you realize this, but eggs go bad after a month and we ate them. You were in that room for the last seven or eight days. We ate all the eggs and the cereal that was there. We are now on to the soup cans and freeze dried foods."

Robert walked back and sat on a chair. He was dumbfounded by what Sydney had just said.

Sydney opened the cabinet and took out three cans of Spaghetti O's with Franks and poured them in to a pan on the stove and lit the burner with a lighter. She took out five paper bowls, spoons, and soon had them filled with warm food. She handed one to each of the kids including Ciara whose face lit up with a smile.

As Robert sat down to eat a piece of bread and some canned peaches it donned on him the girl had been with a father and he had given her brother the granola bars.

"Ciara, where is your dad and little brother."

"I don't know."

"What do you mean you don't know?"

"Me and my mom was sick and they went in to town to get soup. They never came back."

Robert got a concerned look on his face. "When was that? Today?"

Ciara held out her fingers and started counting each one. "One, two, three, four, five, six. Seven days ago."

"So what did your mom do?"

"We went to town to look for them."

"Did you find them?" Robert said hoping she didn't say yes.

She was busy eating spoonfuls of food but paused. "I don't know."

"What do you mean you don't know?"

"Cause mommy didn't tell me."

Robert left it at that and continued eating.

Sydney just stared at Robert for a minute then shook her head. "Ciara it looks like your mommy got a few ouchies but it looks like she is going to be alright."

Sydney looked at Robert. "She got hit in the arm, a hand and her knee so she won't be walking anytime soon. I feel so bad. Really I do."

Chapter 10: Who Can You Trust?

For the past week Allison had been caring for Ciara's mother Gina. Things had been pretty quiet and the bear bells actually looked like they were collecting a little dust. Robert had finally gotten the crutches out of the root cellar and adjusted them for Gina. Today would be the first day that Gina got out of bed and tried to walk. Even though she had been shot by Sydney she had apologized profusely over and over again for the way she came on to the property and how sorry she was for not thinking. Gina was thankful that she was still here for her daughter and was able to be nursed back to health.

Robert was down the hill in the root cellar sorting more things he had gotten from the Wesley's house when he found the phone book he had found while he was there the second day. He found himself sitting on a chair at the kitchen table in the mobile home flipping pages of the phone book a few minutes later. Hallie had talked about her grandmother several times over the past few weeks and Robert saw her on the floor playing with her dog Fetch. It was one of the few times she and Trevor weren't sitting together playing the Battleship game.

"Hallie, what is your grandma's name?" Robert asked.

"Grandma Wesley."

Robert flipped to the W section. Rita Wesley was on the top of the list of Wesley's. The address for her grandparents was on Highway 242 which runs right through downtown Sisters.

"Hallie, your grandma lives on Highway 242? Rita is her name?"

"Yup. Next to the playground."

"What playground?" Robert inquired.

"The one right next to the high school."

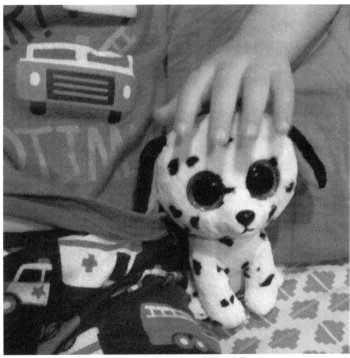

Hallie's stuffed dog "Fetch".

Robert's eyes lit up. The high school is where the emergency shelter was. Robert had learned to love Hallie and Steven but if there was a relative who could care for them that would be best. Robert was worried that they didn't have enough diapers anyway. Not only that having the extra mouths to feed would stretch their food estimates. Also most of all the space in the small mobile home was being used and they could use a little more. At nights when it was bed time there was several times where kids had to be moved to create adult sleeping space. It was becoming very closed in with wall to wall people at nights when everyone was sleeping.

Robert asked Sydney to go for a walk with him. She blushed and thought Robert just wanted to spend some alone time with her. Which he did want some alone time but he wanted to discuss taking a ride in to town with Hallie and Steven.

Before Robert could walk out with Sydney, Gina walked out and asked Robert if she could talk to him privately in the bedroom. Robert followed Gina back in as she slowly hobbled on crutches in to the back bedroom and closed the door.

"What can I help you with Gina?" Robert asked.

Gina sat on the bed facing Robert. "I know I am getting better and I know I was wrong and it wasn't your wife's fault that I got shot and I want to sincerely apologize to you for the situation and ask if my daughter and I could stay with you people."

Robert paused for a moment, thinking of his words carefully. "Gina, we won't put you back out until you are better but we don't have the resources to support you two for a lot of time. We are stretched thin as it is."

Gina put her finger up stopping Robert from talking. "I don't know what kind of deal you and Allison have going but I am telling you that I am willing to do anything to stay."

"You mean work and contribute?"

Gina paused for a moment. "Anything." she said slowly as she winked at Robert and pointed at herself starting with her chest and all the way down to her legs.

"Gina, I have a wife and there is no deal with Allison. Especially for that. I am one hundred and ten percent faithful to my wife. Allison has a special skill set and we feel we need her here. I think you just need to get better and find other family or friends to live with." Robert said angrily as he turned around and walked out of the room slamming the door behind him.

Gina picked up a crutch and through it down. She opened the door. "Don't walk away from me! We can work something out. You just can't put us out in the street!" she screamed.

Robert just kept walking down the hall.

"What was that about?" Sydney inquired.

"Oh wow, we will have to talk about that on our walk." Robert stated. "You're going to be mad when I tell you. You might want to shoot Gina again." Robert laughed with Sydney as they both walked out of the sliding glass door.

As they got outside Sydney persisted. "So why don't you tell me now Robert."

"To sum it all up. Gina asked me if she could stay indefinitely and I told her she would have to go as soon as she was better because we don't have the space or food to support her. She basically made it clear that she would sleep with me if I let her stay and I said no. She thought I had some arrangement with Allison to do the same. I told her that she would have to go."

"That's crazy. You don't have an arrangement with Allison do you?" Sydney half heartedly joked.

"No!" Robert emphatically responded.

Sydney smiled and started flirting with Robert as they were walking. "Good I'd like to make that arrangement though. I'd like to be your sole vendor for that type of thing. Can we arrange that?"

Robert smiled back at her. "That can probably be arranged."

"Good because when we get back I will probably deliver."

Robert walked with Sydney for about a half hour. They both decided together it would be best to see if Hallie and Stevens grandmother could take the kids.

When they returned Sydney was still flirting with Robert and he couldn't help but smile as he poured gas in to the motorcycles fuel tank and started the motorcycle. Sydney had already put the kid's things in a bag along with Hallie's pillow. She left Fetch out so Hallie could hold on to it. She had made a bed in the back of the trailer for Hallie and Steven to lay on while they traveled in to town. Robert started the motorcycle as Allison came out with Steven wrapped in a blanket and Hallie following. Sydney took the baby and laid him gently in the trailer. She picked up Hallie and put her next to him then covered them both with a gray wool blanket.

"So where are we going?" Hallie asked.

"In to town. We are going to see if we can find your grandma." Sydney said as she made sure they were snug and the blanket covered their necks. "Hold on to your little brother. It might be a bumpy ride."

Allison ran back in to the mobile home because it was so cold and she was wearing only a shirt and pants. Robert and Sydney were both wearing large snow jackets and Sydney unzipped hers because she was getting so hot wearing it. After making sure the kids were okay, Sydney got on the motorcycle seat behind Robert. Robert pushed the night vision goggles down so he could see the display and started moving toward the gate. Trevor was already at the gate and had opened it so the motorcycle could go right through and then he quickly closed and locked it as they left. He had done this without even being asked. Good kid Robert thought to himself.

It was about a three mile ride in to town and Robert never saw anyone for the first two miles. He turned his head to see if he could see anything toward the Wesley's house as he passed. It was pitch black and there was no signs of life as he drove by. As Robert got ready to turn on to the main highway and make a right to go in to town he stopped and looked left. There was a road block and it was manned by at least four people with guns.

The men at the road block could hear the motorcycle and turned to look for what was making the engine noise but couldn't see him in the darkness. Robert immediately turned around and drove up a few hundred yards from the main road. He stopped and looked around until he found a grove of trees just off the road. He drove up the hill and parked the motorcycle behind some trees out of site of the road.

"What are you doing?" Sydney asked.

"If I bring this in to town someone might try to take it from us. You couldn't see but in my night vision goggles I saw that there was a road block about a quarter of a mile down the main drag if you take a left. All the men there had guns out and were looking for the sound of the motorcycle."

Sydney got off the bike and told Hallie they were going to walk the rest of the way. Robert carried the kids duffle bag and a backpack of his own. Sydney carried the baby and Hallie carried her pillow and snuggled with Fetch as they walked. It was only about a quarter mile to town and a mile to the school.

As Robert walked through town he noticed about thirty people walking in different directions. Almost everyone had a three inch glow stick around their neck on a string. Each one was pretty powerful and could light up a few feet in front of the person who was wearing it. Robert and Sydney actually looked out of place using a flashlight to guide their way as everyone else was using a glow stick.

As they walked an older man with two kids tipped his hat to Robert and Sydney as he walked by. Robert took the opportunity to stop the man and introduce himself.

"Hi sir, my name is Robert and this is my wife Sydney. We live on Cedar Road. We haven't been in to town in weeks. Can you tell us what's going on? Any latest news?"

The man was balding and skinny and looked to be about sixty. He looked Robert and Sydney up and down trying to assess if they were a threat or not. The old man was dirty and his clothes looked like they hadn't been washed in weeks. Robert and Sydney on the other hand looked like they had just showered and put on brand new clothes.

"Well you look like you're doing pretty well fer yourself there Mr. Robert." the man said.

"We had about a month of supplies but we're now running out." Robert told the man. "Is there food in town?"

The man chuckled. "There's a couple o' choices. If'n you want to get sucked in the FEMA trap you apparently gets three meals a day."

"What do you mean?" Sydney asked.

"If'n you got nothin then you can come live with FEMA and get a cot with thirty thousand people at one of they's brain washin camps. You go there though you aint never to be seen or heard from again in this here town though."

"So what do you do?" Robert asked the man.

"Well Sherriff's got food from some outlaws, a few trucks on the road, grain silo's and stuff and he gives a box of food fer ya family once a week but you gotta work fer the city."

"What do you have to do for the city?"

"Well ever thing. Be a police, man check points, shoot back at the bad guys, bury the dead, raid houses the Sheriff tells you to. It all depends on your skills and the Sheriff decides the job you'll do. Sheriff's puttin together a militia cause there's big gangs stealin food and robbin people like some motorcycle dudes that up'n got themselves killed ere tryin it earlier in the month."

Robert tried to process all the old man was saying. "So if you're old would you have automatically gone to a FEMA camp? We are looking for our grandmother who lives in town."

"Nope. No way. Them government bastards won't take anyone over 65. Pretty much I think they think you aint worth trying to keep alive if'n yer old. Not sure where'd the person your lookin fer be but the Sheriff's been sendin food to the Meals On Wheels fer the seniors so they gots some food. But not much I'll tell yer that."

Sydney grabbed Robert by the shoulder. "Thank you sir, you have been a big help!"

The man tipped his hat. "Anytime ma'am. By the way you's can call me Billy."

As the man walked away Robert held Hallie's hand and looked at Sydney. "The cities road blocks are the reason we haven't had very many people trying to get on our property and robbing us lately."

Sydney just shook her head yes as they walked towards the high school. As they got in front of the high school Robert could hear lots of people talking inside. It was a loud roar and he saw several police offices and other men in jeans and a jacket holding rifles out front. There was a line of about fifty people outside the building waiting to get in and an old prison bus in the parking lot.

It took about five minutes to pass the school and Robert and Sydney traded Steven for the packs Robert was carrying as Sydney's back was starting to hurt from carrying the baby so long. It was only about three hundred feet past the school when Robert shined his flashlight on the numbers for grandma Wesley's house.

There wer no lights on inside and Robert knocked on the door. There was no response. Robert knocked again louder. Again, there was no response. Robert tried turning the door knob.

A loud scream emanated from behind the door. "What do you want? I have a big gun."

Hallie screamed. "Grandma it's me, Hallie!"

Robert could hear locks on the other side of the door start to turn and the sound of a chain hit the back of the door. An older gray haired lady who was obviously already in tears leaned down as Hallie jumped through the door and in to her arms.

"Oh baby, I thought you were dead. I was so worried about you guys." the grandmother said as she held Hallie.

The grandmother had assumed when opening the door that Robert and Sydney were her son and daughter in law with the baby. She was startled as she aimed her flashlight on Robert's face. She stood up when she realized they were not her family.

"Who are you people?" the grandmother snarled.

Sydney tried handing the grandmother the baby. She took Steven as Sydney tried to explain the situation.

"I am so sorry to have to tell you this but a biker gang robbed and killed your grand kid's parents."

The grandmother looked down at Hallie as she shook her head yes.

"We have been taking care of the kids for the past two weeks at our house and we recently found out where you lived. Here is their things." Sydney handed the grandmother the duffle bag full of the kids things, some food and diapers that Sydney had generously packed for the grandmother.

Grandma Wesley was standoffish. She grabbed the duffle bags one by one and through them behind her. "Thank you I have no food." Then closed the door quickly and locked it.

Robert and Sydney just stood at the door pondering and Sydney spoke what they were both thinking. "That was it?"

They could both hear Hallie crying to open the door but the grandmother yelled at Hallie. "Don't monkey with the locks. They might be bad people."

Sydney just grabbed Robert's hand, picked up their backpack and started walking back down the road past the high school. They agreed with each other that they had both just done a good thing and the kids were back with family.

Instead of walking home they took a detour and walked over to the Sister's City Town Hall. There was a whiteboard out front that listed news and another that listed rules. In big red letters the sign said:

"The city is out of asthma medicine, antibiotics, all heart medications, and diabetic supplies. If you have any medical conditions and you need medicine you MUST go to the high school so FEMA can help you."

Sydney tapped Robert and pointed to a note on the board:

"Starting the next Saturday and every Saturday after that there will be a Farmers Market in the Baptist church parking lot. Bring Trade or Barter. The Sheriff's Militia will provide security."

Robert laughed.

Sydney smiled too. "Why are you laughing?"

"Cause I don't even know what day it is."

As they were talking a man walked by with a small child.

Sydney spoke up. "Excuse me sir. Do you happen to know what day it is?"

"Monday the 21st." the man replied.

"Thank you." Sydney replied back.

Robert and Sydney started walking back to the motorcycle. About twenty minutes later Sydney had her arms wrapped around Robert on the back of the bike. They were both now two miles from the mobile home.

Sydney and Robert were acting as though they had just been on a perfect date. Laughing and joking as they pulled in to the gate of the property and drove up to the mobile home.

As Sydney and Robert walked up the steps of the mobile home, immediately Sydney noticed the cracked sliding glass door. Robert who was putting the kickstand down on the motorcycle noticed Sydney's reaction and immediately ran up to Sydney who was already opening the sliding glass door with her .22 revolver in her hand. She started to open the door quickly in a panic. Robert ran up behind her and could see a person's adult legs sticking out on the floor from behind the kitchen table. He had no idea whose legs they were though or what was going on but he saw Allison flopped over on the couch with her long hair covering her face.

As Sydney opened the door Rylee came running up from the couch and jumped up in her mother's arms. Sydney picked Rylee up and put her head on her shoulders and slowly walked over to the adult lying on the floor. As she approached she saw it was Gina and noticed a handgun clutched in her hand. Sydney put Rylee down and felt Gina's neck. There was no pulse as she saw Robert run to the couch to check Allison.

She saw blood on the inside of the night gown Gina was wearing and tore the front of the gown open breaking off several buttons to reveal a gunshot wound just above the heart.

"Robert! Gina is shot and she is dead!"

"Sydney, I think Allison's shot too. She's breathing though. I hear it." Robert looked around to see if there was a kid who could explain what had happened. He only saw Rylee though. "Where is Trevor?" Robert yelled.

Sydney stood up above Gina and picked up her .22 from her the floor next to her and slowly made her way down the hallway toward the back bedroom. She paused in the hallway, quickly scanned the bathroom and checked the shower stall. They were empty. Then she opened the door to the bedroom slowly and turned on the light. She saw nothing but heard a sniff and then cry from the other side of the bed. Sydney slowly went around to the other side of the bed and saw Ciara crying with her thumb in her mouth rocking back and forth.

She didn't move when Sydney came over and scoop her up in her arms. She held Ciara on the bed and rocked her back and forth for a minute or so.

"It's clear back here!" Sydney yelled down the hall to Robert.

"Oh, Ciara it's going to be okay." Sydney said as she cradled her and rocked her back and forth on the bed. "Do you know what happened?"

Ciara kept her thumb in her mouth and shook her head yes.

"Can you tell me what happened? Did a bad guy come in here?" she asked Ciara in a soft voice.

Ciara shook her head no this time. Then spoke up. "My mommy pointed a gun at miss Allison."

"Did miss Allison shoot your mommy?"

Ciara shook her head no. "Trebor did it."

"Where is Trevor now?"

She shrugged her shoulder as if she didn't know. "He ran out and Addison followed him."

"Who shot miss Allison?"

Ciara put her face in to Sydney's chest. "My mommy I guess."

Sydney immediately laid Ciara on the bed and ran out to Robert who had Allison on the floor.

"Robert, Gina shot Allison, and Trevor shot Gina. She said Trevor ran out of the trailer after he shot her and hasn't come back. It sounds like Addison might be with him."

"Trevor probably thinks he is in trouble." Robert retorted.

"Robert, the kid is twelve and he is probably traumatized. What's wrong with Allison?" Sydney asked as Robert was pushing her torso forward on the floor and lifting her shirt.

"I don't know. I can't find where she is shot."

Sydney came over to the couch and helped Robert take off Allison's clothes. First her shirt, and then her pants. Both diligently scanned Allison's entire body and rolled her over several times but couldn't find any injuries. Sydney started going through the hair on her scalp trying to see if she could find any bruises, blood, or a bullet wound. Neither could find any injuries at all.

"What happened to her Robert?" Sydney cried.

"I don't know. Maybe she got hit in the head? I don't know!" Robert said in a panic while lifting Allison's arms to recheck the back of them.

Sydney leaned over and lifted Allison's breasts to check underneath when she sensed there was someone behind her and turned to look. It was Ciara with a brown prescription bottle with a white cap. She handed it to Sydney. "My mommy put this in miss Allison's drink. I saw her do it."

Sydney took the bottle and struggled to read it in the limited light.

Robert looked over. "What is it?"

"Ambien. She might just be sleeping."

"That makes sense." Robert said as he put Allison's right leg down after scanning every inch of the back of it for injuries.

Robert grabbed one of the kids blankets off the floor and covered Allison's midsection. He then stood up and walked over to the kitchen table and put the strap on his head for the night vision goggles.

"You going to go find Trevor?" Sydney asked.

"And Addison." Robert said as he leaned down to take the handgun out of Gina's hand. He felt her chest to make sure she was dead as well. As he walked out the door he saw Sydney in the chair rocking Ciara and Rylee standing next to her mother with the her head on Sydney's shoulders.

He thought about redressing Allison but that would have to wait. She could do it herself when she woke up he thought to himself.

It took about fifteen minutes of searching but Robert finally found Trevor sitting in a corner under a shelf in the back of the root cellar. Robert came up to him and sat next to him. He noticed Addison sleeping in her blanket on the larger blanket that was laid out on the floor during the time the kids were in the root cellar hiding from the fire. A flashlight was still on in little Addison's hand.

"Are you okay?" Robert asked in a soft voice.
"Yes."

Robert put his arm around Trevor. "You did the right thing little man."

"Gina turned evil." Trevor cried. "She told Allison that she gave you every chance in the world but she was not going to leave and Allison had to die. Oh, and she said she was now in charge. Not you."

"I know." Robert said and let Trevor talk. Robert questioned himself why he had just said that but let Trevor continue.

"Gina told Allison that she could join her and do what she said and she would get to live. Allison couldn't move anymore and just laid paralyzed on the couch. Gina said it was because she drugged her. When Allison said she would never help Gina, Gina said she was going to kill her and she was never going to wake up."

Robert listened and held Trevor closer with his arm around Trevor's shoulder.

Trevor started to cry and he paused as he wiped away tears from his eyes. "Gina told me to take the kids out of the room cause we didn't want to see her shoot Allison. I got the kids out of the sliding glass door and I grabbed the gun from behind the chair next to the door and I shot Gina." Trevor started to tremble and cry harder. "I had to do it. I had to do it."

Robert put his hand on Trevor's cheek covering his ear and pushing Trevor's head down slightly in to his shoulder. "I know. You did the right thing. You saved all of us. You're a hero Trevor!"

Trevor stopped crying long enough to smile after Robert told him he was a hero. "You're a hero too."

"You want to stay here or go back in the house?" Robert asked.

"Let's go back in."

Robert picked up little Addison and carried her back in the mobile home still sleeping. He grabbed the blanket off of Allison to make a bed for her which caused Allison to suddenly wake up. She realized immediately that she was naked and got the look on her face that she was just being assaulted by Robert.

She put her legs in front of her chest on the floor and hit Robert in the arm.

Sydney noticed what was happening. "Allison!" Sydney yelled loudly. "It's ok. Let me get you some clothes."

Sydney ran to the back of the trailer quickly and brought out a white robe. Allison took it quickly and covered her front on and pushed herself up on to the couch with her legs.

"Can someone tell me why I have no clothes and what happened to me?" Allison asked suddenly noticing Gina laying on the floor of the kitchen.

"Gina drugged you with Ambien." Sydney said.

"And she stripped me?"

"No, I did that's because I thought you had been shot and I couldn't figure out where you had been shot. We weren't here when this all happened." Sydney blurted out knowing Robert had helped as well but didn't want to mention that part.

"Oh." Allison said. "What happened to Gina?"

Trevor smiled. "I shot her because she was gonna shoot you!"

Allison looked over at Trevor and tried to focus her eyes on him. "Well thank you Trevor. Getting shot today would have really messed up my whole life. I don't remember a thing but that's what Ambien does to you."

"You're welcome." Trevor said as he smiled.

Allison got up to go to the bathroom pausing to lean over and check if Gina had a pulse not realizing she was the third person to check her.

Allison got up from the floor, looked straight down at Gina. "All my hard work fixing her all up and she goes and ruins it." Allison snarled as she walked down the hall to the bathroom holding her white robe closed with one hand.

Robert got up and started dragging Gina out of the sliding glass door by her arm pits. Trevor jumped up and tried to pick up her legs but couldn't keep a grip on both at the same time and kept dropping them one at a time until Sydney came up and took over.

"Where are we taking her?" Sydney asked Robert.

"Outside for now. We'll have to bury her tomorrow I guess. Tonight I am going to have to get some plywood and fix the sliding glass door."

Trevor laughed. "Sorry about that. I forgot the door was closed when I shot her."

Robert smiled and so did Sydney.

"It's okay Trevor. You did lots more good than harm. You're a great kid! Windows can be fixed but people can't be replaced."

Chapter 11: Society Tampers With Being Civilized.

In an effort to bring people and supplies together the local Baptist Church along with the bishop of the local Church of Jesus Christ of Latter-Day Saints organized a Saturday Market to help people trade supplies they had, get to know the needs of those in the community, and trade or barter services. They had somehow obtained the use of a diesel generator that was installed in an old AMT ambulance and was powering strings of lights for the folding tables lined up in rows. The man with the ambulance was trading charging a single battery for two hours for a single can of soup that was not more than three years out of date.

The cost was also a single canned food donation to the churches to reserve your own table to sell or barter on. It was on a first come, first serve basis. The church provided a few reams of computer paper and black markers so that every table could make a list of what they were offering and things that they needed or wanted to trade for. Robert expected it to be pretty much the same thing for everyone but was surprise when he visited every table and other than food and bullets all but three tables were asking for something completely different. Every persons needs seemed to be completely different and virtually everyone there had a large amount of something they didn't need and would trade or barter for.

He scanned down the first of the two aisles of tables and looked at the "wants" for each table. One person wanted just heavy tractor oil, another wanted tampons, another wanted Tide Laundry Detergent and no other brand because of an allergy, one wanted just cooking oil, another wanted a fire pit grill, another needed just toothpaste and dental floss, another needed hot pads, one person needed a kid's coat, a few wanted bleach, antibiotics, or battery chargers.

In the next row which had quite a few empty tables, the needs were foot cream, tweezers, Borax, fishing line, and a woman who couldn't be more than twenty who sat at the very last table was asking for condoms or birth control.   Most people chuckled when they read her sign but she acted completely serious.

For a farmers market there weren't many fruits and vegetables. Because of the lack of sun light the only fresh vegetables for sale were sacks of potatoes and peanuts which grow underground. There was two tables trading for eggs which were in dozen cartons cut in half.

Because of Roberts forward thinking he had a surplus of virtually every item they were asking for. Robert didn't want to take advantage of people but most were offering double or more of the value of the item they needed if you were lucky enough to have a spare and could trade.

Robert slipped away from the Farmers Market and rode his motorcycle back to the root cellar. He took out a backpack and placed virtually every item people were wanting inside except for the heavy tractor oil which he didn't have or ever have a need for as far as he knew.

He quietly returned and visited many of the tables. Only a couple of the people at different tables had found what they needed and had made trades before he got returned. When he was done trading the items he had brought back with him, he had what he estimated to be thirty times the value of the items he had brought back with him. People gave him just about anything they had for some items since there just wasn't any others available. He had four ounces of silver coins alone he had been given for trades. That was worth twenty-five times the value of what had been in his whole backpack had this been two months earlier. He made a lot of friends that day as most of those receiving the items had felt they needed what he to give them more than what they traded it for.

For a while he also felt like the richest man in the world. He had traded twenty-five of his five hundred Cipro antibiotic pills to a man who gave him a five gallon can of gas and a twelve pack of cans of beef raviolis. He hugged Robert four times thanking him as he quickly cleaned his table and ran home to give the Cipro to his daughter who had a very high temperature and an infection. The father had taken a chance that someone at the market might have some super antibiotics and save her but he didn't think it would ever be possible. He thought he was going to lose his only daughter. Cipro was hard to find even in good times and she needed a strong antibiotic to save her life. Robert was glad he could help him.

Robert traded another twenty Cipro pills and ten .22 bullets for a thirty day supply of Mountain House Freeze Dried food in a bucket and twelve MRE's. He had also traded a normally $17 dollar jug of Tide to a woman for two ounce of silver coins. That would be $340 in coins two months earlier. Who knows what the true value of the coins were now. Probably much more.

The battery charger he had traded for eighteen eggs and five pounds of unsalted peanuts. He traded a single pound of Borax for five pounds of potatoes. He felt the man who had the potatoes had no idea of their value. On the other hand the man had a very short time to trade all fifteen or so bags that he had on the table or they would go bad. In terms of getting more value for his trade, this was the one transaction that actually seemed like equal value and a fair exchange.

He got another ounce of silver coins for a box of thirty six condoms from the girl asking for those or birth control. She seemed excited for the trade and even more excited when she saw the expiration date on the box was still another year away. Her boyfriend who came up as she was talking to Robert seemed just as excited as well. Robert wouldn't really be needing condoms for quite a while as Sydney was pregnant and still he had another couple hundred in his stockpile in the root cellar.

When he left the market his backpack was full of new items and both of his arms were holding boxes of food as well. He struggled to carry the two bags of potatoes hanging from his hands under the boxes. He liked going to the Farmer's Market and he was becoming a professional negotiator. At least he thought. But really the process was more like he saw what each person needed or wanted and named the price. The person paid it or negotiated something of equivalent value to what he was asking for. Very few people turned down what he was asking. More likely than not, they were so desperate for the items they were advertising for that they would pay anything they had to get them. Up until Robert got there, there wasn't many people who had any of the items they needed or wanted and were willing to trade for them.

Most everyone there at the Farmer's Market must have been pretty self sufficient before the Farmer's Market Robert thought. Most were only after the few things that they really needed more than anything. There was only three people advertising for just about anything and those were the ones that really had nothing to barter with except for skills. One person was trying to trade weeks of work for food. Of course it was the first Farmer's Market Robert thought to himself. The word will get around.

Robert pulled in to his property and noticed his night vision was not working as well as it had been. He stopped and took them off to see what was wrong. He thought he might need a new battery. He took them off and noticed the wind had picked up and he could actually see without his night vision goggles or a flashlight for the first time in almost three weeks. He looked up and the sky was brown with light shining though. Not a whole lot but letting enough light through that it looked like dusk. When he walked up to the deck of the mobile home the kids were outside playing house and looking up at the sky. It had been a long time since Robert had seen them playing outside.

Sydney was proud of Robert for his trades when Robert explained everything he had traded for. The only thing she commented on was wondering what they would do with silver coins and he should have traded for more food. Robert told her that he could always trade for more food at future Farmer's Markets when they were even more valuable. Sydney commented back that the food would be more valuable not the coins.

The week had been quiet and other than chores Robert, Sydney, Allison and the kids had been outside a lot during the week enjoying the little light they had. They had mostly been cooped up in the mobile home the past three weeks as there was no light whatsoever outside and it was cold. The temperature had gone from being about thirty degrees the prior two weeks to being forty to fifty degrees this week. Well below the seventy degree average for the time of year though.

There was only excitement once during the week when a police officer on a dirt bike had sped past the house shouting at an old orange truck to stop. It passed the house once with the officer chasing it away from town then about ten minutes later the truck doubled back without the motorcycle following it. Robert was worried the men might have harmed the officer on the motorcycle but the officer came flying past the gate about five minutes later. He stopped on the road a little ways down where a passerby had told him that the truck had sped back toward town.

Robert had looked outside the gate the entire week and there started to be people walking back and forth during the daylight hours. Most carrying empty jugs and getting water from somewhere in town. Robert had stopped one person who told him that they were able to get water from the lot of a company that drilled holes for wells across from the Town Hall. The company had apparently installed one as a demonstration unit and the city had connected it to a generator to get water from it. An engineer in the city was installing a water tank on the well so that it could be filled at nights and keep more water available for the residents to use. Right now they were only allowed one gallon per day.

Robert also learned that the city officials thought that only about one hundred residents had well water and of those only about ten percent now had anyway of powering their pumps to get water out of the ground. Robert wished he had a well. He expended a lot of resources to boil the water they drank and was using up his supply of bleach quickly although he still had eight cases of bleach left on hand. Each case contained four gallons.

No one had gotten sick from the creek water yet and Robert was counting his blessings. They still had over thirty gallons in five gallon water jugs, another twenty gallons in stackable water bricks, and four cases of unopened bottles of water he stored away for an emergency. He laughed to himself when he realized right now was an emergency then told himself it was for a bigger emergency.

Saturday morning he was all geared up to go to the Saturday Farmers Market for the second time. Word had definitely spread because there was now hundreds of people and five rows of tables. Not only that but there was now people with their own tables on the side of the road in front and a sign pointing people to another area in the back of the church for more tables. Many more armed guards stood looking out as well.

Robert had traded all the items he had brought with him just in the first row. People's 'wants' and 'needs' had extended to needing kitchen utensils, pots, pans, aluminum foil, soap, disinfectant, rat traps, nets, cages for trapping, blankets, diapers, pillows, Coleman Fuel, propane canisters, school books, medical books, lice shampoo, chainsaw parts, and one person was even asking for crayons and games for a three year old child.

Robert went to one table and the man wanted ice. Robert laughed and thought to himself there was no way he would get that. But shortly after he left the table a man walked up with a small cooler full of ice and traded it for a few pounds of potatoes.

Addison ran up and hugged Robert's leg. His arms were full and he looked down. He didn't see little Addison over the things but he saw Hallie. "Hi Hallie, how are you?"

She was followed by Billy, the man whom Robert and Sydney had talked to the week before on the way to take Hallie and Addison home to Grandma Wesley's home.

Billy shook Robert's hand followed by Grandma Wesley who was right behind him.

"I need to say sorry for slamming the door on you when you brought the kids home. I had no idea you had cared for my grandbabies for so long or that you had been so generous with the food and things you gave us. I was in shock when I opened those bags." Grandma Wesley said to Robert Joyfully. "I really thought that you wanted to get paid for bringing the kids back and I really had no food."

Robert smiled. "It's totally okay. I am so glad we found you."

The other man introduced himself again. "I met you's and your wife the other night but didn't introduce myself proper like. Ima Billy and just so happen to be a good friend of the kids's grammy here."

"Nice to meet you again, Billy. I caught your name at the end of the conversation the other night." Robert said.

"Your name's Robert right? If'n you got's some time I'da like ta sit down with ya and talk to ya about some stuff goin on here in Sisters." Billy said eagerly.

Robert looked at him. "Is it about working for the Sheriff?"

"No siree Mr. Robert. Sheriff got shot up two days ago. He's not dead yet but they say he has a hellava infection today and he aint gonna make it. I wanna run for the Sheriff and put my own posse together."

"Sounds like a dangerous job." Robert replied.

"Well as fer as I can tell juss talkin with ya I can tell you're a pretty smart cookie. You's can tell by the bellies of the men who's gonna survive this thing and who aint. You have energy, you gots stamina, and your bellies growin not shrinkin like most evr' body elses. Meaning your thrivin when evr' one else aint."

Robert looked around and thought about what Billy had just said. He started noticing all the people around him barely moving and most were very frail. Even the police officers and other men posted as guards looked pale and sickly. He realized that he, Hallie, and Steven stuck out amongst the crowd and looked different than almost everyone else. In fact he thought most people might even be dehydrated from lack of water. If they were handing out water in single gallon jugs that wasn't really very much water for each person especially if they were going to a family and the family was taking it back home to cook and clean as well.

He started to see what Billy was saying. All the kids were skinny and frail but Hallie and Steven were full of energy. Robert could see the difference between those who had eaten well and drank well compared to those who had not the last month and a half.

He started feeling bad that he had traded things he had too much of to the only guy who had been trading eggs and potatoes. And he had gotten more than half the eggs the man had to trade. The past week his family and guests had ate eggs with potatoes for many of their meals. Adding several cans of SPAM meat which tasted like ham over the week made for a pretty healthy meal. And mixing the eggs in to scrambled eggs, fried eggs, omelets, or hard boiled made the meal a little different all week long. No one at the house had certainly complained and Robert traded for two dozen eggs this time and another two bags of five pounds of potatoes.

He was about to trade fifteen more Cipro pills for four more cans of Bacon and Cheddar SPAM and a five pound bag of peanuts. He was negotiating from twenty to fifteen when Addison came up and hugged his leg. As he was talking with Billy however the man had traded the last bag of peanuts to another taker.

"Hold on Billy." Robert said.

Robert looked over at the table and decided to just give the man the twenty Cipro pills for all six of the cans of SPAM he had on the table before another taker came along and got those too. Robert seemed to be the only person who had any antibiotics and people he didn't even know kept coming up and offering items for the antibiotics telling him how someone had strep throat or someone had a cut and now an infection. One lady told Robert she thought her daughter had an STD. He had given fifteen to a police officer for a handful of 9MM bullets because he needed them for the Sheriff.

Robert had started with five hundred Cipro pills in his food storage but had divided them in to plastic bags of twenty five this past week and was now down to less than three hundred pills. He had taken first one hundred and stashed them away for himself and his family just in case he needed them. He had decided he would never trade those away.

Robert collected his things and turned to Billy. "Let's go have that chat now." he said as he handed one of the cans of SPAM to Hallie who looked at it and smiled. Her eyes lit up and her tongue went from one side of her lips to the other.

As they were leaving the table area Robert noticed a table selling two cases of Kraft Macaroni and Cheese on his way out. The man was asking for five bullets, .22 or .44 caliber shells only for every box of Macaroni And Cheese. Robert stopped and gave the man behind the table a handful of .22 bullets from the side pocket on his backpack.

The man behind the counter counted out eighteen bullets and gave Robert four family sized boxes and shook Roberts hand. The whole transaction went without a word being spoken. Robert put three boxes in his backpack and handed Hallie the last box. Her eyes lit up again as grandma Wesley looked at the box and said she would have to share that with her little brother when they got home.

The four of them found an empty picnic table behind the church in a barbeque area and they sat down to talk. As soon as they sat down they saw the men standing guard start to listen to their radio which sprang to life. A radio on a man near him started bursting with yelling. "FEMA, FEMA. They just rolled past the checkpoint."

Robert could see people at the tables behind the church start throwing things in to bags and backpacks.

Women and children start to scurry and leave. Billy stood up "We gotta go!"

Robert looked at him. "Go where? Why?"

"FEMA wants the food!" he yelled ecstatically.

Robert looked up and he was on the other side of the parking lot but could see men in National Guard uniforms start to come off the trucks that had just pulled up. Robert followed Billy as they ran down a trail on a dried creek bed behind the church.

Robert could hear a loud speaker telling people to put their hands up and drop whatever was in their hands. Billy was about ten feet in front and going up the other side of the dirt hill they were traveling on when suddenly he doubled back.

"Hide your stuff in the brush! Now!" Billy said quickly.

Robert complied with Billy's request and threw his backpack and the sacks of potatoes in the tall brush next to the trail. Four men dressed in National Guard camo clothing came from behind where Billy had just run from and two others came from the opposite side all leveling M16's.

"Hands up now!" one of the guardsman yelled as the guards shined flashlights on them.

Robert and the adults complied.

"Drop your food little girl." the same guardsman demanded.

Hallie complied and put her hands up as another guardsman picked up the box of macaroni and cheese and the can of SPAM and put them in a burlap sack that looked half full. Hallie started to cry.

The guardsman that seemed to be in charge looked at Robert. "Shame on you sir for handing food to your kid and thinking we won't take it."

The senior guardsman took the butt of his M16 and hit Robert above the left eye. Robert fell backwards and instinctively got right back up in a fighting stance. All five of the guardsman leveled their weapons simultaneously at him. He immediately put his hands back up again. He could feel his eye swelling shut almost immediately.

"Turn around and face the trees. All of you!" the senior guardsman demanded. "Keep those hands up high!"

He started frisking Robert until he found Roberts handgun and took it. He hit Robert in the back of the head again with the handle of his own gun. "What is this?"

Robert said nothing.

"Well its mine now." the guardsman said as he put the gun inside of his waistband.

They finished frisking the adults. One of the guardsman took a small .44 handgun from Billy and a steak knife from Grandma Wesley's waistband. She also had a pocket knife she had concealed in her bra. The guardsman had no qualms about searching there.

"You can go now. Don't come back or you'll be shot." the senior guardsman told all of them. "If you want food, do it the legal way and go to the camps like everyone else!"

The adults quickly ran up the hill pulling Hallie. As soon as Robert saw that the guardsman had gone the other way toward the church he quickly ran back down in to the creek bed and retrieved his backpack. He left the two bags of potatoes and told Billy to go back for those later. They were his if he wanted them.

Billy asked Robert is he would go to Grandma Wesley's house to talk but Robert told him he would come there tomorrow between ten and noon when things had cooled down. He took out another can of SPAM and another box of macaroni and cheese and handed it to Hallie before he started running toward his motorcycle he had hidden in the trees down the road.

Robert struggled to see out of his one good eye on the way home. His injured eye was watering and he could feel something wet on the back of his head. He put his hand on the back of his neck and wiped. When he pulled it back he could see it was blood and not just sweat. He pulled up to the gate and opened it. He was relieved when he was back on his own property. As he walked the motorcycle up to the back of the mobile home Allison came running down the steps.

"Robert! What happened? Sydney!" Allison yelled.

Sydney came running out of the sliding glass door and down the steps. She had a dish towel in her hands and immediately used it on the back of Roberts neck.

"FEMA or the National Guard I might say, raided the Farmers Market for food and guns." Robert said as he held the dish towel up to his neck and walked up the steps.

Sydney picked up the backpack. "What the heck do you have in here?" as she opened it up to see eggs, SPAM, two boxes of macaroni and cheese and other things Robert had traded for. "They must not have gotten your food."

"Oh they got food. I lost the potatoes, a can of SPAM and worst of all my second to last 9MM." Robert said. "Glad I didn't take my Glock. Really glad I didn't take my Glock." he repeated.

"How did you get hurt?" Allison asked.

"One of the senior guardsman basically hit me for no reason at all. Then hit me again because he found my gun while he was frisking me."

By now Roberts eye was completely swollen shut. Sydney opened the freezer to get some ice and Allison led him to the couch to lay down.

Sydney sat next to him with the ice. "We should lay low and not go in to town for awhile."

"We can't. I met Billy the bald guy who helped us the night when we took Hallie and Steven to their grandmothers house."

Sydney looked at him. "Yes."

"He's running for Sheriff and we were about to talk about some stuff when FEMA came barging in. I promised him I would meet him at Grandma Wesley's tomorrow between ten and noon."

"He knows Grandma Wesley?" Sydney asked.

Robert smiled. "I think they are dating."

"Well you better be careful tomorrow. I actually wish you would just not go. I will be worried about you all day." Sydney said.

"I will be fine."

Farrell Kingsley

Chapter 12: What Makes a Hero?

Robert was walking on main highway on his way to Grandma Wesley's home sporting a very dark black eye. He had just turned the corner toward the high school and he could see it from a block away now. It seemed every day the light from the sun showed through the clouds a little more. Today it looked like it was going to rain but it was actually just the haze in the sky still trying to block out the sun.

As he passed the high school which just the day before had been used by FEMA and for the cities make shift emergency shelter he noticed it appeared to be closed and no longer running. There was no one outside and no cars in the parking lot. This was somewhat strange Robert thought to himself as he passed. Just the day before the guardsman had told him to check in there to get food.

He walked up to Grandma Wesley's and knocked on the door.

"Who's there?" Robert heard from behind the door.

"It's me. Robert."

The door came open.

There was a man dressed in camo pants and when Robert first saw the pants he thought it was a National Guardsman. but then saw the man was wearing only a t-shirt.

"Come on in dude." the man said.

Robert followed the man in to the living room where he saw twelve other men. Hallie got up from the floor and ran up to Robert and hugged him. She stopped for a moment long enough to run back and get her blanket and Fetch. Then she ran back and got on Roberts lap as he sat in the only empty chair.

Billy got up. "Here is our platoon Robert."

"Platoon?" Robert replied. "What do we need a platoon for? Protection? We can't take on the National Guard."

"Those National Guard troops are fake." the man who answered the door said. "I was in the National Guard here in Oregon and they lost contact with the Governor's office, the capitol in Salem has been burned down and troops raided the barracks of supplies and weapons and took off. All of them."

Robert got an astonished look on his face. "So those guys who took our guns and raided the Farmers Market yesterday weren't real Guardsman?"

Billy spoke up again. "They's real but nows they juss take stuff from peoples. They been raidin the towns around here for their supplies."

"How do you know this?" Robert asked the group.

The man with the camo pants spoke first. "I am Tucker, they call me Ranger though. Up until two weeks ago I was a Sergeant in the Guard stationed in Salem. I only work one weekend a month but got some orders to keep control and stop looters after the volcano erupted. Then FEMA came in about a week later and took control. The governor didn't like them just taking the food and controlling the water. They wanted the governor to go to one of the camps too so he ordered the National Guard to kick FEMA out. FEMA came back with Bearcat Armored Vehicles and their own army basically and took out one of our mechanized divisions guarding Salem and tried to take over. A few other divisions including the air division came in and started to repel FEMA troops until we started having losses and mass defections. Many chose not to fight the government. It was chaos and when the top general refused to fight the government and troops. Most of the divisions simply disserted and refused to fight and left.   Some decided to go home and help their families. In the end FEMA and the government leveled Salem pretty much and killed everyone in the Oregon government I heard. I personally took what I could and left Salem for home. No one knows who is in control of Oregon."

"When was this?" Robert asked.

"Three weeks ago." Billy said.

"What about the FEMA camps?"

"Never was no camps. Dem troops pretended to be runned from FEMA." Billy responded.

Another guy from the group spoke. He was a short stalky guy with a military style haircut.   "Hi I'm Andrew. My wife and I checked in to the high school to go to a camp. They fed us some food at the high school but when we got on that prison bus they took us forty miles out and just dropped us off in a parking lot. They said another bus would come for us but a day later we were still there. A bus never came. We had to hike back forty miles."

"So does anyone have any news on what is happening with the government? Who is in charge? Anything?" Robert asked the group.

Everyone shook their head no.

"So what are we going to do?" Robert asked the group.

Billy spoke up. "We knows where them guys camps at. Their camps bout thirty miles out yonder in the boonies. They's got's bout fifteen of em and they been stockin up on our stuff from our town. They's gots four semi trucks full in fact."

"So you think we're going to go in there and get it?" Robert said half jokingly.

"Yup! Hittem hard and fast. No one's challenged em an they are gettin cokky and soft! We's able to sneak up'n takem out. Bring our stuff back to our kin folk. They is only gots one guard at night." Billy stated.

Robert immediately spoke up. "What do we have for weapons?"

Tucker smiled. "I think this is the time we adjourn this meeting and reconvene at my compound."

"Your compound?" Robert inquired.

Billy spoke up. "Wait till you's see dis place! Mr. Robert."

Everyone stood up and started piling out the door. They walked down the street and on to a trail. Robert followed while looking around to see if anyone was watching. He didn't see anyone. After they had walked through the dried creek bed they came out to a clearing where Tucker and Billy started removing several large green tarps to reveal 7 four wheelers.

"Where are we going again?" Robert asked before he got on one of the four wheelers."

Tucker paused what he was doing to come start the four wheeler Robert was standing next to. "I have always been kind of a prepper and I made a three story compound out of shipping containers and secured it all the way around. Its only about a twenty minute drive up the backside of this mountain. We are going to go there and show it to you. It is our base of operations and we have plenty of hardware there to choose from. Not to mention food and water. It's basically a safe house."

Robert shook his head as he was excited to see what another prepper had done for preparations. He still had not made up his mind as to whether or not he was going to help them in their quest to attack the fake National Guardsman but he was keeping his options open.

The trail went around the back of the mountain and there were several places where the trail continued but Tucker stopped and moved fake bushes made using gates and trees to reveal an unseen trails that they took instead of the main trail. The rest of the trail sides were thorny bushes and black berry bushes keeping people on the main trail and nowhere else. Such a good idea Robert thought. Had he had the forethought he could have planted those thorny bushes all around his property in front of the fences.

Tucker's cement block walls and shipping container made in to his fence around his compound.

As they came upon the property hidden behind several thick row of trees he was met with a huge obstacle. There was eight feet of cement of cement blocks that were ten feet high. In between each of the eight feet of cement blocks there was an eleven foot shipping container.

Tuckers four story fortress viewed from the outer chain link fence.

Tucker opened one of the shipping containers by putting a key in a secret concealed key hole. When they walked through the opened shipping container he opened the other side with another key. When he opened the hardened steel door everyone walked out to a five foot open area with another twelve foot chain link fence topped with a line of chicken wire then topped with razor wire.   Through the chain link fence Robert could see a giant tower made from nine shipping containers, four stories tall and with a ten thousand gallon water tank in the center of the stacked containers. Just amazing Robert thought. There was stairs and even railings installed on top of all the containers at the third and fourth levels.   Robert stood there just staring at the fortress until someone grabbed his sleeve as they were moving on.

Everyone slowly made their way around to the other side of the compound following the fence until they came to a gate. Tucker removed a large chain and a super heavy duty lock and let everyone in to the open area where the fortress resided. Robert just stared at the huge fortress noticing how incredible it really was. The gun positions, wench to haul up heavy things at the top, and welded railings. He was even more amazed when tucker had a person at the top drop down retractable stairs.

"It goes down two floors underground too." Andrew said to Robert as he chuckled and moved in front of Robert in the line and started walking up the stairs to the third floor.

As they approached the top of the structure on the stairs he followed Andrew who had been following everyone else down a ladder that led in to a shipping container on the third floor. That container led to two other containers on each end. First they walked to the shipping container on the right side and there was a complete HAM radio station with video monitors that showed every direction around the complex from hidden cameras.

"How do these work?" Robert asked.

"Oh, shipping containers block electromagnetic pulses. Nothing electronic I had in these containers ever got effected. Same with my motorcycles and ATV's. I had to replace some cameras but that's about it. The tractors I have down there are all built way before 1996 so they weren't hurt either. That's not what I wanted to show you though Robert. Please follow me." Tucker stated.

View from the far side of the fortress showing the wench and retractable stairs.

Robert walked them out of the room and to the other side and opened the door. Inside was a huge arsenal. Handguns, ammunition, rifles and more. Robert scanned the walls. There was 30-30's, shotguns, AK-47's, Russian made rifles, and eight .50 CAL sniper rifles. Robert was taken back. All of them locked to the wall with bicycle locks run through the triggering mechanisms.

One wall of Tuckers gun arsenal.

Robert was completely taken back.

"So you in?" Tucker asked.

"I gotta see your plans before I commit to anything. I have night vision goggles. Just out of curiosity, where did you get all these guns?" Robert asked.

"Many of them I collected over the years. I used to sell guns at gun shows. I was in the National Guard until it fell apart a few weeks ago and I grabbed a few extras there."

"A few? You mean a few cases?"

Tucker chuckled. "Pick one and join us Robert."

"So is Billy really running for Sheriff?" Robert asked.

"Sure is!" Tucker excitedly said. "He's gonna win to. Everybody knows Billy here in town. Especially after we take care of these National Guard fakers here and start controlling our own destiny."

"Okay. I'm in. But I am an excellent sniper and I want to be the lookout and sniper. I'll take one of those fifty CALs up there." Robert told Tucker.

Tucker immediately started unlocking the guns and took off the first sniper rifle and handed it to Robert. Tucker opened the drawer underneath the gun and took out a green steel ammo canister and handed it to Robert.

"When are you planning on doing this? Robert asked.

"We gotta go tonight before they move their camp. We know where they are. We scoped it out last night and I think we should hit it about three in the morning. On our quads it takes about forty to fifty minutes to get there. So we should go about two." Andrew told Robert.

Robert looked up at Andrew and Tucker. "I think me and whoever went last night should go about midnight.

Let us scope it out. We can watch the camp to make sure we know exactly what is going on when the main team gets there. The first thing we should do is snipe the on duty guard and that should be the signal to go in." Robert said commandingly.

Tucker smiled. "I like the way you think man. Okay. We all meet back here at midnight then. You better shoot that gun a few times, lock up the scope, and make sure your spot on. Cause you're sniping the lookout Robert."

Robert shook his head yes. "Okay to shoot here?"

"Sure! Right off the balcony here if you want. You can target the empty water buckets out back. I put some happy faces on them. Shoot them in the forehead." Tucker exclaimed.

Robert took a handful of shells and the gun up the ladder to the third floor. He went up to the rail facing the water buckets. Everyone was curious as to how well Robert could really shoot and followed him up to where he took his position. Everyone stood behind Robert as he laid out face first on the roof of the third floor shipping container. It took Robert a few minutes to figure out how to load the ten shot clip in to the rifle. He cocked the hammer back and it shot forward loading a shell.

He looked behind him and saw everyone standing there. Suddenly he was nervous.

"Just shoot the closest one." Tucker said excitedly.

Robert stopped adjusted his scope a few time. Looked again, and readjusted. Then he changed positions.

"Well you gonna shoot before it gets too dark Robert?" Tucker questioned.

At that moment Robert pulled the trigger and the fifty caliber shell obliterated the closest water jug. He couldn't even be sure where it hit because the water jug was an empty shell and pieces of plastic were all over the ground next to it.

Andrew spoke up and put his baseball hat on. "I'm good. I will see you guys at midnight."

Everyone started leaving and Robert stood up. "Can I borrow an ATV Tucker?"

Billy spoke up. "You's can have one of em fer wheelers. They's got a lot more at theys camp and we intend to take ever one of em."

"Thanks!" Robert said as he started walking down the stairs to go back home. As he walked down the stairs he couldn't believe what he had just committed to or how he was even going to sell the idea to Sydney. He wasn't even sure why he was going to do this. But now he was all in and gave his word. Plus he felt he wasn't in a very dangerous position. He was the sharp shooter and could stay two or three hundred yards from all the action.

Sydney met Robert outside the mobile home as she had heard the ATV coming. She had heard the motorcycle pull up so many times before. She knew the engine noise of the approaching four wheeler's engine was not the sound of the motorcycle.

Robert signaled to Sydney to get on the back which she did. "I gotta go pick up the motorcycle and have you ride this back."

Sydney yelled in Robert ear. "Okay!"

When they got to where Robert had concealed the motorcycle just outside of town, Robert got off and pulled the motorcycle out and followed Sydney on the four wheeler all the way back to the property.

"So where did you get a quad runner Robert? Or should I say what did you trade for this?" Sydney asked having assumed Robert traded something very valuable for a quad runner that she didn't think they would need. Of course it was nice to have another vehicle though she thought.

"I traded labor." Robert said as he pushed the motorcycle and trailer up behind the mobile home. I have to tell you what is going on. Let's go inside."

Robert took Sydney inside and explained to Allison and Sydney about everything that had happened during the day. When it came to Roberts involvement that evening, Sydney was reluctant to allow him to go but didn't think his part in the plan was too dangerous as long as he didn't get involved in the fighting. She was going to worry every minute until he returned though.

At about eleven o'clock Robert woke up and went out to the secret room in the root cellar. He put on a black sweatshirt, tactical pants, steel toed boots, Kevlar vest, and this time he loaded it with the thirty pounds of armor plating. He then painted his face with black paint and put on a black ballistics helmet. He looked virtually invisible in the darkness.

Next he loaded his Glock and extra clips just in case and put a survival knife on his belt. He then took out a pepper spray canister and put it in his pocket. Lastly he picked up a tactical flashlight, the night vision goggles, and he was ready to go. He jumped on the ATV and sped off using his night vision to see where he was going. He decided to go cross country and it only took him about twenty minutes to get to Tuckers compound. He look at his watch it was only eleven thirty five when he arrived. He was early. But better than being late he thought.

He flashed his flashlight up to the tower.

"Who is it?" A yell emanated from the tower.

"Robert Ralston"

"Okay hold on." the voice replied.

A few minutes later Tucker and Billy were there.

"Here's some water and we's loaded ya some extra clips fer ya." Billy said.

Tucker handed Robert a Baofeng FRS radio and put a headphone in Robert's ear. The cord attached from the radio to the ear piece had a button Robert could use to speak in to without touching the radio.

"We are all going to be on channel 144.450 Robert. I wrote it down on the back if you accidentally mess up the channel but its programmed in as channel 1. Billy and I are both going to go with you and help you scout a position." Tucker told him.

Tucker took over driving Roberts ATV so that he could hold the AK-47 Tucker was bringing and his own fifty caliber rifle on the way. Robert laid the butt of the rifles on each sides foot pegs and then just held the barrels. Robert thought it was strange that Tucker and Billy immediately drove through the back of the property and out on to the main highway. Neither was even trying to conceal themselves at all. In fact Billy had turned on the front headlight.

Both drove straight through town heading on the main highway toward Salem. Robert knew about the checkpoint just past the Shell Station and he wondered about it since they were just passing the now lifeless and dark Shell Station which was on the left. As they approached the checkpoint two of the men manning the checkpoint opened a barrier for the two quad runners to go through. Slowly Tucker and Billy drove through the gate as all the men stood up on truck hoods and cheered as they drove past them.

About five miles down the road, the quads turned off and on to a trail. They started going a lot slower for about thirty minutes then stopped. Tucker and Billy shut off the engines and got off.

"We are here?" Robert inquired.

"About a mile away. We need to hike the rest from here." Tucker stated.

Robert heard Tucker speak in to the microphone on his radio.

Robert whispered back in to his radio microphone. "I am going to follow behind you with night vision. I can see things you can't."

"Good idea'r." Billy said on the radio.

Billy and Tucker walked ahead with flashlights while Robert trailed behind. Robert occasionally walked in the tree line instead of the trail. About fifteen minutes later he heard Tucker in his ear piece. "Okay. We are here. Just over this ridge is where they are camping. Three hundred yards at two o'clock."

Robert walked up past them quietly moving from tree to tree. As he looked over the ledge of the hill they were on above the camp he saw several Coleman lanterns burning on a picnic table where four men were playing cards. There was another person, probably the one who was supposed to be the lookout standing with a rifle under his folded arms watching the game.

Robert pressed the button on his ear piece and spoke in to the radio whispering. "Four subjects sitting at a table playing cards another subject with a rifle watching. Can't see any guards or any movement."

Robert put on his night vision but couldn't see anyone else.

"Everyone else must be sleeping." Robert said in to the radio. "There are two large tents down there. No lights on."

"Anyone walking around?" Tucker asked.

"Negative."

"Okay. Well there was last night so keep your eyes peeled." Tucker stated.

"The guy watching the game has a rifle. I bet he's the sentry." Robert replied.

Robert watched for a while and then over heard the radio spring to life.

"Team 2 turning off the road. ETA twenty minutes."

"Team 2 just come up to the camps seven o'clock. Let us know when you're four hundred yards out." Robert heard Tucker reply.

"Ten four."

Robert watched for the next twenty minutes but the only change was when the man standing walked over and got coffee.

He heard on the radio. "Team 2 four hundred yards out."

"What's the status sharp shooter?" Tucker said.

Robert realized he meant him. "Nothing has changed."

"Can you take out five guys?" Tucker asked.

Just at that moment Robert watched as the man standing and watching the game picked up a radio and held it to his ear. The man then walked up to the front gate and took his position in a chair.

"The sentry just took a position in a chair right next to the gate. Can you guys get close enough to take him out and I will take out the guys at the table as fast as I can. Get your guys to back me up with cover fire on the two guys in front sitting at the table. I will take out the back two first." Robert whispered.

Tucker got on. "Okay. I will take the guard out. Team 2 get to five o'clock just beyond the trees. Take aim at the guys at the front of the table. Take them out. Chris be ready with those lock cutters to get the gate open."

"Team 2 copy."

About five minutes later Robert could feel his heart pounding in his chest when he heard Tucker. "We go five seconds."

Robert took aim at the person farthest back on the left sitting at the table thinking Team 2 would be shooting the forward guys first. Robert aimed and as Tucker screamed "go" he fired. The man on the back of the table dropped and shots fired but the guard didn't drop. Robert noticed the man put the radio to his mouth and fired a shot at the guard. He still stayed standing as Robert fired another shot that dropped the guard.

"My gun jammed, my gun jammed." Robert heard Tucker scream over the radio.

Robert saw everyone at the table was now on the ground. As he scanned in his scope he noticed the man who was sitting at the front of the table slowly moving backwards like a crawdad and taking out a handgun. He fired several shots towards the trees before Robert got in a good firing position and hit him in the chest. The man kept moving. Robert took another one and aimed for the head. The man flopped over. He must of had body armor on Robert thought.

He saw a man run out of the trees toward the gate and put a lock cutter on the fences gate. He struggled to clamp down and break the lock. Robert could see him trying to cut the lock over and over. But couldn't get it budge.

"Keep your eyes open for others!" Tucker screamed in the radio.

Robert from his high position saw something bright in his night vision. He took them off to see that lights were approaching from behind the trees about the camps three o'clock.

"I see lights three o'clock and maybe 100 yards from team 2."

"Oh... crap. " Robert heard in the radio as the truck stopped.

Gun fire started from outside of Robert's view. Robert moved his position farther left to about seven o'clock on the compound. He looked over and could see troops taking cover around an armored personnel carrier. One guardsman was being dragged away while another was shooting cover fire. Robert took aim at the person providing cover fire and fired. The man dropped while the man who was dragging the injured guardsman laid down the injured man and looked around in disbelief. Robert aimed at him but the man got under the truck and Robert couldn't see him anymore before he could get a shot off.

A moment later Robert heard more shooting in the trees out of his view. He tried to see in his night vision but couldn't.

"Billy there's two guys on your six!" Tucker screamed on the radio as Robert heard the crackle of gun fire. Then more gun fire from a different gun. Robert watched as Tucker and another man with him backed out of the trees and started backing up the embankment to their original position firing along the way. Robert saw two other guardsman come out of the brush firing. He cited the one in front and fired. The man dropped.

He pointed at the next one and tried to fire but all he heard was a click. Robert quickly grabbed another clip and inserted it. By this time he looked up and saw in his night vision that there were now three men pursuing Tucker and another two coming up the far side of the compound obviously hunting Robert and coming up from his eight o'clock position.

Robert picked up the gun, switched to night vision and walked backwards in to the trees. He fired at the first man at his eight o'clock. The man fell to the ground. The other man started firing indiscriminately at Roberts old position. Robert fired again and the man fell down the hill. Quickly he turned in to the trees to cut off the ones giving chase to Tucker and the other team member. He saw Tucker go by in his night vision and as a man came up over the embankment in pursuit, Robert only saw his forehead and fired. The top of the man's head disappeared.

"Was that you Rob?" Tucker said in the radio.

"Yes. At least two left." Robert said.

"I am doubling back to about the compounds five o'clock. Cover me." Tucker said.

Robert laid down just before the embankment right about the compounds seven o'clock again. The men in pursuit had been at around six o'clock. Robert saw two men at the gate trying to unlock it.

"Two men at the gate." Robert said in the microphone.

"Take em out if you can! If they get through that gate their going to have a lot better weapons." Tucker yelled quickly.

Robert fired twice hitting the men and they dropped. He simultaneously noticed the guardsman who had hidden under the truck get up and start running for the gate. He stopped in his tracks as Robert shot the two at the gate. The man turned around and started running back for the truck. Robert turned the rifle and fired. The man immediately dropped to the ground.

Robert didn't know how many rounds he had left and he decided to replace the magazine he had anyway with a fresh ten rounds.

"Tucker where are you?" Robert asked.

"Checking on Billy. I am back down by the trees at the gate." He said. A few seconds later. "Billy's dead. Chris is dead. Andrew is alive but shot."

"Wow. What do you want to do now?" Robert asked.

"Cover me while I clear the personnel carrier." Tucker said.

"Okay. Give me a second to change positions." Robert said in to his microphone as he changed positions. "Okay go."

Robert watched as Tucker walked around the carrier. "Clear!"

Tucker got in to the truck and pulled it in front of the gate. He got out and looked at the lock then got back in. Backed up and then drove forward knocking the gate and several feet of fence to the ground.

"See anyone?" Tucker asked.

"Negative."

"Okay. Cover me while I clear the tents." Tucker told him.

Robert watched as Tucker basically shot up the tents instead of checking them, one by one. Next he walked up to the guys at the table and checked to see of each one was dead. He fired several shots in to the men.

"Okay you can come down. It's clear."

Robert wasn't letting his emotions come out. "I'll just stay up here and cover you guys."

"I need you down here. Scotty and Andrew have been shot and I need help loading them. We will have to come back for this stuff later." Tucker said almost crying.

"Who's left on our team?" Robert asked dismayed.

"I think just you and I. Eight dead and Andrew and Scotty are pretty bad. See what we can do for them anyway."

Robert ran down the hill. Tucker had already backed up the personnel carrier to the tree line. Both started picking up bodies one by one and placing them on the back of the troop carrier. When they got to Andrew, Robert could see he had been shot in the groin area, chest, and left shoulder. He was screaming in pain. When they got to Scotty he had already died. Robert carried Andrew on his back up to the cab of the truck and Tucker started driving.

Robert opened the shirt Andrew had on and realized he was wearing body armor. The only bullets to pierce him was the groin and the shoulder. It's not as bad as it looks Robert said to Tucker as he approached the main road.

"Hang in there Andrew. Help is coming." Robert assured him.

As they approached the checkpoint Tucker told everyone what had happened. Everyone seemed glad. Especially when Tucker told them Robert was the actual hero and had taken out twelve of the sixteen guys on the other team. They all gave Robert a thumbs up as they drove from the checkpoint.

"Turn here Tucker!" Robert said as he pointed right.

"We need to get this man to help!" Tucker exclaimed.

"I know and I also know right where to go for it."

Robert directed him to the gate on his property. "This is my compound he said. And we have medical help!"

As they approached the mobile home Sydney was outside with a rifle. It scared Tucker for a second until Robert screamed out.

"We need Allison! Have her get the trauma bag and start the generator." Robert yelled out.

Sydney ran in while Robert and Tucker carried Andrew by the shoulders in to the living room. They quickly picked up the kids and moved them to the back bedroom. Trevor stayed to watch what was going on in the living room.

Allison put on latex gloves and started cutting away Andrews pants while Tucker excused himself and said he had to go. Robert was kind of surprised how quickly Tucker just left Andrew. He knew though that there was so much that needed to be done though.

Sydney helped Allison clean the wound near his groin and noticed he had a bullet wound actually to the inside of his leg and the bullet had only pierced the bottom of his scrotum. Robert winced as he imagined the same injury to himself.

"Robert he's going to need some of those pain pills you got out there!" Allison said loudly.

Robert headed out to the root cellar. When he returned with a bottle of Hydrocodone he gave Andrew two of them while Sydney gave him a glass of water to drink. Allison sprayed Lidocaine used for giving tattoos on the open wounds on his leg and other areas just before Andrew screamed out loudly from the first needle Allison stuck in to suture his wounds.

Robert got up to walk away because his stomach started getting queasy from seeing the wounds. As he got up Sydney stopped him.

"So what happened?" Sydney asked in a disturbing tone of voice with her arms folded.

"It wasn't good." Robert said. "Right after we attacked the camp an armored personnel carrier showed up obviously back from a raid. It was horrible timing."

"So is he the only one who got hurt?" Sydney asked.

"Tucker, Andrew and I are the only ones who made it."

Sydney's eyes opened and her jaw dropped for a second or two. "You mean to tell me out of twelve or thirteen of you, you're the only ones who made it back? Are they going to come after us now?"

Robert shook his head no. "They are all dead. We took them out. In the end we won."

"Did Billy go with you guys?" Sydney asked.

Robert shook his head yes. Sydney immediately knew what that meant and shook her head no and walked to the back room where the kids were sleeping leaving Robert the only one standing in the living room. Robert heard her crying in the bathroom a few minutes later.

Robert laid down on the couch about six in the morning and closed his eyes.

Around eight Allison woke Robert up. "There is honking down by the gate Robert."

Robert grabbed his gun and started running up to the gate. He could see the top of the troop carrier as he ran up. He opened the gate and the troop carrier which was hauling a green camouflaged covered 10x30 car carrier drove past him and up to the mobile home not even stopping.

By the time Robert had ran back up to the mobile home he saw a tall skinny blonde haired woman hugging Andrew on the floor and crying.

Robert turned to Tucker who was standing off to the side. "The wife I assume?"

"Yes sir!" Tucker said smiling. "I got some things for you man for all you have done." as he pointed out the sliding glass door.

Robert followed Tucker out the door to the back of the car carrier on the back of the personnel carrier. It took Tucker a few minutes to open the lock but when he opened it the car carrier contained two pallets of MRE's, one pallet of teriyaki beef jerky, about twenty rifles laid in a pile, at least 20 five gallon water jugs, hundreds of rounds of ammunition, a giant medical kit including Morphine and drug packs, and in the back corner Robert couldn't believe his eyes. Three huge spools of five hundred feet of razor wire.

"Want me to leave this right here?" Tucker asked.

"No. Can you drive it down the hill a little to the root cellar just behind the deck and leave it?"

Robert ran in to get Trevor. When they got back out to the trailer Tucker had already unhitched it and Robert opened the back door.

Trevor's eyes lit up. "There must be five hundred boxes in here!" Trevor exclaimed. "Can I eat some of the beef jerky?"

Robert smiled "All you want man. Don't touch the razor wire. Wait for me to take care of that."

Trevor nodded his head yes and started trying to pull on the shrink wrap around the first pallet. He struggled but made no progress until Robert handed him his survival knife.

Tucker drove off again and was gone by the time Robert walked out of the trailer carrying the trauma bag and the Military Field Emergency Medicine Supply Kit and the drug packs. He walked up to the mobile home and opened the door. As soon as Robert walked in, Andrew's crying wife put his arms around Robert and hugged him and wouldn't let him go.

"What was that for?" Robert asked as he half heartedly chuckled.

"Everyone says you're the reason Tucker and Andrew came home last night. They said you killed twelve guys and there was only sixteen. Tucker said his gun jammed and never was able to even get a shot off." Andrews wife said.

"Is that true Robert?" Sydney inquired.

Robert shook his head yes with no excitement on his face. "Something like that."

Sydney then took Andrews wife's place and hugged him too. "You're not just my hero, your pretty much the whole towns hero hun." she said with a smile.

Trevor ran in. "You have 288 cases of MRE's dad! There is thirty six in each one so that's um...that's 10,328. We are set for life!"

"288 cases Robert?" Sydney asked with a shocked look.

"Yes. But did you just call me dad Trevor?" Robert asked with a smile.

"Well you kind of are now." Trevor said as he ran back outside with excitement.

Robert looked at Sydney who just smiled.

"So Allison what's the prognosis for the patient on my floor? When can I move him to replace my carpeting?" Robert asked.

"Well I think he will live if we give him some of your antibiotic pills and send him on his way." Allison said.

Robert almost forgot about the bag he was carrying. "There might be what you need in here." he said as he handed Allison the Army Trauma bag and drug packs.

Allison took the bag and was dumbfounded. "Oh wow! There's Morphine, sedatives, Adderol, this is about all the injectable drugs a hospital would have. Oh here's Penicillin! Turn over big boy." she said as she took out the vial and poked a needle in to the top of it.

Andrew said nothing as she poked the needle in his left butt cheek and squeezed down the plunger.

"Okay you can go now." Allison told Andrew as she pressed the needle down on the floor to bend the needle so it couldn't be used again. "I'm done with you!"

Robert took the headphones out of the radio he used the night before. "Tucker you out there?...Team 2?"

The radio soon sprang to life. "This is Johnny. Tucker is on his way out to the camp. Something I can help you with? I am Tucker's best friend."

"This is Robert. When he gets back can you let him know Andrew is ready to be picked up?"

"Oh, man Robert. I heard you're awesome dude! The town's planning a celebration in yours, Tucker, and Andrew's honor. Ever thought of being Mayor or Sheriff?" Johnny said.

"Nope. Not really." Robert replied.

Johnny spoke up again. "The election starts this evening and with the Sheriff dead and Billy gone it's a write in only ballot. You better pick one and run!"

Another person came on the radio. "Robert this is Mik. I hear you're the real hero in this whole thing last night and I am voting for you for Sheriff spread the word!"

Robert thought he had heard a growl at the end of the transmission. Suddenly the radio sprang to life as Sydney and Robert listened. It seemed the whole town knew about the radio channel and person after person got on praising the men from the night before and thanking Robert for all he had done. Even Hallie got on the radio right after Grandma Wesley praised Robert and stated how sad she was that she had lost Billy. Hallie called Robert her uncle and told everyone listening to vote for her uncle, her hero for Sheriff.

Captain Johnston from the Sisters Police Department got on the radio. "Robert I am the Captain of the police department here in Sisters. I want to personally thank you for all your efforts on our behalf last night! Already we have hauled enough food from those low life's camp to feed the entire city for at least a year and we are still not done hauling things back. We just brought a semi back which was originally destined for our city and Bend with sixteen pallets of MRE's. And there are two other trucks we haven't even opened yet! Robert, you and the men last night will be remembered in this town for years to come!"

Sydney looked at Robert. "Wow! I had no idea what you were doing was this important." she smiled razzing him. "Hero..."

Robert turned down the radio as more and more people from town got on and declared their allegiance to Robert as Sheriff and Tucker for Mayor.

Andrews wife got up. "What about Andrew? He got shot helping." she said seeming very annoyed he wasn't being mentioned at all.

Robert got on the radio and reminded everyone of the losses and about Andrew who had been shot taking part in the action as well. That stopped the sheriff and Mayor chatter for a few minutes but then the chatter returned to everyone declaring their votes for Robert and Tucker.

Andrew's wife just put her hands up in the air. Andrew pulled her down next to him. "Don't worry about it hun."

"I guess you're right." she said as she put her head down on Andrew's chest.

Robert sat in the chair and closed his eyes and went back to sleep. He awoke later in the afternoon to the sound of Tucker coming through the door.

Andrew and his wife Shannon stood up and slowly walked to the truck as Tucker told Sydney and Robert they needed to go with him.

Robert stretched. "I'm not in any condition to go out now. I am so tired."

"Well put on a hat hero man. You're going in to town. We are the main celebrities. The entire town pretty much is in the Town Hall Plaza and waiting for us to get there." Tucker said. "Oh and if you hadn't heard yet you're the new Sheriff in town."

"What?" Robert said amazed.

"Oh yeah. I might be Mayor but it's too close to call right now." Tucker said excitedly.

Sydney just stood there. She had been dressed and ready probably hours before. Robert grabbed his backpack and both of them followed Tucker out the door to the truck and drove in to town.

As soon as they pulled up in front of the Town Hall four police officers came up to the truck and opened the door for Robert and helped him down. One shook hands with him while two others put their hands out to move the crowd and to clear space for Robert to walk. As he shook hands with someone in the crowd the fourth officer clipped a Sheriffs Badge on his belt.

Robert looked down at the badge which was gold and said "Sheriff. Officer #001". He looked around the plaza which was filled with hundreds of people and almost everyone of them had a big white case of thirty six MRE's. Some had individual MRE's in their hands holding them up in celebration. He could see the end of a white semi parked at the end of the lawn and three men off loading MRE's to people in line.

A man walked up to Robert. "Hi Mr. Ralston. I am the City Manager Craig Tyler. I was wondering if we could have a meeting tomorrow morning sometime?" he asked.

"Walk with me Craig." Robert commanded as he shook hands with people he didn't even know.

"Yes sir!" the man said saluting Robert.

Robert turned to the officer walking next to him. "Can you find me Hallie Wesley and her grandmother Rita?"

"Yes sir!" the officer said as he scooted away and in to the crowd.

A loud speaker could be heard asking for the Wesley's to come to the front. The officer returned. "They are at their home Sheriff. I sent a car to go get them."

Robert shook the officers hand and said "Thank you" as he approached the podium setup in the plaza. Robert had not yet gotten used to being called Sheriff.

As Robert was about to pick up the microphone, Craig leaned over to Robert and whispered in his ear. "Tucker didn't get enough votes for Mayor."

Robert looked over to Craig. "That's too bad. Then who is now Mayor so I can announce it?"

Craig got a concerned look on his face. "You're the Mayor and the Sheriff."

"Is that possible to be both?" Robert asked the City Manager. "Is it legal?"

"Possible yes. Legal yes. You were legally voted in and the city elections chair has entered it in to the official record. So officially you are the first Sheriff and Mayor ever elected at the same time. Never has this happened before in all of history." Craig said. "Anywhere as far as I know of, but I don't have the Internet to confirm that."

Robert handed Craig the microphone. "You would be the better person to announce all that to everyone."

Robert didn't see Tucker or the personnel carrier anywhere. Maybe Tucker already knew he thought.

Craig picked up the microphone. "Hello everyone, I am here with Robert Ralston the new Sheriff."

The plaza erupted in cheers. So loud that Craig had to stop speaking for several minutes for the crowd to die down.

"We have a very interesting situation here folks! Our little city is making history with a new Mayor! Your Sheriff Robert Ralston has also been voted in as your new Mayor!" Craig said and then paused.

There was dead silence for what seemed like an eternity as people tried to process what they had just heard. Then the cheering erupted again.

As Robert picked up the microphone Hallie and Grandma Wesley came up on the stage. They were soon followed by an officer carrying little Steven. Sydney grabbed little Steven out of the officers hands. Steven who had been crying looked when the officer was holding him looked up to see who had taken him. He saw it was Sydney and smiled, quickly hugged her, then laid his head on her shoulders.

Robert picked up Hallie and held her with one arm as he spoke in to the microphone. "As your Sheriff and Mayor I sincerely hope that I can meet all of your expectations. I would like to introduce my wife Sydney. We have a son named Trevor and a daughter named Rylee. We come from Portland, Oregon but own property here in town. I look forward to serving you!"

The crowd again erupted in to applause as Robert put Hallie down as he picked up his backpack and walked down off the stage.

He turned to the officer who had helped him once before. "Do I have an office somewhere close?"

The officer paused for a minute. "Yeah. I guess you have two of them."

"Just take us to the Sheriff's office." Robert said.

"The Mayor's office is nicer and you have a bigger conference room." The officer said.

"Okay. Let's go there. Oh, and can you get about five cases of MRE's and deliver them to the Wesley's house. Make sure they get back home safely also."

"Yes, sir."

Robert, Sydney, Craig and four police officers left the podium and walked through the front doors of the City Hall where it was quiet. Robert looked around but did not see where the Wesley's had gone or the officer he had told to make sure they got home. He did hear a commotion outside and someone yelling for help. He figured the officers outside would take care of whatever was going on.

The officer he was walking with Robert would later find out was Captain Johnston who led them to the conference room where they all took a seat.

Robert looked at Craig. "Where do we start?"

Craig thought for a moment. "I guess we should make appointments."

"What are appointments?" Robert asked as Craig retrieved a binder from one of the shelves.

"That's who you assign as advisors or as heads of departments." Craig replied.

"Are they paid?"

"Of course." Craig said to Robert.

"Do they get housing?" Robert queried.

"They get whatever you want. You are the Mayor. So long as its within reason. The city council can overrule anything you do with a unanimous vote." Craig informed Robert.

"Does the city have housing?" Robert asked Craig.

"About twenty apartments, four repossessed mobile homes, eight or nine vacation homes...I can get you a list. The city has a lot of properties we have gotten from failure to pay taxes over the past few years. We have held on to them to sell them when the real estate market gets better. It helps to have those properties on the books for collateral to get loans for the city."

"I see. Okay so who do I have to assign?"

"Well that's appoint. We can go down the list. Just give me a name. Assistant Deputy Sheriff."

"Tucker."

Craig spoke up. "You know Tucker used to be the Fire Chief?"

Robert got serious. "So what happened? Why is he not Fire Chief anymore?"

Craig said in a serious tone. "Because you just made him your assistant."

Sydney laughed but no one else did.

"Okay. Finance and Budget Director."

"Skip for now."

"Okay Parks and Recreations Director."

"Hold on." Robert said. "How many of these are there?'

"About twenty."

"Is there a medical director?" Robert asked.

"Of course."

"Make it Allison Turner" Robert said. "And she and her little girl are going to need an apartment."

"I wouldn't want that job." Craig said.

"Well why not?" Robert asked.

"The city is pretty much out of every medicine. Even Insulin and Morphine used the most at the hospital and the two elderly care homes. Those places are a horrid mess and the buildings are going to just need to be demolisged and rebuilt when this is over. At last check we had forty or so Insulin dependent people who are going to die soon." Craig said.

Captain Johnston spoke up. "We were taking a wait and see approach and now it's more like a watch and die approach."

Robert pushed the palm of his hand on to his forehead. He started thinking that him being there was the most craziest things he could of have ever imagined. He thought to himself that he certainly was no hero like the city thought he was. Now he was making all the decisions for not just his family and guests but now for the entire city and their guests.

Sydney spoke up. "I am curious who shot the old Sheriff?"

Craig looked at her. "The old Mayor did."

Roberts eyes lit up. "The old Mayor shot the Sheriff?" he said in disbelief. "And the Sheriff shot him?"

Craig shook his head no. "No, the old Mayor is just fine. He shot the Sheriff because the Sheriff ordered the Mayor's son to be shot for looting and robbery without consulting the him first." Craig paused. "It's something you are going to have to deal with as Sheriff now."

"So is the Mayor in the jail?" Sydney asked.

"Nope. He left the building and Deputy Mitchell picked up a resignation letter from him to the city council that evening."

Robert looked up at Captain Johnston. "Why has no one arrested him?"

"Because the Sheriff or the Mayor has to give the order. We are still under Martial Law." Captain Johnston said. "The county prosecutor is not issuing arrest warrants. The Mayor and the Sheriff give the orders in Martial Law."

Robert gave his first executive order. "Do it! Arrest him." Robert looked around the table. "Anyone have a problem with that?"

No one said anything. Craig and Captain Johnston both shook their heads no.

"Craig just give me a list of appointments and give me your recommendations for each position if you have any." Robert said as he stood up to leave.

The door opened up to the conference room and an officer handed Captain Johnston a radio, handgun, holster, and two extra magazines. "We got about twenty radios that actually work from the camp attack last night. They are all charged up and we are going to start using them. Here is one for you Sheriff. Here is also your service weapon sir."

"Thank you." Robert said as he clipped the radio to his belt, then clipped the handgun holster next to his new Sheriff's badge on his belt and holstered his new gun.

"One more thing" Captain Johnston said. "What are we going to do about Salem?"

"What about Salem?" Robert asked as he sat back down.

Craig interrupted. "Salem is a big city. They are out of food. It's virtually lawless. Refugees are coming for food and their numbers are doubling every day. There is a rumor that there is a huge gang going house to house. They're killing and plundering everything and no one can stop them. The groups are much larger than the eight or nine bikers who overran our checkpoint a few weeks back. What concerns us is even though Salem is a hundred miles away, we are not prepared in any way for them or any other organized group that comes here."

Robert thought for a moment. "What kind of weapons are we getting from the National Guard camp?"

Captain Johnston spoke up. "Not too many. But food was our focus."

"Get officers up there right now to take over and inventory what is coming back. We need to post guards and help clear that huge camp out as quickly as possible. Get me a list of what's there and try and get Tucker to tell us what he has already gotten for weapons. There are about twenty rifles at my house that Tucker delivered to me." Robert stated.

"Yes sir!" Captain Johnston said as he left the room.

"Craig." Robert said. "How many officers do we have?"

"You mean how many do you have? Sixteen deputies, two detectives, one captain, and a lieutenant."

"So twenty?" Sydney asked.

"Yes."

Deputy Mitchell who had been escorting them all evening walked in to the conference room and looked at Robert. "Sir. Are you related to the Wesley's somehow?"

Robert looked at Sydney. Then looked at the officer. "Yes. Why."

"Well I am sorry to tell you this but Rita Wesley has passed away. The officers think she had a stroke as she was coming off the podium this afternoon, sir. Possible from the stress from the loss of Billy maybe."

Sydney got tears in her eyes "Oh, no."

Officer Mitchell looked up "What do I do with the kids sir?"

Sydney got up. "Let's go get them." she said as she walked out with the officer.

A minute later Sydney stuck her head back in the conference room door. "Robert I am going to need Allison home with me. If you make her the medical director that's going to be a problem." She closed the door and walked down the hall.

Craig looked at Robert. "Scratch Allison Turner for medical director?" he said facetiously.

Robert looked at him. "Yup." Humorously. He sat back in his chair and sighed.

Robert was amazed at how well he got along with Craig. He also liked Craig's spontaneous sense of humor. He gave Robert the information he needed to know but always seem to leave out that one piece of information that Robert would ask about and he would rhetorically say it and it would be something funny or strange about the situation. He suddenly remembered that with Craig's balding hair and glasses he reminded Robert of the school principal in the cartoon TV show "Handy Manny". In fact Robert repeated to himself. That's exactly who Craig reminded him of.

Robert spent the next half hour going over city government appointments. Robert had kept Tucker as the Fire Chief and assigned Andrew as the Emergency Services Director. For his assistant he assigned Captain

Johnston. A better choice thought by both Craig and him both. For most of the other positions they thought it best to reoffer the positions to the incumbents and let them just continue in their positions.

As they finished the meeting a long haired teenage girl walked in the room carrying school books. Craig looked at her. "Oh, Sheriff Ralston. This is Mikayla. She is an intern from the college that has been here since she was sixteen. She helps out a lot around here and we really should think about offering her an official position with the city. Right now her only pay is double rations for her and her family."

Mikayla spoke up. "Completely worth it right now. You already know of me though Mr. Ralston."

"I do?"

Mikayla shook her head yes. "Do you remember two weeks ago when you traded my dad twenty Cipro pills to help his daughter recover from an infection?"

Robert shook his head up and down.

"That daughter was me. Those pills healed me up in two days. I would have been dead in two days had you not had those. Thank you."

Craig handed her the list he and Robert had made. "We need letters typed up for each of these people on the list and have them hand delivered. If they have a red star it means they need to accept the letter of intent. The rest just need a letter notifying them that they will continue in their old positions with the new administration."

Mikayla looked at the list and started walking out of the room but stopped. "Did you mean to put on Chris Norton for Treasurer?" She said in a sorrowed voice.

"Why?" Craig asked.

"He died yesterday in the raid." she said. "At least that is what I had heard anyway."

Craig looked at Robert who shook his head yes and then looked at Mikayla. "Ignore that one for now and we will discuss it."

Mikayla walked out of the room.

Craig took out another page with a list of nine names. "We really need to talk about compensation and how we are going to feed the families of those who died in the raid last night." Craig told Robert.

All but one had a wife and kids and are all long time residents of this town.

Just at that moment Officer Mitchell rushed in the room. "Sheriff. There is something bad happening at the checkpoint sir. They radioed in that they were in a fire fight with unknown subjects. They were turning away a group of people and several of the refugees started shooting at the checkpoint officers. They are calling for help!"

Robert got up and picked up his backpack. "Do we have some better weapons than handguns?"

"Yes sir. Follow me."

Robert and Officer Mitchell ran to the gun locker and opened it. There was not as many guns as Robert thought a city should have but he grabbed a shotgun and an M16 and three thirty round clips which had already been loaded.

They ran out to the back lot and got in to an old white Chevy El Camino and raced out of the parking lot towards the checkpoint. As they got closer they could hear shooting. Robert asked to be let out just before the gas station and ran in to the forested area confusing Officer Mitchell who continued on to help.

Robert continued through the forest as fast as he could run. As he got closer to the shooting he opened his backpack and took out his night vision goggles. He ran up to the trees just above where the shooting was happening. Robert could see the officers pinned down behind two trucks used to block the road as two assailants fired. He watched them as they changed positions to the other side. Robert took a position behind them and started creeping up on the two.

They slowly closed the distance as one attacker fired on the truck while the other moved closer to the truck in a tactical fashion. Robert closed his distance twice as fast and waiting until he was only fifteen feet from the attackers when he opened fire with his M16 immediately silencing both attackers.

Robert yelled out. "It's clear!" Robert noticed about five other people on the ground hiding from the chaos or were shot. He couldn't tell in his night vision.

One of the officers yelled from behind the truck. "Who are you?"

Robert overheard Officer Mitchell yell to the man. "Its Sheriff Ralston you goof."

Both men got up and walked out with their guns drawn.

"There are six people on the ground at your eleven o'clock and fifty feet up. There are four more at your one o'clock and seventy five feet. The shooters are down on the ground twelve feet in front of you at ten and two o'clock." Robert yelled.

The man who was with Officer Mitchell quickly asked. "How does he know that? How does he know that?"

Robert yelled back. "I have night vision goggles."

The man retorted. "Dang! We need some o' those!"

A moment later Captain Johnston and two other officers showed up on motorcycles. Each helped to frisk the men and women on the ground and investigate who the attackers were.

Robert had them all brought back to the police station and have them interrogated. He wasn't going to do that until he found that one of the people laying on the ground was the sister of one of the dead attackers and thought this might be something bigger than just the two people attacking the checkpoint. Especially when he found an AK-47 underneath the heavy jacket she was wearing. She also seemed pretty unbelieving that her brother was dead.

She made one comment when Officer Mitchell was questioning her that really stuck out. She said. "This never happened before."

All three officers heard her statement and immediately knew this group had attacked other places before and they needed to know more.

Captain Johnston had them all placed in handcuffs and brought back to the jail at City Hall. Before they had even made it back to the jail the story of how Robert had single handedly killed both attackers was told on the radio. As he walked in to City Hall Mikayla, Craig, the jail guards, and the officer at the front desk were wanting high-fives from Robert or to shake his hand in congratulations.

Sydney, Hallie, and Steven were in the conference room when Robert walked in. Sydney had her head on the table sleeping with Steven on the table in a blanket. Sydney's arm was reached out and holding on to Steven while Hallie drew on some computer paper. She had made quite a mess at the end of the table with scissors, ink pens, and the computer paper. In all the mess Robert really couldn't make out anything she had made but a mess of cut up paper with scribble marks and pencil hole marks.

    Robert let everyone know that he was going home and asked for a ride. Captain Johnston told him he could just take a maintenance truck from the yard and handed him the keys. Robert picked up Steven while Hallie and Sydney followed.

Chapter 13: Overwhelming Circumstances.

From Robert's research long before the crisis began and Yellowstone erupted, he learned early on that one of the best skills to acquire was adaptability. He learned that overcoming any crisis requires you to do things that you are in no way accustomed to doing. Not only that but being able to adapt makes it easier to adjust your life and your mental outlook to make the uncomfortable become comfortable.   Just one area of adaptability was the financial collapse after the volcano erupting, the earthquake, and the EMP that struck. Having the ability to find new ways of doing things, changing your lifestyle, accepting that what you have is as good as it's going to get, and dealing with it kept Roberts mental outlook up.

As Robert walked in to the conference room a line of people were there to tell him their problems and see if he could find a solution for their problems. Robert learned very quickly that everyone expected a solution even when there was no possible solution. In fact the second person he let in to see him threatened him after he told the person there was no way to get a high volume of water weekly to his property nine miles away. Robert volunteered to get him ten gallons delivered which was nine more gallons than the limits set by the previous Mayor. It wasn't enough the man insisted before Robert had him removed from the conference room.

Lieutenant Betsen was next to come in. He was a burly old man who had gray hair and Robert had actually met him before at a restaurant a year or so before Yellowstone erupted. The officer looked so much different after losing so much weight. He was still wearing his uniform from when he weighed at least fifty more pounds and it had never been resized.

"Sheriff my name is Mark Betsen and I need to talk to you about the people we brought in last night." he exclaimed.

"Well let's talk about it." Robert replied.

"It's bad." Mark said.

"What's bad?"

"After questioning the sister we learned that all of those arrested last night were involved. They were the scouting party for a much bigger gang coming from Salem." Mark stated.

"How big?"

"They say three hundred. And that's not the bad news." Mark stated.

"What's the bad news?"

Mark grinned. "They are armed to the teeth. They have been raiding houses, the police stations, even the State Troopers barracks."

Robert shook his head yes and started to process what he was saying.

Mark continued. "The girl we brought in says that the gang may have attacked two other checkpoints. They use an ambulance to approach with the lights on. When they are waved in and talk to whomever is stopping them the back and side doors open on the ambulance and the men inside level everything and everyone with their heavy weapons. Then the rest of the gang comes in."

"Well we know what they do how are we going to combat them if they come here?" Robert asked.

"We need to get the militia ready. We need a lot more men and better weapons. A better warning system wouldn't hurt either." Mark said.

"What put a scouting party up the road somewhere?"

"Exactly." Mark replied.

"How did you get them to talk?" Robert inquired.

"We told them they would be executed under Martial Law unless they were agreed to help us. I want to execute them anyway. But I need your authorization." he said to Robert.

Robert had thought about the fact that he had to now authorize any executions. This was very hard on him. Someone on his property trying to kill him and his family he had no problem shooting and if they lived or died after he stopped the threat he didn't care. These were people who had been a threat but no longer were. Also the people in the jail were not actively participating in the fire fight the night before. They could have easily gotten involved and maybe have changed the entire outcome. But they chose not to.

"Who has been cooperating?" Robert asked.

"The sister of one of the shooters and the other brother." Mark said.

"There was another brother there?" Robert questioned. "Interesting."

Mikayla opened the door to the conference room. "How much more time do you need? I have about ten things you need to address and need to know how many more people you can see today."

Robert turned to Mark. "For sure the ones not cooperating were involved?"

Mark shook his head yes. "Both the brother and the sister's answers matched. They named who they were and what they did for the gang."

Robert shook his head no. "I can't believe I have to make this decision." he paused for a moment. "Okay. Execute the ones not cooperating with us and I want to talk to the other two later."

"Yes sir." Mark said as he got up to leave the room.

"Wait." Robert said. "Make sure the brother and sister know their friends are being executed for not being helpful."

"I see where you are going with this. Big psychological impact to entice them to keep providing useful information. Huh?" Mark smirked. "Do you want me to have them executed in ear shot or be able to see them?"

Robert thought for a moment. "It's up to you. It doesn't matter. Oh, on the other topic. Let's see what we can do to fortify the checkpoint and get as many people as we can armed and on call for something bad to happen."

Mark shook his head yes and walked out as Mikayla walked in.

"You are a very popular person today. I am going to triage your backlog and make sure only the most important see you first!" Mikayla said to Robert. "Normally the water department would be the last person on the list but in this case I think he is the second most important."

"Who is the most important?" Robert asked.

"You just met with him." Mikayla said. "If nothing else I need you to talk with Dr. Simmons about an emergency issue and after that Officer Hammond who is in charge of burying the dead right now. If you have time we really need to address food security and distribution now that there is food again."

"Any others?" Robert asked.

"You don't want to know sir." Mikayla said. "There is Tucker and Barrett who want to talk about stuff they found at the camp, there is Captain Johnston who wants to talk to you about now putting up another checkpoint on the Bend side, there is Edith Pond who wants to talk about getting help at the hospice, Mike Rudy wants to talk to you about security for the Saturday Market...Should I go on?"

"Just start sending them in. I guess we can address them one by one. Might as well get them out of the way today because tomorrow there will be all new issues. Can you send Craig in too? He can help me I am sure." Robert said while he mentally prepared himself to deal with all these people.

Just as Mikayla opened the door he heard a gunshot.

"What was that?" Robert said as he stood up.

Dr. Simmons who had been waiting by the door looked in. "The town just got back to killing their no goods!"

Robert looked at him in bewilderment.

"Do I gotta spell it out? They just executed someone!" The doctor yelled.

Doctor Simmons was an old school doctor in his seventies and he obviously spoke his mind and didn't care what others thought. "You ready for me son? I got lives to save!" He yelled in to the conference room at Robert.

"I assume you are Dr. Simmons." Robert said. "Come in and sit down. What's on your mind Doctor?"

"What's on my mind?" He grumbled.

The doctor sat down. "You better sit down Sheriff or Mayor or whoever you are now."

Robert complied.

"We are in for a mass die off in this town unless I get some help." Doctor Simmons said.

"What do you mean?" Robert said.

"Well let me start from the beginning. The first few days after the EMP hit we had a large number of people die off. Virtually everyone who had a major medical problem or was in ICU at the hospital died. During that period those on automatic feeders and on ventilators, well there was nothing we could do without power and there was too many of them for the medical services we had. Some of those on feeding tubes we were able to keep feeding up until now by feeding them liquid foods and mainly Ensure which we got from a warehouse nearby. Well my friend as of last night we are out of Ensure and have nothing really to feed them but MRE's."

"Okay." Robert said.

"MRE's can't be fed to a person who can't stomach solids. That's just the beginning. In the next two weeks we will be out of Insulin and cardiac medications. Already we haven't been able to keep the Insulin cold enough due to the many power outages and the potency of the Insulin is about one-third. This means that the supply we do have is starting to be used up three times faster than normal."

"What else?" Robert asked.

"Oh, Mr. Ralston you don't want to know." Doctor Simmons said as he paused. "Mental medications are completely dispensed and everyone's last two week supply is going to run out in the next week or so. Psychotic drugs, those to control depressions, schizophrenia, depression, you name it. I estimate there are about two hundred or more in the town who are diagnosed with serious issues and being treated. And not to mention those coming here from other cities."

"What do can we do?" Robert asked.

"If we can't get more medicine there is nothing we can do other than deal with the people humanely." Doctor Simmons shouted.

"Humanely?" Robert asked.

"Yeah. Meaning you need to quarantine them and you can't just put them against a wall and blow their brains out!" The doctor yelled. "If I can get some pig's pancreases I might be able to make some low grade Insulin. But who has any pigs?"

Robert shook his head no. "I have no idea but I can see what I can find. Insulin comes from pig pancreases?...who knew!"

Doctor Simmons looked at Robert. "Yeah. You do that. Insulin nowadays doesn't come pigs but the first insulin ever created did." He said rhetorically. "Next there is a problem with the water."

"The water?" Robert asked.

"Yes we have eighteen deaths from Cholera and I suspect we have waterborne parasitic diseases such as Amebiasis, Cryptosporidiosis, Giardiasis in the water and Naegleria Fowleri." The doctor said.

Robert laughed. "I have about zero understanding of what you just said but I take it those things are bad. Is it from the creek water?"

"I thought originally it was but now I am seeing most of the cases come from people getting water from that well." said the doctor.

Robert shook his head. "Oh brother. How can we purify it? That's the town's main water source!"

"Well bleach is the best way but there isn't a disinfectant, bleach bottle, or anything else owned by this town left. We are completely out! That's why the kitchen we are cooking food in for everyone in town is having a severe problem with ETEC." The doctor said to Robert.

"ETEC?"

Dr. Simmons took a deep breath. "Oh, in easy English Enterotoxigenic E. Coli bacteria. We have three seniors who I suspect died from E. Coli in the past three days. Diarrhea is running rampant and I have no medications left to treat it. And I am down to one case of twelve IV's and I only got that because it got delivered by Tucker from that camp you guys raided. Meaning next week people are going to be dying from dehydration. It's bad Mayor or Sheriff or whatever you want to be called."

"What can I do doctor?" Robert said seeming very concerned.

"Send some people up to Salem. Get us some medications, some IV's, find a way to clean the water. If you don't you can probably cut the numbers of people you have to feed next month by half." The doctor yelled as he opened the door to conference room and left.

Robert put his head on in to his hand with his elbow resting on the table. "What have I gotten myself in to?" he thought to himself.

Craig walked in to the office. "You look beat up already Sheriff."

"Craig how many people are in this town?" Robert asked directly.

"About three thousand permanent residents and another four thousand who are vacation residents." Craig replied.

"How many have died since the volcano erupted." Robert asked.

"Do you really want to know?" Craig asked.

"Well as of three days ago we had buried eight hundred and sixty four, there were over fifty bodies in the grade school auditorium waiting to be buried. However twenty eight weren't residents at all. They were killed at the checkpoint." Craig said.

"How many from natural causes?" Robert asked.

"Maybe one or two I would think. That's about the average in a given month. Seventeen were executed by Martial Law. I know that." Craig replied.

"So about eight hundred died from lack of medicine or diseases?" Robert stated.

Craig paused a moment. "Well I wouldn't say that. About a hundred or so died from acts of violence. Another fifty died from accidents. Probably somewhat related to the power being out or the fire that tore up the back country. We also had two house fires that killed eight total. Oh, we had five bear mauling deaths too. Funny thing is that until this event there was never a recorded bear mauling death that I know of. But of course I don't..."

Robert interrupted. "don't have the Internet to check it. Yada Yada Yada. Doesn't this city have history books?"

"Well I don't know sir. I could check for you." Craig said trying to help.

"You go do that!" Robert said sarcastically.

Immediately Craig left the conference room.

Robert had a few moments to ponder. "Nine hundred people are dead in this small little town." he said to himself. "Many of the people probably bugged out to their vacation homes so that is probably around twenty percent in only a month and a half."

He stopped pondering this as Mikayla brought Robert in a bowl of tomato soup and a Philly Cheese Steak Sandwich with actual bread and steak. He took one bite and rolled his eyes in the back of his head. It was the best sandwich he had eaten in a month. The taste of fresh meat was incredible. Right after he took the first swallow he remembered what Dr. Simmons had said about E. Coli.

"Mikayla" He asked her as she held the conference room door open.

"Yes sir?"

"Where was this sandwich made?" He asked nicely.

"Right here in the kitchen. I know you probably heard about the bacteria issues at the schools kitchen. But I have been hiding anti-bacterial wipes and been wiping down the kitchen from top to bottom every three days. No one here has gotten sick." Mikayla said smiling.

"What about the water?" Robert asked.

"We have about fifty cases of bottled water at the jail. It's not coming from the well. Don't worry." Mikayla led Officer Hammond in to sit down.

Officer Hammond extended his hand to shake Roberts. Robert shook his hand but then squirted hand sanitizer on his hands he had gotten from his backpack when he was done.

Robert looked at his chest and read his name tag. "What can I do for you today Officer Hammond?"

"Two issues which are my assignments." Officer Hammond said. "First off we need to decide how to distribute 188,000 MRE's, fourteen hundred pounds of beef jerky, and twelve thousand three hundred pounds of powdered soups in five gallon buckets. We had issued ration cards but when we stopped using them many people probably tossed them."

"Can we make new ones?" Robert asked.

"I don't know if we have the means to print them." Officer Hammond responded.

"Mikayla." Robert yelled. She immediately opened the conference room door. "Do we have the ability to make and print five thousand or so ration cards?"

"If the generator holds out." She replied. "We have enough paper and ink. They won't be laminated like the others."

"What's wrong with the generator?" Robert asked.

Officer Hammond spoke up. "We have plenty of fuel. In fact we got two hundred gallons from a farm a few days go. However it is using a belt from a Volkswagen which doesn't fit and will probably break again anytime. I found another one but it takes a day to take the generator apart and put a new one in."

Robert took a deep breath. "Okay. Mikayla please work with Officer Hammond here to print what he needs on the ration cards."

Robert turned to Officer Hammond. "What about the burials?"

Officer Hammond shook his head. "Major problems. We are about eighty bodies behind. The tractor we were using to dig holes broke down."

"So what do you need officer?"

Officer Hammond looked Robert right in the eyes. "Sheriff I need your authority to commandeer one of Tucker's tractors! He has three working tractors and we cannot dig holes for eighty people with shovels. Secondly half the work crew is sick. The other half were working for double rations for their families and now that they have a bunch of food from the MRE's they aren't showing up. I need to use inmates. I was going to suggest using the ones you arrested the other night but before I got in here Johnston killed three of them!" Just as he said that another gunshot was heard. "Okay four of them."

Robert ran out the door and out in to the foyer where an officer was escorting two more of the eight inmates. "Officer take the inmates back and hold off on shooting them."

"Yes sir Sheriff." One of the officers responded. Robert heard the officer telling one of the men who was crying that they had just gotten a reprieve.

Robert walked back in to the conference room as he heard another shot ring out. He stopped and just couldn't help but shake his head and roll his eyes.

As soon as he sat down Captain Johnston was opening the conference room door. "What's up Sheriff?" he said as Mark Betsen walked in behind him.

Robert looked at Captain Johnston and Lieutenant Betsen. "Have a seat please."

"Officer Hammond brought up a very interesting thing. We need labor to bury people and inmates would work out splendidly for that. Instead of executing the rest I think we should sentence them to hard labor for their crimes." Robert told the men.

"Yes sir." Captain Johnston said. "Is that all?"

"No. Why would we need a check point on the other side between here and Bend?"

Mark spoke up. "We have received some threats Sheriff."

"What threats?" Robert snapped back.

"First it's gotten back to them that we have food. Secondly the town of Bend is telling people we have food and to come here to get it. Third they are pushing their mental patients out of their check point and sending them here. Fourth they have a bigger police department, bigger militia and a rumor that they are going to come and take our food by force."

Robert just sat back in his chair. "Could anything else be wrong in this town?"

Robert thought for a minute. "Okay. In exchange for food for families all men sixteen years and older must work for the city fifty hours per week. You two decide on each person's skill sets and where they would best be placed. Let them know along with their families getting food they will personally get double rations."

Both officer shook their heads yes.

"Now. Let's get a checkpoint setup at the edge of town. Somewhere where we can control and have the high ground. Do we have any night vision equipment?"

Both officers looked at each other with their heads down. "Yes."

Robert looked concerned. "Why do you say it like that?"

Both officers looked at one another again. Lieutenant Betsen spoke up. "Tucker brought back two pairs last night. We each kept one pair of night vision goggles."

"So what's wrong with that?" Robert inquired.

Captain Johnston spoke up. "We took them home with us. We were going to keep them sir."

"Well we need a pair at nights at both checkpoints. When this whole thing is over you can have them. For now we need them."

Lieutenant Betsen stood up and saluted Robert. "Yes sir!"

"Before you go. Let's get six guys at each checkpoint. Ten to twelve guys constantly patrolling downtown with a radio. We can make them our quick reactionary force. Let's keep as many officers rested up here at the Town Hall and jail as possible ready to get in to body armor and to either checkpoint in three minutes. Then let's get a radio to whoever is heading the militia force. How many do we have there?"

Captain Johnston looked up at the ceiling and started counting. "Okay forty five or forty six now that eight of them died at the Guardsman's camp."

"Okay that is our reserves however we need to get a bell or something in town that can notify all of them that we need help." Robert said in an excited tone. "Where is the food being stored at?"

"The food we got from the camp is mainly being stored at the City Warehouse. It's being guards 24/7 by three officers taking shifts."

Robert thought for a minute. "I have an idea. But it has to be a secret. Only we can know what is going on."

Mark looked at Robert. "Ok I am all ears."

"Here is what I want to do. I want you to bring three pallets of MRE's for the food we are going to give away this next month. Move that food to city hall and place the pallets in empty jail cells. Then I want you to remove all the MRE's and Beef Jerky from the boxes on the other pallets and place them in all those empty fifty-five gallon drums outside of the city warehouse. The ones I see stacked up every time I drive by. Then I want you to have the inmates place a shovel full of dirt in every one of those empty boxes and reseal the boxes. Then take the boxes full of dirt and restack them on the pallets, shrink wrap the pallets as if they had never been opened and put them right back on the truck. The very last pallet on the truck I want to have actual MRE's. Just on the top back row facing the back door of the semi. For those four or five or six boxes only! Are you with me so far?"

Both officers shook their head yes.

"Okay. Now I want you to take the fifty five gallon drums that are filled with food. Label them as 'Non-Potable water' or 'Used oil' and then place them in the caged area for maintenance vehicles. Put one kid guarding the semi at the City Warehouse and tell him if any trouble happens to report it and run."

Mark started writing down everything Robert told them so they wouldn't forget.

Robert continued. "I want you to get a city maintenance worker to build a guard house on the hill right above the vehicle maintenance yard by tomorrow. Get a tow truck or tractor from Tucker to move all those non-working vehicles in front of the fence with all the drums so it would take hours to move them to get to the food. Anyone attacking us would never think to bring a tow truck. Put the guards up in the towers and tell them their job is very important. Their job is to guard the valuable running vehicles. Call for help if anyone or any group visits there. My guess is even if we are attacked they would never go there."

Captain Johnston just shook his head. "You just thought of all this in the last ten minutes? Wow."

"Yes! And you guys better get going. Pull in any resources you need to get this done by tomorrow! My family can help move the food later tonight. I want the knowledge of the foods location to be left only those in this room."

Both men got up. Both saluted Robert and started to walk out. On the way out of the conference room door Mark stopped and turned to Robert. "Are you sure you weren't born for this job?"

Robert smiled. "I certainly hope God had other plans for me."

Robert walked out of the conference room doors. "Mikayla?"

A few moments later Mikayla appeared. "You needed me, sir?"

"Yes. I need Tucker."

"Um. He's probably at the fire station sir." Mikayla responded.

"Well can we find someone to get him?" Robert asked bluntly.

"Um. Hold on. We have a radio now." Mikayla said as she stuttered.

She leaned behind the front desk and pulled out a radio. "Is Chief Tucker on? City Hall to Chief Tucker. Come in."

A few moments later the radio came to life. "This is Chief Morrison, Mikayla. What's up?"

"The Sheriff wants to see ya pronto." Mikayla replied.

"ETA is twenty or so." Tucker said.

Mikayla turned to Robert. "He'll be here in twenty minutes sir."

"Very good." Robert said and returned to the conference room. When he walked in Sydney, Rylee, and Trevor were sitting in the conference room. "Hello my family what a great surprise." Robert said with a smile.

"We thought we would come visit you on your first day of work. How are thing going?" Sydney asked.

Robert laid back in his chair and smiled. "If I told you your head would explode."

Sydney smiled. "Actually you haven't cleaned any water so I decided to come up and get some."

Roberts eyes lit up. "Don't drink the water from the well!"

Sydney got concerned. "Uh okay. Why not?"

"It might be contaminated. At least Dr. Simmons thinks so."

"Who is Dr. Simmons?" Sydney asked.

Robert suddenly thought to himself. Who was Dr. Simmons to the city? An advisor? He never thought to ask.

Robert just replied to Sydney. "He is the town doctor. You can drink the water but put a cap full of bleach in the water and wait for thirty minutes before drinking it. On second thought. I need all of you including Allison to go see Captain Johnston. I have a secret project for all of us to work on tonight." Robert paused for a moment. "Mikayla." Robert yelled.

Mikayla opened the door.

"Can you get a case of water bottles and bring it in here?"

"Yes sir."

"One other thing. I thought there were a lot of people to see me." Robert asked Mikayla.

"You spent hours with the others this morning they either left, got tired of waiting or I scheduled them for tomorrow." she said.

"Okay. Thank you. What about the water department guy?" Robert asked.

Mikayla got a strange look on her face. "Didn't Dr. Simmons bring that issue up?"

Robert shook his head yes. "But shouldn't the water guy be here to give me suggestions on cleaning the water?"

"Um. There is nothing in this town to treat the water with! Bend and Salem's water contamination is infecting our supply. He says he has no answers." Mikayla responded.

"I do! Tell Tucker to wait here until I get back."

Robert walked out of the conference room and found the detective in the foyer he had met a few days after the EMP happened. This detective had investigated the death of Trevor's father. Robert walked up to him and placed his hand on the detectives shoulder.

"I need you to get a car and meet me out front." Robert began to say as the detective whipped around and threw Robert against the counter and began to aggressively hand cuff him. Mikayla and Captain Thompson came running up to the detective.

Captain Thompson yelled. "What are you doing Myers?"

Detective Myers looked up. "This guy tried to grab me and he's under arrest!"

"Grab you?" Robert yelled back. "I touched your shoulder to get your attention and told you to get me a car."

"Remove the handcuffs now Myers! That is Sheriff Ralston." The look on Detective Myers face was one of sheer terror and bewilderment. He walked Robert over Captain Thompson. Took off his badge. Drop it to the ground and just walked out the front door.

"Detective?" Captain Thompson yelled out.

Detective Myers just slammed the front door open to the exit and walked out not turning around or saying a word as Captain Thompson fumbled with his keys to remove the handcuffs Robert was wearing.

A few moments later Tucker walked in. "What happened here?" As he looked at all the stunned faces standing around and Captain Thompson removing the last handcuff from Roberts wrist. "Did I come at a bad time?"

Robert looked at Captain Thompson. "Thank you." he said as he rubbed the red marks on his wrist. "Change of plans Tucker." Robert commanded. "I need you to drive me to my house really quickly to get some things."

Both men left the building. About thirty minutes Robert returned with eight gallons of bleach. Robert carried four gallons in a case and Tucker carried the other four. He placed them on the counter in front of Mikayla. "Get the water guy to start putting a quarter teaspoon in every gallon we give out until further notice. That should get us by for a month or so until we figure something else out about cleaning the water."

Mikayla picked up her radio and told someone he had never heard of to send the guys at the well to the Town Hall as soon as possible.

Robert then turned to Tucker. "I am glad we came to an agreement in the car. I know you don't want to part with them but its best for the city and you in the long run."

Tucker walked out.

"You got Tucker to part with a tractor?" Mikayla asked.

Robert smiled. "And his guns." he said as he walked away unwrapping one of the last mints from the front counter.

Mikayla just stood there dumbfounded with her mouth open. She yelled down the hall at Robert as he walked away "Detective Myers quit!" and then in a lowered voice knowing no one could hear her anymore. "And he's not coming back. Not that we care anyways. He was a jerk."

Chapter 13: Banding Together.

It was the start of Robert's second week as Mayor and Sheriff of the small little vacation town of Sisters, Oregon. In all his preparations one of things that always stood out was being physically prepared for whatever is thrown at you and being prepared to defend yourself.

Being good at self-defense means that need to have good physical fitness. That Robert felt was one of the most important things in a crisis. He had also learned in his preparations that the most dangerous predators on earth are those with two-legs. He was now involved in a battle with enemies he couldn't see. Viruses, Amoebas, and bacteria everywhere. Not just in the water but on every counter and door handle.

Now he was reading a report that Lieutenant Betsen had gotten from a person trying to in a sense defect to the City of Sisters because they were out of food in Bend and also sick and he stated there were no doctors or medicine there. The citizens of the City of Bend were mainly battling those in city government who had never planned ahead and did not made the necessary preparations to be able to take care of themselves or their citizens in even a short term disaster much less a long term one. The city fathers had turned to declaring Martial Law and forcibly removing all the food and supplies from virtually every citizen.

The difference in that city was they were hoarding everything they took for themselves and not offering anything whatsoever to the residents and they were suffering and dying with nothing.

The city government in Bend was basically living in a fortified bunker at City Hall. Their own looted supplies were now dwindling and Robert who had previously thought their militia was bigger and better might have been wrong. From this report from the man who had tried to defect the night before, it now looked like the militia was only formed to attack their own city to get their food and supplies stolen from them back. The militia had made some strides and retrieved some of the stolen food and water it sounded like but now both sides were running out of virtually everything.

The man trying to defect from Bend had been taken to the Police Station and was being questioned even as Robert was reading the initial report from the night before. The man also had stated that he was the former janitor for the City Hall in Bend and he had learned that the city had sent several scouts to sneak in to the town of Sisters late at night and see what supplies we had. In fact they knew about the semi trucks loaded with MRE's and guarded at the City Warehouse. Captain Betsent had also learned from the man that one of the scouts had actually returned with a picture of all the pallets loaded on one of the trucks with the door opened on the truck.

The report also said that the City of Bend's Police Chief had gotten word back that the trucks were our storage and if the city was attacked the trucks would be moved to another location at the beginning of an attack. Robert realized at that moment that someone in the city was helping the City of Bend. That was the exact story that he, the Captain and the Lieutenant had deliberately let everyone in the city government know.

The work to hide the real food was done entirely at night by Robert, Trevor, Officer Mitchell, Mikayla, Captain Johnston, and Allison. The only people Robert felt he could trust. The boxes were filled with dirt by Officer Mitchell's inmate crew and told the boxes would decay faster if there was dirt inside them. No one other than those seven knew the boxes of MRE's and Beef Jerky in the semi truck were now really filled with dirt or the real location of all the food hidden basically in plain sight.

At the very end of the report was a scribble of notes and one of them said. "Attack Thursday / 4 A.M."

It was Tuesday. That only gave them two nights to prepare. Robert got on the radio and started calling everyone of the police officers in the conference room to relay his plans. As everyone sat down Robert drew a map on the white board.

Robert stood up. "We have information that the City of Bend is going to attack us for our food supplies early Thursday morning."

Everyone except for the Captain and the Lieutenant gasped.

"I have a plan. From 2 A.M. Thursday morning on, we will not man the checkpoint between here and Bend. We instead put a closed sign up until 8 A.M. about twenty yards ahead of the checkpoint by one in the morning. Next, we will place sleeping bags on the two trucks that look like four people are sleeping in them." Robert continued. "They will most likely attack us from the high side coming from Bend and secondarily straight down the road with some kind of heavy vehicle or vehicles I am sure." Robert paused to take a breath and finish his whiteboard map.

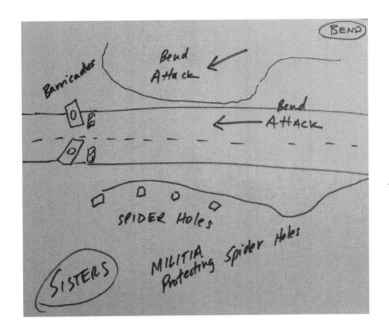

Robert's whiteboard map of his attack plans.

"We are going to setup on the Sister's side of the hill with four sniper holes. I have ten .50 CAL sniper rifles from Tucker each with a scope and two with night vision. We will place four of them in the sniper holes above the check point and four on the roof of the Town Hall. We will bring in the militia to help but their job is solely offensive. They will guard the entry in to the city past City Hall which we will have another manned checkpoint temporarily setup. Also the militia will guard City Hall, guard the officers who will be the snipers in the holes so the they have free reign to engage the enemy without fear of guarding their back side." Robert paused and then turned to all the officers in the room. "We have several goals. One to pick off as many of the City of Bend's officers as we can. Secondly, to let them take a semi of food. The last and biggest goal is to make sure not one of our officers gets injured or killed in the process!"

One of the officers stood up. "I am Officer Rodriguez." He spoke very loudly. "We are just going to let them take our food? That's B.S. man!"

Officer Rodriguez then sat down as many of the other officers shook their heads up and down in agreement.

Robert looked at Captain Johnston and Lieutenant Betsen. Then shook his head yes. "One the City of Bend needs the food and the goal of repelling this attack is simply to reduce their numbers and to make them weaker if they want to attack us again. Lastly, I want everyone in this town to go home to their families."

Robert looked at Officer Rodriguez. "I know how you feel but there are people suffering there in Bend and a full head on assault would cost us too many lives. They out number us by a huge number."

Officer Rodriguez shook his head yes. "Okay. But what if someone comes up to the checkpoint after its closed."

"My guess is that if they are coming to attack us everyone on the Bend side would either know or they would be stopped before they could get here so that no one came down to warn us!" Robert stated.

Robert came over and put his hand on Officer Rodriguez shoulder. "Can I count on you to grab some guys and go up and dig the four sniper holes as secretly as possible tonight?"

"Yes sir." he replied.

"Well get to it then. Thank you for your service! All of you." Robert said.

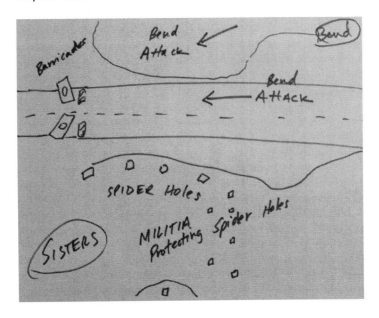

Updated whiteboard drawing of the attack plan.

Before everyone left the room Officer Mitchell started laughing.

"What's so funny?" Robert asked Officer Mitchell.

"Look at your white board! We are making spider holes now and not sniper holes?" he said as everyone but Robert started to laugh out loud.

"You guys know what I meant!" Robert grumbled as he too started to laugh.

By the end of the day on Wednesday not only had the four Sniper Holes been dug above the checkpoint but seven more had been dug on the far approach to the high point. By doing this six militia men could be concealed by green tarps and leaves. These six could surprise anyone trying to come up behind the sniper positions guarding the barricades. A seventh sniper location was Officer Rodriguez idea to place a sniper position on the cliff above the militia men guarding their positions. This sniper would have one of the night vision goggles and Robert volunteered for this position even against the advice of the Lieutenant and the Captain.

To make the situation appear to look more authentic, Robert opened the back of the semi truck so all could see the items inside. He backed up a small pickup and loaded it with about ten cases of MRE's. These cases were really loaded with sand and he placed a dolly next to the truck with another six cases. It looked to most anyone driving by that someone was simply offloading some cases of MRE's and taking them back to the city. Even the officers driving by commented to each other on their way to their positions by the barricades that the Sheriff must not want the city of Bend to get all the MRE's and so he was offloading some before the attack.

By one in the morning everyone was in position. About two o'clock Robert was high above the check point and able to see all the positions. He could see clearly about six hundred yards away with his night vision goggles. It was a nice night and the moon was out giving lots of power to his night vision. About twenty-five minutes later he noticed several dark figures slowly creeping up the tree line on the other side of the road about a half mile down the road.

Robert quietly picked up his radio. "Time to go to bed guys" he said in on the special channel they had established for this attack.

The men at the checkpoint lifted the sleeping bags filled with blankets on to the hood of the trucks and propped an old musket rifle on one of the bumpers. All four men sped off in another truck just as the two scouts got in to view of the checkpoint. Robert had carefully rigged some fishing line to two of the sleeping bags so one of the militia men could periodically move an inflated ball inside a sleeping bag to give the appearance that someone inside had moved. Robert smiled when he saw it move the first time because it looked so real.

Robert saw the two scouts from Bend move in closer to the checkpoint and just sit behind a tree about a quarter mile down the road. One of the scouts sat out of site while the other watched the checkpoint. Robert saw the scout watching the checkpoint get on a radio several times. He didn't speak only pushed keys on his radio.

At about three thirty in the morning Robert saw lots of movement and noise coming from down the road. He started getting scared and his heart started pounding. He had no real idea of what surprises the City of Bend had for them. As he was thinking this he looked in his night vision goggles. To Robert it seemed like five other men just appeared from nowhere from behind the trees and joined the two scouts.

After the men spent a few minutes speaking with the scouts the men appeared to feel as if there was no real threat and stood up and moved around here and there freely even laying their guns down at times. A few minutes later one even lit up a cigarette. Someone must have said something because at the same time all five simultaneously sat down at the end of the tree line with their rifles standing up. Occasionally they would stare at the road toward Bend looking as if they were waiting for something to happen.

Robert whispered in the Radio. "Now seven high side A. Next to the scouts." As he said that he looked down and saw two more men dressed in black come through the trees and creep right up to one of the militia's sniper holes and crouch down actually using the sniper holes covering as a barrier to not be seen. Robert heard the sounds of large diesel engine trucks coming from the Bend side of the highway and saw dust and smoke flying in the air about a mile down the road. He waited about forty more seconds when the noise of the trucks was loud enough to mask the sound of gunshots then yelled in the radio. "NOW!"

Shots rang out from multiple positions. Robert had his eyes on the two down below him and shot one of the assailants as the man in the sniper hole right in front of him shot one of them through camouflage of the sniper hole. Both men were dead long before they even knew there were men hiding right below them.

In Robert's night vision scope he could see the officers and scouts on the other end of the road going down one by one.

Suddenly everyone but Robert's view was blocked to the other side of the road by large semi trucks and trailers cut open to be troop carriers. There were three of them and they came down the road at fifty or more miles per hour. Snipers in sprang from the sniper holes and peppered the first two trucks with gun fire. The backs were opened up and man after man in the back of the trucks came falling out. Most riddled with more than one bullet and shot dead. Some flopped over in the trucks even before having time to realize they were under attack. Two trucks were completely saturated with gunfire. By the time the third semi truck went through the barricade virtually every sniper including Robert was out of bullets and were in the process of reloading.

Everything turned quiet for about three minutes. During that time the radio sprang to life with officers and militia checking to make sure no one was hurt. Everyone had checked in that they were fine. Suddenly everyone could hear gun fire from inside the city. It was clearly a gun battle and Robert feared he had been wrong. City Hall was the target.

Robert got on the radio. "Betsen do you need help?"

"No! The gunfire is coming from the warehouse!" He yelled back. "Who's down there Sheriff?"

Robert yelled back. "Nobody should be there!"

"Well some bodies down there putting up a heck of a fire fight!" Captain Johnston said in the radio.

There were about fifty more shots fired before a huge explosion silenced them all. The sound of a semi starting caught everyone's attention in the dead silence. It could be heard even out at the checkpoint through the silence. Then another truck started.

"Get ready you guys. Semi's coming to you!" Captain Betsen yelled in the microphone.

The first truck to come around the hill only had a driver and was the third vehicle in the convoy when they first went through from the other direction.

Robert yelled in the radio. "Don't shoot the driver we don't want to block the."

Robert stopped. It was too late. The driver had been shot by at least three snipers and the truck veered off and up the mountain side underneath the four sniper holes, overturned and then caught fire.

This didn't stop the stolen semi which held the pallets of MRE's which rammed the other truck out of the way and kept going. At least four muzzle blasts could be seen flashing from the back of the truck which had one door opened as the truck went by. All the snipers including Robert exhausted all of their ammunition in the clips firing at the truck as it drove away.

Robert heard the radio. "Sheriff! Sheriff! Come in."

Robert picked up the radio. "Yeah. All clear here." He said as militia men watched the truck go up in flames and several teams went over to the seven shot on the opposite hill. "So far at least sixteen bad guys dead and none on our side. A perfectly executed plan!" Robert exclaimed.

"Not quite Sheriff." Lieutenant Betsen declared over the radio. "I have eight dead over here. I have Tucker here who says Officer Rodriguez told him and his fire crew to defend the semi truck at all costs."

Robert got irate. "Are you kidding me?" Robert yelled angrily as he started climbing down from his position.

As Robert got on to an ATV he heard Officer Rodriguez over the radio. "We had to attempt to save the food. That's a year's worth of food the citizens of this city need. Over eighteen hundred cases." He yelled defending himself.

Other people on the radio started saying Officer Rodriguez did the right thing until Captain Betsen got on and yelled. "There was only six cases of MRE's on that truck. The rest were all filled with dirt. You just got eight people killed for six cases of MRE's!"

Lieutenant Betsen got on the radio. "Nine now. Tucker just passed away. All officers please disarm and arrest Officer Rodriguez immediately!"

Robert arrived at the City Warehouse and surveyed

the damage. He saw Tucker and eight others dead behind the building. The Bend police force had used sticks of dynamite thrown with a wire attached and detonated it to kill most of Tuckers team. He noticed a box of other sticks of dynamite inside one of the diesel trucks they had come with along with four other dead Bend attackers inside the cab and a few more in the back of the truck. The other truck had plowed in to a fence. It contained only a dead attacker in the back who was obviously killed with a .50 CAL shot. The driver of the truck was not in there and must have gotten on to one of the other semi trucks before they left.

All in total there were twenty six dead officers from the City of Bend and nine dead from the City of Sisters.

Robert was completely silent and processing things but couldn't help but laugh when Captain Johnston said. "I sure wish I could see the look on the faces of the cops in Bend when they open those first boxes and say 'Score!' then start giving them away to people and see the look on their faces when they realize the rest of the boxes are dirt!"

Robert got serious as everyone from the battle gathered around Robert. "This was supposed to be a joyous victory with no lives lost. Officer Rodriguez clearly went around the chain of command and now nine people are dead because of it."

Officer Rodriguez spoke up loudly and crying. "I was only trying to help I didn't know they were dirt. Honest you guys."

Robert asked all the officers to move over to the right side. And all the militia to the left side of him. "Officer Rodriguez is an officer who basically pulled the trigger and got at least one city employee killed. The fire chief."

Robert was interrupted by Captain Johnston. "They are all city employees. The Chief and most of the fire department."

Robert put his head down in disbelief along with most of the officers.

Officer Rodriguez stared pleading. "C'mon guys. You know me I wouldn't get anyone killed."

Lieutenant Betsen spoke up. "You did! You went around the chain of command and people are dead! Not just anyone either. Critical people this town needed for survival. You used people who were not trained for combat either and now you need to pay the ultimate price. Right Sheriff?"

Officer Rodriguez pleaded some more. "Please guys. I have served the city well for ten plus years. I got a wife and three kids. Please listen to me! Please!"

Robert put his hand up and Officer Rodriguez stopped to listen to what he had to say. "I have two options. Life in prison or execution. I will let the jury of your peers decide your fate." he said angrily.

Robert turned to the officers. "All in favor of life in prison for his crimes raise your hand." There were no hands lifted.

Officer Rodriguez pleaded. "Javier we are friends for life man. Kevin we have known each other for years. Our kids play together. Man?" He cried.

Robert watched as both Kevin and Javier slowly raised their hands with their heads down.

"Okay just for a fair vote. How many of you vote for execution. " Robert asked.

A lot of heads went down this time as the remaining fourteen officers lifted their hands and refused to look Officer Rodriguez in the eye. Robert turned to Captain Johnston who had not voted and jerked his head in a yes motion and started walking away back to the City Hall just half of a block away.

Before Robert had even reached for the door handle he heard a shot ring out. A tear came to his eye. Not for Officer Rodriguez but for Tucker who had become one of Robert's best friends.

Chapter 14: The Crisis Ends.

In all of Robert's research being able to teach new skills was one of the most admirable skills a prepper could posses. Regardless of the crisis you face, your children can still be educated and you can teach them how society went wrong. Robert started writing a book based on his notes he had written in his journal for his kids to learn from. He wanted to make sure that his kids' children would learn from the mistakes of the past and be ready in case a disaster or unforeseen event ever happened again. In this disaster the local schools closed down for two years. One of the major differences he had was that as a survivor he and his wife always kept educating his children and the ones he adopted as well.

As it turned out China never attacked the United States at all. In fact no nuclear bomb ever went up in the air. Further studies showed that all the debris in the atmosphere from the volcano stirred around creating a global static build up and it discharged causing a medium level EMP almost worldwide. It may have been exacerbated by a solar event but no one will ever know for sure.

It took another eight months before the City of Salem sent word that it was back in business. Another two months later the first trucks with medical supplies and food rolled past the cities checkpoint in to town.

The City of Bend was completely disorganized during the event and never had a true leader. Although there were over fourteen thousand people in Bend when the EMP struck there was less than four hundred that survived and most were trucked out for hospitals when the relief workers and trucks arrived to care for the people.

Over the past ten months small pockets of survivors had attacked the City of Sisters from Bend and from Salem but none had been successful. The City Of Bend had lost over eighty attackers whereas the City of Sisters had lost only four of their militia defending itself at both checkpoints.

The City of Sisters under Robert's leadership had one of the best records for survivors in the whole country. In the end it was determined that the city had around seven thousand, four hundred people visiting or living in the city the day the EMP hit. Over five thousand people lived to tell about their experiences. Forty six new residents were also born during the ten months including another daughter born to Robert and Sydney Ralston they named Amelia.

Thanks to the good work of Dr. Simmons and the pig farm Robert helped create, even fourteen Type 1 diabetics who were insulin dependent patients were alive and well when the medical supply trucks rolled in. The City of Sisters was only one of three cities in the nation to have any numbers of survivors of this type.

Robert Ralston went on to serve another term as Mayor but left that position to serve as Governor of the great State of Oregon. Three terms, in fact. He adopted Trevor who's mother was never found. Trevor became a doctor and took over Dr. Neil Simmons practice in Sisters Oregon after Dr. Simmons past away about eight years after the event.

Robert and Sydney also adopted Ciara who eventually became a house wife. She married Mark Betsen's only son Cory.

Both Rylee and Amelia went on to marry preppers who worked for their father Robert on his many campaigns for Sheriff, Mayor, and then Governor. Both of their husbands eventually became state senators in Oregon propelled in to office by their father-in-law's many endorsements.

Robert was instrumental in passing new laws that restored many rights removed after 9/11 and a law that every town must be able to provide for the needs of their citizens for at least one year. The City of Sisters however passed their own laws to make it three years.

None of that really mattered because almost every church asked its members to have three years of not just food but everything they needed to survive. Most had learned that it took more than a supply of food to survive. Almost every family started their own food supply and survival supply for themselves and the United States became an entire nation of 'preppers' from then on. It became cool to be a prepper and you were looked down on if you hadn't done anything to start preparing for a calamity or disaster. Completely the opposite from the way things were before the event when many people thought Robert was crazy for preparing as much as he did.

Later in Robert's life Robert he was instrumental in passing several new consumer protection laws that required EMP testing on all new vehicles and all electronics used by city, state, and government. All electronics were from then on to be tested and certified and to be shielded with newer technologies against EMP's.

Robert and Sydney visited their old neighborhood in Portland one year after the eruption. The entire subdivision had been completely destroyed by fire. It would be many years before Sydney ever learn what had happened to their old neighborhood or the many neighbors they had grown to love over the years.

As the years passed Sydney had continuously searched for Claire, Thomas, and even the two girls with no luck. She was able to locate Claire's brother Charlie a few years later who had been in Hawaii with his wife the day Yellowstone erupted. Sydney was saddened to learn that Chuck's wife had not made it and that Claire's brother had never heard from or been able to find any other member of his extended family including Claire. He had promised Sydney he would let her know if he ever found out what happened to Claire or his kids.

It wasn't until fifteen years later when Sydney received a message from Robert that a Thomas Rigby had called the Governors' Office and left a message for her. During a return call Sydney had learned that Thomas had been adopted by another family. He stated that gangs had gone door to door and Claire had told him to take the kids and hide in the creek bed near the house. He had hid there in the creek bed for two days while the gang looted the entire block.

Then they burned every house. Thomas had never heard from his mother again. He asked what Sydney could do to find out what had happened to his mother. Robert sent a special investigator from the Governors' office to go through every report from that time period including the police and coroners reports. Fire investigators were sent to sift through the rubble of the still decaying shell of a house for a body. There was no body found and no record that could be found that explained what had happened to Claire.

The most likely theory was a gang that had looted and pillaged for thirty miles from Newberg all the way up to Tigard had probably taken her prisoner and discarded her when she was no use. The gang was eventually cornered and all the gangs members were killed by the Portland Police and the Portland Militia when they attempted to continue on their path of destruction in to Portland. By then the gang had over three hundred members. All the dead gang members had been photographed and finger printed before they were buried and none of those members had been Claire.

Sydney dreaded calling Thomas to relay the bad news that fateful day when Robert revealed the results of the special investigators report.

Sydney died before Robert at the age of ninety-six. She left behind a loving devoted husband who had been married to her just one month shy of eighty years. Along with that she left three natural children. Rylee, Amelia, and Jacob who was born just two years after Amelia.

Sydney also left behind three adopted children. Ciara, Trevor, and another child Addison who's mother Allison died about a year after things got back to normal of breast cancer. There were also eighteen grand children and twenty-two great grand children and two more on the way when she passed away. Two months after her death the first great great grand child was born.

During the funeral hundreds of people from around Sister's Oregon came to pay their respect and told stories of heroics and good deeds Robert and Sydney had done for the whole community including the night Sydney and Robert had stayed up all night hiding all the cities food in drums right in the plain sight of everyone to save the City of Sisters.

Sadly Robert passed away only three days after the funeral for Sydney. Doctors couldn't find a thing wrong with him. Most felt he just died of depression and missed Sydney so much he had to be with her.

EPILOGUE

Trevor walked in to his living room where he saw his grandson Calib. He was reading an old paperback book from his grand fathers book shelf, "A Leader Not A Hero" by Robert Ralston.

"Hi Calib. What are you doing here? Is school out already?" Trevor said as his ninety one year old frame walked slowly and shook as he tried to hold his cane.

"Great Grandpa, was your daddy really a hero?" Calib asked the frail old man.

"Why do you ask Calib?" Trevor inquired.

"Well our class went on a field trip today to the Sister's History Center and there was an old lady guiding us around. Her name tag said she was Hallie Wesley. She showed us a statue of your dad. I told her that he was my great great grandfather. She said she knew him very well and that I was related to the greatest hero of all time. She said none of us in Sister's would be here today had it not been for him over eighty years ago."

Trevor's face began to show tears. His throat tightened and he could barely speak. "Your great great grandfather Robert Ralston was truly one of the greatest men that ever lived and I personally have ever known." He said as more tears came to his eyes and started to go down his face.

"I haven't seen Hallie or her brother Steven in over sixty-eight years since she went away to her grandparents in Oklahoma. She was going to be adopted by my father but another set of grandparents were found and objected to the adoption. Eventually my father had to send them to Oklahoma and the grandparents sent us letters asking us to never contact them again. It was one of the saddest times my father ever went through. He loved those kids and Hallie was my best friend." Trevor said as he picked up his car controller.

"Where are you going grandpa?" Calib asked.

"I am going over to the Historical Center. Do you want to come with me?" Trevor asked Calib.

"Of course I do!" Calib said running out. He pushed the button on his ear piece. "Tell mom I am going to history center with grandpa great!"

"Door open!" Trevor yelled at the door which slowly opened. He and Calib walked up to the Google Solar Self Propelled Hover Vehicle(SSPHV). He pushed the button on his hand controller and the vehicle doors opened and the unit powered up.

The vehicle dashboard came to life. "What is your destination?" the vehicle asked.

"Sister's Historical Society!" Trevor yelled.

"I have found a listing for Sister's Historical Center. One point eight miles from this location. Is this correct?" The car asked.

"Yes!" Calib yelled.

"Doors are now closing. Please keep all limbs in the vehicle for your safety and do not block the automatic doors." the car said.

A few moments later the hover car lifted over the houses and landed in the parking lot of the Historical Center. The doors opened and Trevor and Calib slowly got out. Trevor made his way up the stairs where an elderly man opened the doors for him.

"Come in. Come in. Please!" the elderly man said as he held old wooden door open.

Trevor walked through the doors and then straight toward a group of people being led by an elderly woman on the other side of the room. The elderly woman stopped talking to the people around her and stared right back at Trevor.

Most of the members of the group stopped and turned around to look as elderly woman walked through the middle of the group directly toward Trevor. Tears filled her eyes as she went straight to Trevor and hugged him.

They both stayed there embracing each other for five minutes until Steven Wesley, the one who had opened the door for Trevor walked up crying and extended his hand. Steven smiled through his tears and said "It has been too long Trevor. We need a rematch on that Battleship game."

Trevor smiled. "We do."

THE END

Farrell Kingsley

Made in the USA
Middletown, DE
10 November 2014